Dynamix at the Roxy

Rob Atkins

Taff Vale Books
Abertillery

Copyright © Robert Atkins 2024

The moral right of the author has been asserted. The story, all names, characters and incidents portrayed in this book are fictitious. No identification with actual persons is intended or should be inferred.

Rob Atkins is the author of:

Playing at the Roxy
Abertillery Kid
Luke, Stranger

He is a retired Baptist minister and teaches French and music privately. He writes and performs songs under the name Frost at Midnight

1

"I expect you've heard of like, the Dynamic Teen Team Scheme, Howard?"

Howard wondered if this could be a trick question but he answered in any case, "I couldn't very well not have heard of the Dynamic Teen Team Scheme, could I, Cathy?"

The D.T.T.S. was plastered all over their publicity: in Howard's view a free holiday in an exotic place courtesy of the Lighthouse Agency in exchange for some upbeat stories from girls in shorts and t–shirts and studious but broodingly charismatic boys on the scrawny side. It had been flavour of the month for a good while by now.

"It's Catti. Yes, it's been like, one of our most successful new innovations in, like, centuries? When we started . . . "

The voice was insistent and positive and there was clearly much more in this vein to come so Howard put the receiver on the desk, leaned over to the bookshelf and picked up a glossy leaflet all about the D.T.T.S. that happened to be to hand on the top of a pile of dusty brown Bibles in a superseded translation. Downstairs, Howard could hear some muffled bangs and crashes as Paquito got ready for a hard day's scrounging in the porch of St Anne's church with his dented saucepan. Going over to lie on the bed, Howard studied the picture yet again – a dozen young women were in an abandoned ecstasy playing beach volleyball while two young men in the background with tablets appeared to be having a learned debate over a heap of books on a deckchair. Howard had a bit of a thing for the one about two feet off the ground – one of the girls, as it happened – hands clenched in the middle of a blocking shot at the net, blonde hair showered out behind and, as her salmon pink top rode up, a tantalising glimpse . . . Howard picked up the twittering phone again.

". . . when you call it a freebie abroad and suchlike, myself Vicki and Suzi, we prefer to call it like, a gap–year opportunity for hands–on mission at the cutting-edge. Faith spelt R.I.S.K?"

Howard came to with a start. "I'm sorry, Cathy, did you ask me a question?"

"It's Catti, actually. And, no, I was just like, filling you in on the Ditsies. Giving you a bit of a heads-up on the whole idea."

"*The Ditsies*? I don't quite follow . . ."

"Oh, come on, do keep up, will you? I've just been telling you about the rebrand of D.T.T.S., the Dynamic Teen Team Scheme, as *The Ditsies.* Vicki came up with the name. Ha, ha! She got a couple of thousand bonus for that and three days holiday." Howard had to hold the phone away from his ear because Cathy had a laugh that was at the same time a gasp, a pant and a cackle. Howard had decided it was intolerable about the second time he'd heard it.

Vicky, Cathy and Susie were running the Lighthouse Agency operation from a newish industrial unit in Milton Keynes. Howard remembered from his only visit for interview that it was a lavish conversion. They had their own industrial kitchen in there and a dedicated cook on weekdays at both meal times. There was a gym, a separate games room with table tennis, table football and a *Terminator* pinball machine and a directors' suite as well as all the offices. Out the back there was a hot tub in a little annexe. All three of them had been on the panel when Howard had been accepted by the Agency on the strength of jotting down and then performing a rap about his experiences working with churches in France. He'd remembered just in time that back in the 90s Vicky had famously got the top job as International Director by singing *Tell me what you want, what you really, really want* and that Cathy had been appointed in the noughties as Home Secretary and Press Officer on the back of a spiritual dance based on *Rolling in the Deep* by Adele. Howard wondered what Susie, the finance Director might have sung. Maybe that *Periodic Table* song to show she was able to cope with detail, Howard speculated, or maybe the accountancy side of it was too important to appoint on the basis of a gimmick.

Howard wondered when the current trend for trying to entertain and delight the panel of trustees had begun. Maybe it was when the Agency moved from the Strand and Joe Marple took early retirement. On the whole he decided he'd far prefer to be interviewed for a job rather than have to audition for it but he realised you had to go with the flow these days or you were on the scrapheap. So, a rap it had been. The Lighthouse

Agency had come a long way since its foundation in 1887 as the Combined Varsities Mission for the Improvement of the Unreached Heathen (Overseas Division). Howard often wondered why the agency was called after a lighthouse. In his view a lighthouse was designed to keep people away not to attract them and If you follow a lighthouse you end up on the rocks. It's only by keeping as far as you can away from the lighthouse that you stay safe, he mused. Admittedly, a lighthouse is a guide but that's another idea altogether.

"Anyway, how's the Dynamic Teen Team Scheme going so far, Cathy?" Howard decided he should try to keep up his end of the conversation. "Taking the world by storm, I expect?"

"Catti. The Ditsies? It's going really, really well, but we're just like, rolling it out at the moment?"

"You're *rolling it out* already! Why are you getting rid of it so soon after the launch and just when it looks so promising? I thought you called it an *innovative new innovatory innovation,* a moment ago?" Howard tried to keep the sarcasm out of his tone but without much success.

"Ha ha – very funny." That laugh again, "So, there are one or two teething problems we need to go over with a fine tooth comb and iron out before it'll fly. For instance, the team we sent to Rio de Janeiro? We know they arrived safely because there's clear CCTV coverage from the luggage carousel and even from the taxi rank a bit later on but we're hoping they'll get back to us in the next week or two or at least like, hook up with the Johnstones."

"They'll be all right with the Johnstones – two safe pairs of hands there."

"Agreed – If they manage to hook up with them. On the other hand, the Johnstones may be a bit *too* safe because at Milton Keynes we reckon they are both a bit too much on the er . . ."

"Traditional side, maybe?" suggested Howard, remembering the two decades of church planting following the loggers far into the Brazilian interior that had made the Johnstones' name before their relocation to an administrative posting in Rio as they wound down towards retirement.

"Yeah, they're a bit boring? *A Favelous Time,* was our name for the Ditsies team but it looks like they've vanished with our ten thousand Brazilian *Reals* in used notes? People in the churches keep sending us these emails and tweets saying, *I hope the Ditsies are having a Favelous Time. Get it? Give us an update, please.* They all say that or something like it. So, we've had to send out a blanket email saying, *Thank you for your message; expect a big announcement soon.* But we're beginning to think this trip might be a write-off. The parents are like, hitting the panic button with the Foreign Office but we're trying to push back and hush it up. Our solicitors tell us we can't get us for being *in locus parentae* because they're all over eighteen, thank goodness."

"The Foreign Office – as bad as that? Well, let's hope they coffee up your *Reals really* quickly," Howard laughed but he knew the joke was feeble. You should have stuck with my suggestion, what with two of them being from Liverpool: *Brazilian Wacks.*

"Not one of your best."

"Did I imagine this or wasn't there another D.T.T.S. team with Ivor Morris out in Thailand? *The Stunning Thais*, wasn't it, that one?" Howard remembered seeing a photo on the website showing Ivor beaming alongside the three members of this team only a week or two back.

"*Was* is dead right on this occasion. Granted, *The Stunning Thais* went really, really well for about a week and a half: it was a really, really good learning opportunity for Ivor. It was meant to drag him kicking and screaming into the twentieth century. But then Ivor got a bit uppity about his great chance of getting, like, shaped by young minds."

"What happened? I saw the photo – it looked like a great team."

"There was a bit of a disagreement. Only with one of them – she's called Sali. So, Sali's put up with it for a whole ten days of being told what to do and so on – fetching and carrying – and then she's turned round and she's *lit a candle in the darkness* and she's *told truth to power* and she's directly accused Ivor of being an embarrassing throwback to a more old-fashioned time and doing things in like, old ways. You know, *Greenbelt* type things, if you can believe that in this day and age. Only *literacy* and *advocacy* and *empowerment* and that!"

Cathy was scoffing at Ivor and Howard found he didn't like that much at all; he liked being expected to join in even less. This Sally sounded a bit above herself. All the same, he feigned horror because he had his eye on a posting at Milton Keynes at some undefined time in the future. "I get the picture – you can't afford to let that kind of situation go on festering. Nip it in the bud. It's terrible really."

"The *Stunners* tried to get him interested in the latest worship songs from Mountain Crest and so on but he was, like, *If Graham Kendrick was good enough for the apostle Paul . . .* He said he couldn't understand why *Amazing Grace* needs a chorus, if you can believe that? *My chains fell off!*"

Howard could hear that Cathy was rolling her eyes so he decided to say something after all, if only out of respect for Ivor.

"Hang on, Cathy, there must be another side to the story. Ivor has been out there for thirty–five years at least and he's been doing a great job with that Phuket orphanage for at least twenty of those! He must have a pretty good idea of what he's doing by now. Wasn't there even talk of giving him a gong – an Empire Medal or an M.B.E. at one point?"

"Exactly? Like I said, he's just a throwback? It's Catti, by the way? *The Empire Medal* – that says it all doesn't it? If you look into it, the Agency wasn't founded back in the 18th century to be, like, paternalistic was it?"

"Nineteenth, actually. And just because you run an orphanage, that doesn't necessarily make you paternalistic, Cathy."

Cathy sighed with exasperation, "Look, Ivor is, like, stuck back in the, like, *Victorian* times with the Tudors and all those and he can't, like, make the leap? There's no, like, agile thinking because his mindset isn't granular enough and there's no like, blue-sky stuff coming out? And there's this, like, glass ceiling thing he's got going on about young empowered women like Sali."

Howard looked down and noticed he'd been doodling on the D.T.T.S. leaflet. Oops, that was a bit unsubtle. Still, there were at least a couple of hundred more of those downstairs in a box hidden by the freezer up in the projection room so he tore this one up meticulously, got up and put half the pieces in the bin by the desk and sauntered through to the kitchen to throw the others in the little red bucket under the sink. The telephone wire would just about stretch that far if he held the phone at arm's length.

"Hang on, I meant Ivor has got solid experience after more than thirty years, is what I meant. *Ivor Morris is Thailand is Ivor Morris is Thailand* as far as the Lighthouse Agency is concerned. We've always said that, ever since I was a kid myself and collecting for the *Ivor's Orphanage Fund* when he was just setting the place up. You're not trying to tell me the Dynamix started telling him how to do his job, are you? This, what is it, *Sally* and the others?"

"*Sali?* Howard, you musn't call them *The Dynamix* any longer – that's all wrong now – that's so last year. *The Ditsies* is what we all say here and what we recommend in the churches now the trustees are on board. Only one of the Ditsies started telling him that – Sali. And Emmi and Darren – Dazz for short – just tagged along. It was an emotional roller-coaster for them but they did amazing."

"It doesn't say much for the others that they didn't intervene – try to defuse the situation."

"Diffuse the situation! They had to blow it wide open and Sali's got what it takes to be a leader. She's going to Oxford next year to study, like, Maths, Law and French? Her uncle is the regional coordinator for the south–east in the Lighthouse Agency (UK) – Norman Fanshaw. Maybe you've heard of him? Her dad's a Sir. That makes her the *Honourable* Sali Fanshaw – how long have you been with the Agency?"

"Ah, she's a Fanshaw, is she? I'm beginning to get the picture. Five years come Easter next year."

"So, Ivor, like, he's totally over–reacted to getting dragged into the light by Sali's stern but compassionate critique. He's literally exploded and I'm not exaggerating if I say their feet literally haven't touched the ground and he's like, bundled them onto a plane in Bangkok and Vicki, she's had to go to Heathrow with the chauffeur and she's whisked them up in Larry the Agency limo, like, a week ago?"

"There's an Agency limo? Since when? That's a first for a South London girl like you, surely?"

"Yes, Streatham – and Larry the limo is quite recent. We sometimes rent him out for weddings on a Saturday and in the week for parties but it's a good look for us to rock up at churches in it so it's not available on, like, Sundays? Anyway, the Ditsies have had some quality time with Cassi in Publicity? Photos, interviews, vids, charity single? And since then they've been, like, chilling here in haitch queue Milton Keynes? They're in the Directors' Suite right now watching Countdown? They're on the PlayStation 3 and ordering in, like, pizzas with all the toppings?"

"Sounds like *I'm a celebrity*. Except they probably want to stay around the place if it's that good."

"We're, like, keeping them here in Milton Keynes for as long as it takes? Suzi's literally having kittens about the financial side of it, though? Donations are barely keeping pace with their lifestyle? We've spent the whole repatriation budget a couple of times over, so things are going to have to change in pretty short order?"

"Cassie is for Cassandra, I suppose – the prophetess of doom? Talking about the repatriation budget, I've heard Ivor is coming home as well. How's he getting on in all this? Is he getting over it and getting ready to go back after a well-earned break?"

"What? It's just Cassi, I think. Cassandra. Is that even a name? Doom. Ivor. Yes, Ivor got the sack? So that's all right? It's all working itself through? S.N.W.F.U. – Situation Not Worrying For Us? Suzi says it's a welcome relaxation in payroll."

"What? You kicked him out?" Howard was aghast. If Ivor Morris could get his cards there was no knowing who was safe any longer.

"He had to go? He kicked himself out really, at the end of the day? He only went and called Sali, like, *a foolish child and a disruptive influence*? Sali! So, Sali wasn't having any of that old–style macho shtick so she's got onto Vicki on Skype that evening in a group call with her uncle Norman – the one who's the regional coordinator – and Vicki's, like, totally agreed Ivor's lost it and she's pulled him out straight away? She's made him agree it's been conduct unbecoming towards a colleague? So it's been, like, totally mutual in the end?"

"I can see the reasoning, but it all seems a bit harsh to me, all the same." Howard didn't dare say that it looked to him as if Ivor had been the victim of an outrageous injustice. You had to try to keep sweet with the Milton Keynes lot, after all.

"Howard! This is people's actual *money* we're talking about? When a worker goes stale like Ivor did it's, like, T.I.N.A. – There Is No Alternative? How to give the sack, like, quickly and cleanly, especially to a colleague in the field is, like, an art? Take yourself: If you show any promise, we'll, like, train you up in it? Even take you along for a sacking or two and show you how to do it? Then let you do it by yourself while we watch and then let you train up others, and so on."

"Is that even ethical?"

"Ethical! What's with the big words? Come on, it's a good laugh? Once, a woman got, like, trained up to sack and she's, like, turned round and sacked the guy who trained her within, like, a year? We roared? He's in Milton Keynes now?"

"What? I'm confused. The one who did the sacking? Working at HQ is she?"

"No, the other one: the man? He's collecting trolleys in Milton Keynes Asda. Myself and Vicki put in a word with the manager who we know? But Trudi is coming to Milton Keynes soon to do some time in HR"

"*Aitch* R!"

"Yes, HR, that's what I said."

"So, you decided to take Sally's word over Ivor's without question? That seems odd."

"At the end of the day, like, we gave her the benefit of the doubt? You can't be too careful with the punters' cash?"

"So, farewell, then, Ivor Morris! Oh well, *Sic transit.*"

"What are you on about now?"

"You know, *Sic transit Gloria mundi*."

"What – is that French? No wonder people think you're a weirdo, Howard?"

"Oh, nothing. *O Tempora!* So, what's going to happen to Ivor when he gets back?" asked Howard with concern.

"Ivor? It's not exactly our problem is it? He's okay, though? Being a single man, Vicki's easily sorted him out with a place In Haringey at the Wood Green end in a, like, hostel? We got him a cheap flight and he gets into Manchester early tomorrow at, like, two twenty-three a.m. in the morning? He can claim his coach and his tube fare back all right? So he'll be alright, alright? He can get his benefits till we can get his, like, farewell tour of the churches sorted out? He's, like, really old – like, 63 so he can draw his Lighthouse Agency pension in, like, I don't know, three years under the new rules? I suppose a few of the older baby boomers would like to see him one last time, what with his magic lantern slides and his *typical day in the life of a missionary* and his *let's all say a greeting in Thai* and his *can you guess what I've got in my bag, boys and girls*? Yawn? I expect we'll name one of the offices after him in the end? That'll please the crusty cheque books as we call them?"

Howard was shocked. Ivor had been a figurehead for the Agency for as long as he could remember, even back as far as the days when there'd be a monthly prayer tape on cassette. It had been an exemplary life of service on the margins, as far as he could see, first as a firebrand for social justice and latterly as an elder statesman. Howard had sat there dreaming month after month as a teenager listening to Ivor.

"How long has Vicky been a man, then?" Howard went on.

"What are you on about now?"

"You said, *Being a single man, Vicky's easily sorted him out etcetera*. Sorry, I mean, *and so on*."

"What?"

"Oh, forget it. Anyway, I'll be off now you've brought me up to speed on Ivor and the Dynamix. Thanks for phoning – I'll see you at Conference next year, Cathy."

"Actually, Howard (it's the Ditsies)."

"Yes, Cathy?" replied Howard with just a touch of foreboding in his voice.

"Catti? We were wondering, actually, Howard. It's about this set of Ditsies, the Stunning Thais?"

"Yes?" There was even more of a quaver of trepidation in Howard's voice now, because Cathy was obviously going to call in a favour of some kind. Maybe she was about to ask him to speak at a rally with these young people in the middle of the summer holidays he was hoping to spend at home in Cardiff with his feet up. Maybe even go to Milton Keynes to tell the staff about France as they yawned and gazed at the clock. In the end it was even worse than that.

"Howard, we were wondering how you'd be fixed for having the former Stunning Thais down with you in Bordeaux for a few months? Sali, Emmi and Dazz? Well, I say a few months! Till July, actually? We'd have to think up a new name for the team, of course."

"Here In Bordeaux? It would have to be *The Bordeaux Whiners*. Speaking hypothetically, of course," Howard added straight away. He had to put her off. He shouldn't have given the impression he had bought into the idea by suggesting a name. "Actually, I'm only really just settling in again after all that trouble over the vote in the church meeting," he stumbled and gabbled, "it was a bit tight – I only survived by one vote, actually – and I can't pretend to have seen off all the opposition just yet. And the work with the homeless is good and everything and it's great publicity for the Agency but it might be a bit too challenging for teenagers, you know. So, maybe in a year or two when things are a bit more stable we could start looking at it. Perhaps."

  Howard suddenly remembered it was a mistake to open up to being in a week position. People remembered it for ever if you admitted to vulnerability, whereas they forgot your successes straight away. "Things are very stable, of course – never more so – but a bit unstable in a stable kind of way, if you see what I mean. Plus, you know, this is Bordeaux and all your French publicity has got the Eiffel Tower on it, so it would be a bit of a downer as far as the Agency's image goes to bring them all the way down here in the sticks, Cathy, when you could probably put them in a more glamorous setting in the capital . . ."

  "Catti? Howard?" Cathy cut in. "I think I ought to tell you straight out – The Ditsies are arriving with you next Friday afternoon. Let's see. At a place called Bordeaux Saint–Jean, at fifteen forty, it says here. Let's see, that's, er, twenty to four p.m. in the afternoon, isn't it? They're travelling first class on something called a TGV – you'll know what that is, I expect. I tell you what, I'll send you their photos on Instagram so's you can, like, pick them out when they get there. Actually, you've given me an idea: *Eiffel on my feet!* How about that for a name? How cool is that?"

"Could you send me the the photos as an attachment in an email, please? I'm not on Instagram."

"Is that some kind of joke? Fair enough, I'll send them over like that if you're still living in, like, the Stone Age with, like, knights in armour and fax machines over there."

"*Eiffel on my feet.* It's neat and all that but, Cathy – now, this is always a bit of a niggle with me – this is Bordeaux not Paris and we have our own culture down here which . . ." The line was dead. Friday at fifteen forty. Howard checked the date on his *Cheeses of Wales* calendar and scribbled the time alongside *Dynamix*, in the relevant box.

2

"So, let me try this again, Boss. It's *Ze Dynamique Ten Tem Scam.*" Pascal was undulating his shoulders, doing that funny thing with his lips and staring with puzzlement at the D.T.T.S. leaflet. "Beach volleyball. Nice."

"Easy, tiger. No, I'm not saying it's a scam, not at all, Pascal, at least not as such, but it is, arguably, little more than a bit of a publicity stunt, in my opinion. It's a *scheme.* There are probably some benefits for the churches back home and for the kids themselves, it's life–changing, maybe, but whether there are any advantages for us here on the ground remains to be seen, really." Howard was still trying to convince himself about the idea of having a team but with little success so far. "They'll arrive expecting some kind of religious revival within the first few days and then when it doesn't happen – and it won't, of course – we'll have to keep them going for the rest of the time as best we can. Whenever Lighthouse Agency workers get together, that's what we all reckon. Off the record, so don't quote me. Now, slowly, say after me: *The Dynamic Teen Team Scheme."*

"No, I give up on that, Boss. *Les Dynamiques* will do just fine." Pascal folded up the leaflet and put it in the back pocket of his greasy jeans for future use. "Look, there's a space over there at the far end of the car park. Near that nice BMW over there, look."

"Yes, very nice."

Revving up, Howard manoeuvred the ancient blue tin snail into a place next to the far wall of the station car park and climbing out, tossed the keys to Pascal who always had better luck with the temperamental door lock than he did himself. Old Cornflower the Citroen 2CV had served him well, at least since the back door had been replaced. It was only a red one from the scrapyard, but the whole car had been resprayed at least once in the distant past, so this detail looked like an intentional raffish touch – or so Howard reasoned to himself.

After a few moments fiddling with the lock, the pair made for the station concourse and in the end had less than five minutes to spare before the Paris train came in. Howard had been humming *Hotel California* to himself all morning and now realised why, as he found himself singing aloud but under his breath, *And I was thinking to myself, this could be heaven or this could be hell.* He nervously scanned the sheet of photos one more time and noted Darren, Sally and Emma lounging in Milton Keynes; Darren and Emma lying on a beach in Phuket with Sally and standing on a platform in Westminster Central Hall, singing something to Sally's guitar accompaniment.

"Let me see the pictures again, Boss," said Pascal, undulating still more. Howard handed them over. "Emma,

Darren, Sally. Emma, Darren, Sally. I don't fancy yours much. What do you know about them?"

"Next to nothing apart from the incident with Ivor Morris in Thailand I told you about. I found out they've all got 'A' Level French, so that's a start, I suppose – for instance, if I need any easy translation from French to English done." Howard checked his watch against the indicator board. "Bum! There's almost time for a coffee but not quite – let's go and sit over there, then. No, there's not even time for that now." He looked down the line and far away in the distance saw a glimmering light as the TGV approached.

"I've got the flask with me, Boss," said Pascal reaching into a ragged *Carrefour* bag for life.

"Hey, that's *my* flask you've got there."

"*And* it's your coffee but you're not complaining, are you, Boss? There's only one cup but you can have that and I can swig it out of this."

"Pig. Pour mine out first, then."

"Fancy one of these fig rolls, Boss?"

"Those are my fig rolls! No wonder I've never got any . . ."

"Hey, look, it's drawing in." Pascal wiped his mouth with the sleeve of his sweatshirt then sucked at the residue. "So, what are we going to find to do with them, Boss?"

Howard had been asking himself the same question ten times a day – it was sometimes difficult to fill his own days let alone have to invent activities to entertain teenagers eager for novelty and instant results. "In the long term, I don't know. Help with Paquito and the other homeless people, I suppose. A bit of leafleting, maybe. Beach volleyball. Some drama, street theatre, a bit of music, who knows? But first up, put the bags and stuff in the Roxy. Then do a quick tour of Bordeaux in Cornflower and then the champagne reception at Heseltine's this evening, then kip down. To be honest, I can't wait for that last bit."

"There's a champagne reception? *Quelle horreur!*" Pascal did his full–on Heseltine impression but it wasn't very convincing.

"Not really. The Heseltines are putting on a bash but it'll be low key, I expect. Just us, the Dynamix, Daniel and Suzon – and Véronique, of course, if they can coax her out of hiding from up in the dark tower. You'd think she'd be half sick of shadows, wouldn't you?"

"No, you've lost me there. Remind me why you call Daniel de Moulinet *Heseltine*, Boss?"

"It's just a British thing – most people over there would recognise the reference and draw their own conclusions. It's partly a political thing: born to rule, lordly bearing and all that – but it's mainly the faded blonde hair with the widow's peak and the blue blazer, brass buttons. No? Oh, forgot it – it's just something that keeps me going."

"He's like Sarkozy, is he?"

"Much taller."

The train was on time and a few moments later the concourse was teeming with passengers and rides. Howard wandered round, then, suddenly, in the crowd, he saw her. He had never been so sure of a nickname in all his years of practice. Sally, dumpy and vivacious, dull blonde and red–

cheeked in a check shirt and jeans, laden down with no luggage and striding ahead of the panting Emma and Darren who were bowed down heavily, was beyond a shadow of a doubt, Bunty.

Howard made himself known and was rubbing his damp hands together. "Well, gather round, you three. Welcome to Bordeaux, Dynamix. Let me introduce ourselves, myself. Let us introduce ourselves: I'm Howard Morgan, the leader of the church here and this is my member, Pascal." Pascal undulated gently as he went to shake hands with Darren who gave a guffaw of shock. Emma drew back behind Darren as Pascal closed in for the *bise,* leering at her even though she wasn't much to look at really. She was dressed just like Sally but was mousy and retiring with no vivacity to speak of.

"We're actually called the Ditsies, not the Dynamix, Howard," Bunty was wagging a stern index finger, "Everyone enrolled in the scheme is a Ditsy and *Eiffel on my feet* is the name of this team in particular. You see, it's a question of corporate identity and *Eiffel on my feet* is a stroke of genius and I jolly well told Catti so. I thought Vicki, Catti and Susi made all those PR matters quite clear to you the other day – I did ask them to. Cassi's quite categorical – it says Ditsies on the front of everything the Lighthouse Agency produces at the moment and the money comes rolling in on the back of it, you see. We need to be consistent with the brand."

"Okay, thanks, er, Sally, quite so. You are Darren – welcome, Darren – so you by a process of elimination – ha ha – must be Emma."

"I'm vegan."

"So it's true what they say?"

"What do you mean?"

"Nothing." Howard smiled to himself. "Well, listen, er, you guys, I thought I'd take an hour or so to drive you round the city before you get settled into the Roxy. Show you the sights of Bordeaux – the Cathedral, the *Pey Beyland* Tower, the *Quinconces* as the trees turn, all that. The *Quinconces* is one of the biggest city squares in Europe – a terrific sight at this time of year. It's a great place, Bordeaux – very atmospheric in autumn. You fell on your feet . . . if you like. Then we have a bit of a do tonight, nothing fancy but it's in a nice setting in a church member's *chateau* out in the vines. Daniel and Suzon de Moulinet and their daughter Véronique."

"Oh, Howard", Bunty scolded, "there's no need for any of that. You see I know Bordeaux very well indeed, as it happens," said Bunty with what sounded to Howard like scorn. "I can set the others right on foot later on – maybe I'll get round to it in the morning. It would be good for Emmi and Dazz to see a street market, for instance and there are none of those at this time of the afternoon, you see. It's their first time in France and they didn't dare go out when we were in Paris so I do so want their first impressions to be positive."

"What? I don't quite understand how you can, can have . . ."

"I know – if a man or a woman is tired of Paris, he or she is tired of life as Montaigne might have put it."

"No, I mean I can't see how you can show them round Bordeaux." Howard was stumped. "You've only just arrived and this is my turf. This is my manor."

"It's like this, you see: Daddy's a vintner. You'll have heard of Fanshaw's." Bunty looked Howard up and down. "Maybe not you, but people have heard of Fanshaw's in some higher circles than those in which you move. So, Bordeaux is the main place for Daddy, this and Burgundy, oh, and the Beaujolais of course, so I've spent almost as long over here as in my school at Brabourne Acres as a matter of fact, certainly during the hols. And as for staying at the *Eglise Evangélique de Bordeaux Centre*, that really is a *no* from me. I've seen it if only from the outside but I can tell at a glance it's the most awful dive – a real fleapit. It'll be fine for these two, of course." Bunty indicated a cowering Emma and Darren who gave a guffaw.

"Where do you intend to stay then, Sally?" Howard took a step forward. "A hotel? Sorry, an hotel? What do you think this is – some kind of free holiday or something?"

"It's like this, you see: Daddy knows Daniel de Moulinet really well from what he does in the wine trade and so I shall be staying up at the *chateau* with him and Suzon, you see. Come along, all of you – I've a lot to do before this evening's entertainment."

They had arrived in the car park by this time, following a striding Bunty. This was an unexpected dynamic altogether and Howard was at a loss but he decided to be conciliatory at this early stage and managed to stumble out, "That's all fair enough, I suppose, um, Sally, isn't it? So shall I just run you up to the *chateau de Moulinet* after I've shown Darren and Emma here around the Roxy? Would that be all right by you, Sally?"

"Actually, there's no need, Howard. You see, Daddy's been kind enough to arrange some wheels for me – I got the keys in the post the day before yesterday from Daniel and Suzon before we set out from Milton Keynes." Bunty looked around for a few moments before indicating a brand new BMW i8 Roadster in black, parked up and gleaming. "There she is – come to mama, you proud beauty."

"They bought you that? But it must be worth about . . ."

". . . 124 000 euros plus VAT," said Pascal."

"Don't be foolish, Howard: it's only a lease vehicle, for goodness sake."

Clicking her fingers, Sally grabbed her suitcase from Darren and a matching Armani shoulder bag from Emma, trotted over to the BM, porky legs pumping, stowed the luggage, climbed in, adjusted the mirrors, gunned the motor and zoomed off with a cheery wave. "Toodle pip. See you later, Ditsies."

"Nice," said Pascal. "The car, I mean."

"So, Darren and Emma, how was Thailand? No, don't answer that. Just climb in here and we *will* have a drive around after all." Howard was defiant and beckoned the Dynamix towards Cornflower. "Pascal, you jump in the back with Darren. It's good really that Bun . . . that Sally's got her own transport: this thing is a bit cramped with five up and the luggage – all those guitars and so on. Hold tight, everyone: it's a very unusual ride – very up and down, more like a boat or a hovercraft, really."

3

"And, finally, this is the Roxy Christian Centre, 36 to 40, *Rue Jean Jaurès*. The *Eglise Evangélique de Bordeaux Centre* the de Moulinets will insist on calling it but I'm holding out for *the Roxy* for obvious reasons." Howard drew up in front of a dilapidated art deco building in dirty plaster which Howard indicated with a proud, proprietorial gesture. "The big X in the neon sign was my idea. As you can see, it's a converted cinema – it was built in the 30s as far as we can gather, when this was quite an upmarket part of the city. Then for a while in the sixties it was an art–house place and then, um, another kind of pictures."

"What's that smell?" asked Emma, holding her nose.

Howard sniffed the air. "Cabbage, I think but there's a bit of coffee in there, too. Yes, the area's a bit run–down these days, as you can see, but it does come to life at the weekends – in the evenings mainly, well, at night, really – and they say it could be up and coming some day given a fair wind from Madame de Pigalette and the City Council. I normally put those oil drums over there to save the parking space but the customers at the *Aigle d'Argent* over there tend to move them –

again, at the weekends mainly." There was dance music pounding from the *Aigle,* a bar almost directly opposite. "It's all just getting going, see?" Howard made a few robotic movements but the others didn't laugh. "Do the honours, will you, Pascal?"

"Sure thing, Boss. Heave them onto the pavement, yeah?"

"Yeah, go on. Watch out for that bloke on the carboard, though. Don't want to wake him up or he'll be sponging on us like a shot. Oh, it's only Paulo."

"Mr. Morgan, are we, like, living *here?* Sally's going to be living in a *chateau* and we're staying, like, here?" Emma was trembling and pouting on the edge of tears.

"Call me Howard. Well, Emma, I have to live here, so it's not too . . ."

"It's just, like, it's so dark and dingy? It's, like, only a back street? I was hoping for something a bit more like, I'm searching for like, the right word? Got it: like, nice?"

"Oh, don't *you* start."

"What?"

"Nothing." Howard decided to leave his rant about grammar for another occasion. "I was Just talking to the car. Cornflower sometimes starts up all by herself. Down, Cornflower – have a nice rest, there's a good car. So, what do *you* reckon to the Roxy, Darren? Isn't it just what the doctor ordered?"

Apart from a sniff and a stifled guffaw, Darren remained silent, for Darren was sitting on his case in tears, gently weeping. Without a word, he got up and gathered his things together and all five went in through the double glass doors into the foyer.

"Now then, here's the cash desk, but there's not much use for that in our operation. An older chap called Paquito sleeps behind there whenever he decides to stay overnight in the Roxy. We allow that." Howard indicated a sleeping bag and some blankets piled up with a half–empty bottle of cheap red wine beside them. "So, just tiptoe past until you're sure he's out. Along here – toilets on the right: Gents, Ladies. Along here is where the two, never known what to call them, cinemas, auditoriums? You can't very well call them screens because the screens are things you project films onto, aren't they?"

"Films?" Emma was puzzled.

"Sorry, *movies* you probably call them. Here's where they are, anyway – the rooms, the auditoria. On the left is the one we use as the church and for the homeless stuff. It's a bit smaller because it's only, like, a small church? Sorry, it's a bit smaller because it's only a small church, you see." Howard didn't correct himself this time even though he made a mental note not to take on Sally's verbal mannerisms. "The smaller one is *Salle Deux* so logically the bigger one is *Salle Une.*"

Howard pointed upwards to a steel door flush with the wall about two and a half metres up. "There's the projection room in the middle but you need this steel ladder hanging here to get up in there. We don't bother much with it except when we show a . . . *movie,* and except for the freezer in there for the homeless breakfast because there are some, er, *unsuitable* films in there in canisters and some old creationist stuff dubbed into French by Americans – hilarious. If by any chance you do go in there, make sure you don't look at one film called *A School for Scandal* because it's full–on right from the start. It's by far the worst of the lot. I've been told. We can just take a peep in there: here's the key, hidden under this corner of the carpet, see? There's only this one, so don't lose it or run off with it. Come on, climb up after me.."

"What kind of movies do you show?" asked Emma, showing some interest at last, "not *School for Scandal* and that?"

"What films do we show? We've tried to run a cinema club but it didn't really take off so we just show one of the Christian classics maybe quarterly and it so happens that we've got *The Biding Place* a week tomorrow. I've got to get the publicity sorted but to be honest we haven't got huge expectations. It's very niche but at least the local people know it's still a functioning cinema as well as everything else we do."

Howard opened the door to reveal a dusty lumber room with two archaic projectors bolted to the floor, shelves of canisters filling one wall and a chest freezer. After allowing the Dynamix to climb in and glance round, Howard sent the others back down the ladder, locked the door behind him, replaced the key and led the way into the larger of the two rooms, *Salle Une*.

"Now, Emma, this is where you'll be sleeping, in this bigger room. We hardly ever use this one except for the odd concert. We've taken a couple of rows of seats out here near the back for you. I'm afraid your bed's on a bit of a slope but you'll soon get used to that and you can decide which side you want to lean on. Or straight down, of course. Or straight up." Emma slammed her bags and guitar down. "That's the way, put your stuff down there. The lights are here – all or nothing, unfortunately, but we can easily rig up a table lamp or something later." Now Emma was crying too. "Yes, I know it's moving to have all this space to yourself, Emma but you can really put your stamp on all this. I'll just let you settle in and then we'll make a move for the *chateau*. Come on, let's go upstairs, Darren. That's where I live in the flat and, Darren, you'll be with me. Darren? Darren?"

"I'm afraid he's in the bog at the moment, Boss. Shall I get him out of there? Or you can do it and I'll stay in here with Emma."

Howard noticed Emma shrink back. "No, I'll go, Pascal. You take his things up to the flat, will you? And keep still, for goodness sake – I think you're making them more nervous than they would be otherwise. Put them on the other bed – the one furthest from the window."

Howard pushed open the Gents toilet door halfway along the corridor and closed it behind him without making a sound. There was a tremulous voice issuing from the farthest cubicle.

"I can't, Catti. It's, like, terrible, it's, like, horrible . . . No, Bordeaux itself is all right . . . Very old . . . Yes, but it's, like, the red light district here . . . yes, and there are these drunks lying round and he lets them in . . . I know . . . I know . . . I can see that, but Sally's different . . . She can speak it . . . I know I've got 'A' level but, apart from a movie we did called *L'Haine* . . . Yes, sorry, I forgot, a movie we did called *La Haine,* it was mainly, like, literature? You know . . . literature: Books? *Tartoof* by *Molliair* and *Volltair's Condeed* and *Lettr der mo moular* by *Alfred*

Doughday . . ." From time to time Darren did a kind of guffaw as he choked back a sob. "Sally? Well, she bosses us round, Catti . . . No, it's much worse than Thailand . . . Well, she, like, tells us what to do . . . We have to do things for her like carry her things and things . . . And she says people, like, keep on thinking she's French . . . Senior? What do you mean, *senior*? I can't . . . Well, I suppose . . . Howard? I don't, like, know if . . . Ivor? No! He's got this creepy man with him . . . Pascal . . . He's got these dirty clothes on and he keeps moving his shoulders and doing this funny thing with his mouth . . . No, there's no sound but if there was it'd be, like, *Mwa, Mwa* . . . Pascal . . . What do you mean, *pascal lamb?* I don't know what you're . . . *bare my claws?* I don't . . . Oh, *bear my cross . . .*"

Howard decided to leave Darren to it, crept out again and followed Pascal up the open stairs through the door with a no entry sign and marked *Sans Issue* that led to his flat. Halfway up, he stopped short. "This is madness, Pascal. I've got to give them one of my full–on pep talks – you know, sit them down. I'll try the Brian Blair thing and . . ."

"The Brian Blair thing, Boss – what's that?"

"You know. The sincerity thing. *I hate what I'm saying; I hate having to say it but I'm having to say it anyway even though I hate having to say it.* That. Come on, let's get them both in *Salle Deux* and I can have a go at least before we set out for the Heseltines' place."

Together, they strode along the corridor. Howard banged on the toilet door and yelled, "Darren, two minutes, along here on the left, *Salle Deux.*" Then he tapped the door of

Salle Une, put his head round and called out, "Emma, we're about to have a team meeting across the way, please."

There was still a stale smell of cigarettes from that day's homeless breakfast as they pushed through the doors into *Salle Deux* so Howard opened the emergency door at the far end, letting in a gust of aggressive music from the *Aigle d'Argent.* He went over to the piano and played a phrase of *Smoke gets in your eyes* with one finger. He switched to *These foolish things* then moved aside the conductor's music stand he used as a pulpit on Sunday mornings as Emma and Darren slunk in. Howard stood up straight and Pascal slouched at his side, undulating.

"Come on, Dynamix, front row. This is where it all happens – this is the nerve centre. We have our services in here and this is where the homeless people have their breakfast, so we'll be spending quite a lot of time in *Salle Deux* one way or another. Are we engaged in a mighty work for the Lord of Hosts? We are. Do we expect hardship? We do. Do we expect to be misunderstood and spurned? We do. Are there rewards out of all proportion to our feeble efforts? There are. Will you join me in this great enterprise? You will. Let us move forward. Together." It wasn't one of Howard's best efforts because he still felt doubtful himself. "Now, before I go on, I expect you'll have some questions? Yes, I'll take yours first, Emma."

"Why does that man keep, like, *looking* at me?" blurted out Emma, pointing at Pascal. "Has he even got a D.R.S. check?"

"I'm afraid there's no such thing here, Emma, although we do have the Ministry of Culture and Sport and also the

Renseignements Generaux – the R.G. – and they both keep a close eye on us. I tell you, once I asked a woman who'd been coming for about two months if she wanted to become a church member. She said she couldn't but I'd understand why not some day. Very enigmatic it was. It turned out she was a spy from the R.G. Actually, it's called something else now. But they're efficient, so dodgy characters are virtually unknown in French churches." Howard laughed at the very idea. "Next."

Darren went on, "Will we have to speak any French tonight?"

"Yes. Next"

"It's just, every time we say anything, Sali puts it right straight away and in Paris we went out just the once for a coffee and she said I sound like a drunken Belgian toddler from the eighteenth century. She told me to shut up because I was embarrassing her. I haven't said anything since then."

Emma added, "But she keeps on telling *me* to, like, speak more? But when I do, she just laughs?"

"That wasn't a problem in Thailand was it? Just try to interact with Sally on the same basis that you did there. You'll soon get better anyway because I expect you already know a lot of grammar from 'A' level. Oh, sorry, I forgot – back in the day we had to learn all about verbs and clauses . . . "

"Actually, it *was* a problem even in Thailand," Emma cut in, "Sali had . . . "

"Enough. It's *Sally*."

"Oh, all right. *Sally* had, like, a pen–pal? Like in . . ."

"Emma, stop, Emma. Try to stop saying *like* all the time, please. And before you go any further, make firm statements.

Don't ask questions all the time. They won't let you get away with that when you get to Uni. Oh, actually, these days I suppose even the younger lecturers coming up through the system have a tendency to . . ."

"Right, so Sally had a pen pal in Thailand for years and years when she was in what she called prep school – that's a kind of junior school for posh people, I think – and as a family they sponsored some children from over there who visited them a few times as well and on top of all that she had a gap year in Thailand between this prep school thing and this other place Brabourne Acres she keeps going on about."

"Yes," Darren guffawed, "She's, like, a year younger than us but she's been, like, everywhere, done everything? Speaks, like, all the languages? Did, like, 'A' levels really early?"

"Well, I feel your pain," Howard went on brightly, "I hear what you're saying, but do try to see this as a great opportunity to start catching up with her. It's a funny thing, life," laughed Howard lightly, "but the advantages of a privileged upbringing and a private school education tend to vanish as you get older. It becomes a level playing field where we can all compete equally. No, scrub that. It's like this: people like the Honourable Sally Fanshaw get what they want and the rest of us just need to make the best of it and try to get some of the scraps as they fall from the top table. It can still be worthwhile going on living even if those people do get all the finer things in life right off the bat. Another question?"

"Have we got to go out tonight? Won't it wait till tomorrow sometime? After all, Sali said earlier on . . ."

"You're going to have a great time, Darren. Stand up straight, walk in confidently, take a glass of champagne from the butler in full livery and settle down on the *chaise longue* for a game of Charades before moving to the dining suite where you will be careful to choose the correct cutlery for each course." Emma flinched and Darren gave a guffaw. "That was a joke. It'll be relaxed: just have a nice drink, a whisky or something, settle down and enjoy the setting."

"Neither of us drink, Howard."

"Neither of us *drinks*, Emma."

"That's a coincidence, neither do we." Emma gestured at Pascal. "I thought he smelled a bit of . . ."

"No, *we* drink. After all, *when in Rome.* You shouldn't turn down people's hospitality in France and that's often expressed in the offer of a drink – a bit like a nice cup of tea with us. But okay, in this case just say, *Limonade* if you must. You'll be a vegetarian, Darren, I expect?" Darren nodded. "I thought so. That can be a problem in France, too."

"I'm vegan," pointed out Emma.

"You did say. But whatever you do, don't forget to say, *merci* and don't forget to say, *s'il vous plaît* or actually just, *s'il vous plait* without the circumflex accent is fine nowadays because they're dumbing down over here as well as much as they dare. As for me, I'm wedded to the circumflex until my last breath, I'm afraid. So, *Limonade, s'il vous plaît, Monsieur.* And give it *Monsieur* and *Madame* as much as you think you can get away with without looking like you're taking the . . . making fun of them. And don't let Bunt . . . er, don't let Sally intimidate you. Why! She's going to be just as nervous as you are deep down."

"She's not," said Emma.

"Circumflex accent?" put in Darren.

"Little hat over the letter. No, I suppose Sally won't be nervous," Howard agreed. "Time, Pascal?"

"Seven fifteen, Boss."

"Right, we're off. Exactly twenty minutes it is – door to door."

It was already dark by the time Pascal had moved the oil drums back into the road, jumped in and rubbed his hands clean on the back seat where he was with Emma. In the mirror Howard saw Emma shrink away so he got Darren to change places with Pascal although there was some complaining from Darren about having to sit on the oil stains. The faithful Cornflower fired up on only the third attempt so Howard was relieved that there was no need to use the starting handle, at least this time.

4

By the time they had finished negotiating the narrow city streets and the boulevard and reached the ring road, Howard decided it was time to get to know the Dynamix a little better – they had driven in silence so far – so he glanced over his shoulder and switched on what he thought of as his most charming manner.

"This is the life! That's the turn-off for the airport just there and ours is the next but one. Now, there wasn't all that much info about you two from the Lighthouse Agency, in fact none apart from the photos – all the documentation must have got left back in Thailand – so, where is it you come from exactly? Why don't you start, Emma?"

"Like, Preston? Sorry, Preston."

"Oh, yes. I've never been there but I'm told it's very . . . well, I've heard of it because of, because of, Tom Finney. You know, he was a footballer from the olden days. And the bus station. Tell me, do you have any brothers and sisters at all?'

"One."

"Oh, yes? Is it a sister?"

"A brother."

"A brother – do you know, that's wonderful! It's nice to have siblings, isn't it? You learn a bit of give and take as you rub along together, as it were. No airs and graces in family life."

"No."

"Preston!" Howard continued, "yes, you know I felt sure I could detect a bit of a Freddie Flintoff accent going on there in the background. I've just remembered he's from up there, isn't he? A fine wicketkeeper – one of the best since, er, since records began."

"Yes."

"So, tell me, Emma, have you moved around a bit, or have you lived in Preston all your life?"

"Yes."

"All your life? All your life! I expect you'll have seen quite a lot of changes there in all that time?"

"Yes."

A long silence ensued as Howard turned off the ring road onto the *Route Nationale*. The plane trees flanking the road on either side whipped slowly by at a resolutely moderate speed as Cornflower plunged up and down along her length. Howard even managed to get the car into top gear although every vehicle that came up behind chose to overtake almost straight away and sometimes unwisely. Howard began to think of the dozens of times he had taken this road, sometimes in hope of a word of encouragement from Daniel – an acceptance of what he was trying to do – and more often in fear of a blazing row. He wondered what the outcome of this latest trip would be. He flushed and grasped the outsize steering wheel still harder as he remembered the time he'd driven this road on a rainy night to try and placate Charlotte, the niece from Paris. In many ways that evening had cemented Heseltine's opposition. Howard had been played for a fool by Charlotte that night, for sure.

"So, I understand you're going on to Uni, Emma? That'll give you a chance to spread your wings a bit after this, I expect won't it? Where are you going, exactly?"

"Preston."

"Oh yes? Well, it can be quite a bit cheaper staying at home than going away. Less of a wrench, too, sometimes."

"Yes."

"So, What subject are you going to be doing?"

"Media Studies, I'm doing."

"That'll be interesting. You're doing Media Studies, eh? What is it that attracted you to that course in particular?"

"I don't know, really. Lots of things."

There was another long silence as Cornflower trundled along the *Cantonale* at a steady forty and still with a regular rise and fall. There was no other traffic now as they headed into the vines. Howard could make allowances for the fact that the Dynamix were getting wound up about meeting the de Moulinets but all the same he felt they could make more of an effort so after a minute or two chatting with Pascal he decided to try to break the ice again.

"I'm from Cardiff myself," said Howard. "Splott," he added, laughing. "Some people say *Splo* for a joke, you know, like *Ponge*. Oh, yes, *Splo,* they say, some people."

Cornflower sped steadily along through a series of featureless villages. All the shutters were already closed. Somewhere in the distance, a dog barked. Somewhere even further in the distance, another dog barked.

"So, how about you, Darren? What subject are you going to be doing? When you get to Uni, I mean."

"Media studies."

"Media Studies? Well, well, that's quite a coincidence. It's good, though: you'll be able to have a lot of interesting conversations with Emma about that, won't you? You'll both be able to have a think about the French media for your dissertation, I expect. I've got a telly in the flat and you'll find the wylus is very interesting here with lots of interesting . . . wylus programmes."

"Yes."

"You noticed I said *wylus* then, I expect."

"Yes."

"I expect you'll be wondering why?"

"Kind of."

"Well, I'll tell you: It's from a classified ad for a car I saw once in Cardiff. *All mod cons: sat nav, sun roof, wylus.* Well, I laughed. And are you going to be living at home when you start Uni, Darren? It can be quite a lot cheaper than going away, you know. Going away can be a bit of a . . . a bit of a wrench, sometimes. To go away."

"Yes."

"And where is that again?"

"Nottingham."

"That's a great University! D.H. Lawrence and, er, D.H. Lawrence. It's got a great reputation, has Nottingham. I had a friend who went to Nottingham University. We lost touch."

"Nottingham Trent."

"Oh yes? Still, all the same. I expect you've seen quite a lot of changes in Nottingham over the years, haven't you – if you've been living there all your life, that is?"

"Yes."

"I thought I detected a hint of a Jake Bugg accent going on there in the background. He's from Nottingham, isn't he? A great actor! The way you say, for instance, *yes*."

"Yes."

"Sisters? Brothers?"

"A Sister."

"A sister – that's great! It's nice to have siblings, I think. After all, you're bound to learn a bit of give and take like that as you rub along together. As it were. No airs and graces in family life. So, you're originally from Nottingham?

"Yes."

"Cardiff, I'm from. Splott. *Splo*, some people say. You know, as a joke."

Howard decided to give up but by this time they were already quite a way along the rutted road between the vines leading to the *chateau de Moulinet* so Howard got Pascal to put down the flask he'd been drinking from, lean over into the boot and pick out one of the cheap boxes of Aldi chocolates he bought by the half dozen and kept in there for dinner invitations, because he invariably forgot the flowers until it was just too late. Soon, the headlights picked out first some terracotta statuary of Bacchus and his pards flanking the entrance gates, then some barns and other outbuildings and at last the courtyard and horseshoe staircase leading to the main doors of the de Moulinet Residence, resplendent in its Second Empire finery. Most of the shutters hadn't been closed yet, so dripping chandeliers could be seen in a number of windows, including the one in the turreted tower in the east wing that was Véronique's sanctuary from a bewildering world.

"Right, I'll lead the way," said Howard cheerily as he bounded up the steps and leaned into the the bell push. "Now, whatever you do, follow close and don't forget, there's nothing to be afraid of: they're just very rich and refined people with a large and successful wine business, an extensive property portfolio, many of the finest artworks, a taste for gourmet cuisine and huge influence in the French arm of the Lighthouse Agency. They're simple souls – you'll just have to take them as you find them."

"Oh, hello, it's *you lot.* You'd better come in, then." Howard was surprised that it was Bunty who answered the door in an ankle length cerise silk dressing gown. "I was just getting an hour or two of piano practice done."

"Piano?"

"Yes, you see, I've been awarded an organ scholarship and a few other minor musical bursaries so I want to get my F.R.S.M. out of the way before I go up to Balliol for Michaelmas."

"What's Michaelmas? What's the F.R.S.M?"

"Oh, Howard! In no particular order, F.R.S.M. is Fellow of the Royal School of Music. It's the highest diploma of the

Associated Board of the Royal School of Music and I mean to keep my record of distinctions and medals at every grade and in the other two diplomas if I have anything to do with it. This is an ideal situation, you see: it's so unusual to come across both a Bösendorfer 290 Imperial *and* a Fazioli F308 in a private home and in a suitable acoustic environment. Of course, the banqueting hall can seat two hundred comfortably, you see. Moving on, *Michaelmas* is what people like us at Oxford call what people like you probably call *the autumn term*. Hilary and Trinity, the others are."

"Hillary – named after the climber, is it? Bosomdorfer and Fascioli – these are Pianos, then, are they? Good ones, are they?" Howard failed to keep a truculent note out of his voice.

"Hilary of Poitiers. A Saint . . ."

"What did she . . ."

"A man. These are only the best pianos in the world – personally, I rate them even above all but the very best Steinways although there's a consistency in those that one simply has to admire. Mummy and Daddy have a matched pair of Bechsteins in Weybridge but I feel they lack warmth and require careful handling, especially in the Romantics. I'm always nagging our technician to calm down the hammers. You see, they only really come into their own for Ravel and Messiaen, in my opinion." Howard was surprised by a rare touch of humility. "In our Dijon place we have to make do with two horrid Yamaha uprights but the less said about them the better. One of them is even brown! Such vulgar, vulgar beasts. Brabourne Acres has many fine pianos, too, of course."

"Véronique really fell on her feet when she came here, then."

"Oh, she did! I simply *love* Véronique; she's such a dear and a very talented musician – for a French person! We've just now been playing through the Wieniawski *Fantasia* Opus 42 while her mum and dad have been getting ready. Do you know it?"

"Not offhand, no, although I might recognise if I heard it."

"Somehow, I doubt it. What are your own tastes in music, Howard?"

"Very eclectic," replied Howard.

"Somewhat varied, too, I expect," Bunty scoffed. "Where are the others? Oh, I see you've brought *him*," Bunty gestured towards Pascal who was now by Howard's side, undulating. "You might have made him change out of those dreadfully ragged duds. Is that oil on his sweatshirt, for goodness sake? Just think of the fine silks and the rare upholstery in here."

"Yes, it's oil and coffee mainly. Emma and Darren are down there in the shadows. Come on up, Dynamix."

"We call them *the Ditsies*, Howard. This is a final warning before I get onto Catti to give you a stiff wigging. I say, come and meet these English people, Véro," Bunty shouted inside, "they're a little on the shy side, like yourself, but they mean well and they'll have their uses, I'll warrant. You'll find the way they speak rather quaint and very amusing. Howard and this other dreadful fellow you know, of course, from church," called out Bunty in perfect, idiomatic, unaccented French. Véronique crept nervously into view and she and

Howard exchanged the *bise*. Véronique had to stoop quite a bit for that even though Howard wasn't all that short.

"How are you? It'll be nice for you to have someone to play piano duets with to a high standard, Véro."

"Oh honestly, Howard," Bunty was scolding again, "Do stop patronising her."

"Patronising, me? I hate Britain!" Howard said lightly, remembering something one of his school friends had said and that he had been using ever since.

"What a feeble play on words. What's more, they are not *piano duets* as you call them. You see, with a few honourable exceptions – Schubert's *Wanderer* is an obvious example you may have come across, and the Debussy, of course – *piano duets* are uncomplicated domestic works for four unsophisticated hands at one modest piano. We, on the other hand, play masterworks of the two piano repertoire. This is why *everyone* needs two fine concert grand pianos side by side, you see."

"I haven't got any pianos at all, not here, not at home, not anywhere."

"Somehow, that doesn't surprise me."

"Except the one at the Roxy Centre."

"The one at the *Eglise Evangélique de Bordeaux Centre*? Now that's a boneshaker honkytonk and make no mistake, or so I've been told by Véronique and she's not given to being critical at all, as you know. Come on, you lot, cook has decided to push the boat out with devilled kidneys on toast as it's only an *apéro dinatoire* rather than a dinner engagement as such. There's a walnut salad with sherry vinaigrette too. Divine."

Darren started to say, "I'm veggie . . ." but Bunty was already far ahead and bustling through the hallway into the more intimate dining area.

"Come on, you lot, through here. Uncle Daniel and Auntie Suzon, allow me to present Emmi and Dazz. They're the other two Ditsies. Pascal and Howard you'll know already."

"*Quelle horreur!* I meant that for *those two*, the so-called minister and his sidekick," roared Heseltine, tossing back his greying blond mane and shooting out his cuffs. "Of course, I'm delighted to meet you, Emmi as a friend of Sally's and, what was your name again, young man?"

"*Limonade, s'il vous plait, Monsieur,*" Darren blurted out.

"I'm vegan," put in Emma.

"Typical!" Bunty tossed her head. "It's Dazz, Uncle Daniel: short for Darren, you see. I'm afraid they don't really speak French yet but I'm working on getting their inarticulate grunts into some kind of structure. They did do our 'A' level which is a bit like the *baccalaureat* but less searching, certainly less wide-ranging – altogether less stringent. They only got a B grade, too – decidedly mediocre – while I, on the other hand, managed to get the Bloundell prize for languages while still in the fifth at Brabourne Acres. My *Phèdre* was written up in the Guardian by Michael Billington, partly – but only partly as he made clear in the course of an extensive review – as a favour to Mummy. I feel every school should do a French play. My Hippolyte is in RADA making waves and doing a little stand-up and panel games on Radio 4 to get some pin money to spend in Edinburgh."

Suzon glided forward. "May I take your coats? Please sit down and I'll bring you all a glass of punch. With or without alcohol?"

Pascal jumped forward, "With! With!"

"Of course, Pascal," Suzon laughed with genuine warmth, "I expected nothing less! A large one. For you the same, I think, Monsieur Morgan? And for the others?"

Howard explained what was going on to the Dynamix and some consultation and dithering went on. "That'll be two without, please, Suzon."

"A pleasure. Make yourselves at home, please do."

"Morgan, there's something pretty important I need to discuss with you urgently," barked Heseltine, looming menacingly over the settee where Howard was sitting.

"Maybe later, after dinner, darling? In fact, I'm sure it'll wait until after the service on Sunday morning," purred Suzon. "What a lovely jacket, Emma."

"Thank you, it's *George*. You know, Asda?"

"Oh, all right! All right! *Quelle horreur.* Anyway, you'd all better make yourselves at home. You'll find we're pretty relaxed here." Heseltine handed a tartan blanket to Pascal. "Sit on this."

"Darren," whispered Howard, "we've got kidneys on toast and you'll eat the lot or I'll serve them up at every meal until you go home."

"I can't," Darren guffawed.

"I'll have a stab at Darren's kidneys, Boss," Pascal whispered, "I'll cause a diversion and you can swap the plates round."

"Er, I'm vegan, Howard," said Emma.

"Two diversions, please, Pascal," said Howard.

"Three plates of kidneys? Bliss!"

"Actually, three diversions, Pascal: you can have mine. I'm feeling a bit off colour tonight," said Howard, sipping at his punch.

*

A little later on, the conversation around the table seemed to be going quite well so Howard had asked to be excused and was wandering around the *chateau*. In spite of Heseltine's implacability towards him, he still had the right to drop in unannounced whenever he wanted within reason – probably because Suzon had put in a word for him – and look around unsupervised. Especially late at night, maybe after a Bible study, he loved to take a look at some of the paintings by torchlight. He particularly liked gazing at the riverside landscapes by the Bordeaux artist Pierre Lacour, and matching the scene in the early nineteenth century with what was left of the waterfront today. They didn't compare well with the two minor Canalettos the de Moulinets also had but it was interesting to see quite a few familiar buildings. He was engrossed in one of them when he heard piano music starting up in the banqueting hall.

He crept up the central staircase and gently opened the door, taking care to peep inside in case it was Bunty who had come up to play and he had to withdraw but it was Véronique at the Fazioli. Howard had already noticed that when she played, a lot of her gawkiness vanished, the long, angular limbs became graceful, the thick specs became studious and the wiry cap of her hair was somehow transformed into a boyish crop. Howard listened for a minute or two at the door, then, as the reflective music drew to a close, went in and sat sideways at the Bösendorfer.

"Was that Chopin, Véro?" Howard felt he was on safe ground because he could make out in the low lighting the word *Chopin* printed on the music.

"You're close, Howard, but actually it's Schumann's portrait of Chopin in his Opus 9, *Carnaval.*" Veronique showed him the front cover.

"But it is like one of the Chopin Nocturnes, isn't it?"

"Yes, that's the point, though. It's an affectionate portrayal of a friend in a thoughtful mood, really. All the movements are portraits. Schumann himself is in there in a couple of contrasting movements."

"Oh, right. Original. How are your own compositions coming along? Did that project of an album of your songs with Didier Deschiens come to anything in the end? You know, *Roxy Musique?*"

"No, Didier decided to go with someone who already had a much bigger profile – a gospel artist from Quebec. He did say I could go over to Toulouse where he was recording and do an overdub of some handclaps, so that was kind of him. I didn't go in the end. It didn't seem worth it to go all that way just for that."

"That was the best he could do after what he suggested for your songs? That sounds a bit insulting to me."

"Not insulting really. I didn't mine – it would have been very stressful. I did come to the conclusion it was all about Didier's career in the end, though. I'm sure he was sincere at the time, but he just got a better offer. He ended up going to Canada a couple of times free of charge, too."

"I suppose that's the French Christian music scene – well, all Christian music, perhaps music generally, ha! Perhaps the arts as a whole – it's all quite incestuous, isn't it? In fact, life as a whole."

"I did play one or two of my songs to Sally last night." Véronique blushed. "She said they were pretty in their own way but she pointed out some technical flaws in the harmony. I was discouraged at first but, as she said, it does give me something to work on."

Véronique was doodling away, improvising on the *Chopin* theme and Howard put in a one-fingered counter melody to it but it didn't really add anything to speak of so he let it trail away.

"Do I gather you already knew Sally before this evening, then?"

"Oh yes, she's been around for years, off and on. In fact, I'm surprised you haven't run into her yourself at some point."

"She's had no reason to go to the Roxy before now, I don't suppose. Do you get on with her?"

Véronique sighed deeply and after due consideration began, "I wouldn't go quite that far because it's the same story as with my adoptive cousin Charlotte in Paris, unfortunately. When you can't have children and decide to adopt, maybe there's always this thing about the child you never had. They treat her a bit like they treat Charlotte and I feel a bit, well, left out. A cuckoo in the nest. You've seen Charlotte in action, of course when she's been down here."

"Unfortunately, yes. That ended badly for me. I don't suppose she'll be back down here as long as I'm around – so much for a whirlwind romance. So, as far as Sally is concerned, that's a *yes, but* answer, is it?"

"Yes, it's good to have somebody to play two piano material with but she's very critical and you can't discuss anything like literature or politics with her because she always has such firm opinions about everything and she won't be shaken from them."

"You surprise me. Suzon seems to glide above it all, though. *Under the thumb?*"

"I hope that's one of your unfathomable English jokes, Howard."

"It wasn't, but I do see what you mean. I'm Welsh, by the way – it's a completely different thing, altogether. Listen, we should really get back down there because it's not fair to leave Emma and Darren in the lion's den with Daniel. I wouldn't mind some piano lessons some time and I'd be quite happy to pay. I can pick out a few things with one finger so I must have an ear for it. I did have lessons for a bit as a kid – I can't read music, though. I used to do everything from memory and the teacher found out. She covered my hands with a tea towel and that was it. *Good money after bad,* my Dad said."

"Here you are then, take a look at this." Véronique handed a child's piano primer to Howard. "I've been using this with a kid but they've grown out of it now. The early stages are fairly self–explanatory. What are your own tastes in music, apart from Didier Deschiens, of course?"

"Quite, eclec . . . my tastes are very varied. The popular classics. Classic rock. I'm a big Bob Dylan fan. Cardiacs is a band I love and I think the leader Tim Smith was a genius. I'm going to join the others. Coming down? You can't hide all evening – we're supposed to be getting to know the Ditsies."

"Oh, I'll catch up with you in a while but I'll just play through the rest of this first." Véronique gestured at *Carnaval*. She began on *Estrella* and by the time Howard reached the dining room, *Reconnaissance* was sparkling away.

"Admiring the paintings, Morgan?" roared Heseltine, "I'm surprised you could concentrate at all with that dreadful racket going on. Those beautiful pianos are wasted on her; it's been such a joy to hear them played properly again today and I say long may it continue, eh, Sally?"

"Yes, some of Véronique's *cantilena* does tend to lack finesse," added Bunty, "and her technique in the most rapid sections is a little ragged . . ." Sally cocked an ear. "I mean to say, just listen to *that!* But I'm absolutely determined to make sure that under my tutelage this year she becomes more refined in her delivery and more communicative in her manner. She's very inward, you know."

"I liked what she was playing and the way she was playing it," said Howard, sticking up for Véronique. "I love Schubert's *Carnival.*"

"It's *Carnaval* by Schumann actually, Howard," said Bunty as Heseltine tossed his head and even Suzon looked at Howard with pity. "This is the conclusion just coming up – you see what I mean about the lack of precision when the music is going like a train. Oh, Véronique, Véronique, what are we going to do with you?"

"*Quelle horreur!* I fervently hope you can achieve something with her. She spends too much time with the wrong type of person, if you ask me," said Heseltine with a pointed look at Pascal.

5

"I told you to stop playing. Stop that wretched, roiling racket, you dolt, I mean my dear sister, *Quelle horreur!*"

Heseltine was leading the service and had just preached a lengthy and bitter sermon all about declining attendance even though in reality the congregation had been boosted to a new high of seventeen by the presence of Sally, Darren and Emma. There had even been a little welcoming ceremony at the beginning with a bunch of carnations for the team and a chance to introduce themselves, accepted with joy by Bunty but declined by the others. Now, Véronique was playing meditatively a version of one of her own songs while Suzon stood by her side, suavely beating time on the piano lid.

"So stop! Stop! That's better. My dear brothers and sisters, before we close the service, let's continue in an attitude of prayer as we enjoy a moment of silent meditation."

The members of the congregation dutifully bowed their heads as Heseltine continued speaking, ploughing relentlessly forward.

"So, as we enjoy this blessed silence, let's bask in the presence of the Lord and relax into a rich realisation of his goodness towards us and even towards those who have seen fit to absent themselves from the precious assembly of his saints beyond which there can be no blessing; in the stillness, let us reflect upon the choice of him who has called us out of darkness into a life of simple living and poverty in imitation of our Saviour who had nowhere to lay his head; at the same time, let us give thanks if we have the good fortune to live in a comfortable apartment, house or, indeed, *chateau*, or in a humble cinema; in the tranquillity, let us also remember our responsibility to oppose ministers who bring this church or any church, for that matter, into disrepute by associating with some pretty disgraceful characters, I can tell you, and by inviting into the holy precincts of this the Lord's house those who have failed in our society and who are obliged to rely on honourable and right–living people to support their dissolute lifestyle; in the blissful calm which we now enjoy, let us thank the Lord for bringing into our midst a very talented team of young . . . a very talented young woman with many gifts of intellect and holy song and who is already known to us personally as a person of integrity unlike some others. *Quelle horreur!* Amen? Amen!"

It had been quite a rant and Heseltine unclenched his hands from the lectern to mop his brow with a puce silk handkerchief taken from the top pocket of his blazer.

"Now that we have enjoyed that moment of reflective silence, let us close this, this *service* or whatever it is we've been doing by singing a song of worship by, let's see, by Rory Ashurst. It's not included in our hymnal, *Songs of the Pilgrim Way* but emanates, so the very gifted Sally Fanshaw tells me, from a South African community church known as Mountain Crest. They are devoted to one another locally and are currently making inroads all over the globe. The words are on the overhead projector, so please join me in singing the, er, song we learned before the service, *Injudicious inclination.* Let's concentrate on the Lord, shall we? Véronique, please."

It was a fairly upbeat number and the moment Véronique began to play in an incongruous boogie–woogie style, a razor thin woman with a garland of red rattling plastic beads leapt to her feet waving a long pink ribbon. Howard leaned over to Darren and whispered, "This is that Angélique I told you about. I've had to promote her to the worship group and give her free rein or she threatened to leave and go back to the Pentecostals and we can't afford to lose anybody at this stage. It's a real buyers' market here." Grabbing the microphone from Heseltine and placing it on the stand, Angélique began to sing wordlessly over Véronique's introduction in a piercing wail. Old Madame Joris was sitting on a cajón drum but she was playing heavily on the first and third beats of the bar instead of the second and fourth, giving the music the leaden feel of a Congolese canoeing song. A guitarist , one of the homeless men called Jean–Pierre – the only musician plugged into the P.A. system – added a confident but rhythmically incoherent wall of sound and Suzon added a tingling, dainty triangle but Angélique's keening cut right through it all:

Injudicious inclination,
Precipitate partiality,

Daredevil devotion,
Is your holy heart,
Is your heart,
Your heart,
Heart,
For me, me, me, me, me, me, me
God

"Ca plane pour moi, moi, moi, moi, moi," Howard sang to himself, quietly. An ecstatic expression on her face and her head thrown back, Angélique was moving across the front of the platform, the ribbon fluttering and the beads clicking. Filled with familiar distaste, Howard found it impossible to drag his eyes from her because every few seconds she cut across the beam of the overhead projector and the unfamiliar words disappeared for a moment, causing a hiatus in the singing.

Temerarious besottedness,
Irresponsible proclivity,
Audacious predilection,
In your holy mind,
In your mind,
Your mind,
Mind,
For me, me, me, me, me, me,
God

    The music became yet more insistent and the pitch rose for the chorus as Angélique's voice became more strident still.

"What's she doing now?" asked Darren with concern as Angélique began to fiddle with the ribbon.

"You'll soon find out. Wait till after the service: about three times out of ten she announces her engagement – a different guy every time. You'll see either this week or next or possibly the one after," Howard grimaced. At this point Angélique leaned down and picked up what looked like a beach ball. The ribbon was fastened around her wrist by now and she began to execute clumsy gymnastic movements with the ball, now tossing it high into the air, now rolling it across the platform and scampering after it.

"I thought that kind of thing went out with the ark."

"Not here in France, because we get everything five years later than you do in Britain, don't forget."

"So, let me guess is there a *shofar* hidden there somewhere?"

"A what?"

"A *shofar*. You know, a ram's horn that you blow? They' were all the rage for a time."

"I expect we've still got that to look forward to, then."

Injudicious, temerarious,
Injudicious, temerarious,
Injudicious, temerarious,
Injudicious, temerarious
God

For the thoughtful bridge section of the song, Angélique stopped dead and raised both hands to the sky, gazing at the ceiling and swaying gently. It was somehow even more difficult not to look now.

Oh, I wish I had a million pens and fifty thousand pots of ink
And scraps of parchment manifold to scribe you what I think;
I wish I had an aeroplane and letters made of smoke
To tell the world about the feelings in my grateful heart
You evoke,
You evoke,
God

    Again, Angélique squatted down and rummaged behind the piano. "You mean there's more?" – Darren was incredulous.
    "Yes, but we're getting towards the end now. Don't say anything afterwards; remember, we need to keep everyone sweet."
    Angélique reached behind the piano and drew out two enormous billowing flags on poles, crimson and aquamarine, embroidered with doves. As she sang, adding spontaneous lines of banal harmony, she began to wave them in enormous arcs above her, to either side, crouching, kneeling, jumping, reaching down, straining up. When the ribbon tangled round one of the poles she was checked and wrongfooted but only for a moment.

Injudicious, temerarious,
Injudicious, temerarious,

"Yes, Lord!" Called out Angélique for no apparent reason.

Injudicious, temerarious,
Injudicious, temerarious,
God

Angélique made a sign right in Véronique's face for her to repeat the chorus but Heseltine was too quick for her this time and stepped in: "And that's all we have time for this morning. Thank you, Véronique and, er, Angélique and, er, the others for, for, er, that. It's good to know we are still at the very cutting edge of hymnody," said Heseltine with evident distaste. "Let's close our all too brief time together by saying in fellowship the Grace to one another."

As one, all the members of the congregation began to shuffle and look aimlessly around, trying not to catch anyone else's eye. "And now, may the grace of the Lord Jesus Christ, and the love of God, and the fellowship of the Holy Spirit," everyone recited confidently but the last line was, as usual, lost in mumbling because nobody was ever quite sure how it was meant to go.

"Please do join us for coffee in the foyer," began Heseltine but before he could continue, Angélique was again at the microphone.

"Everyone, your attention please: I have an important announcement of a sentimental nature to make. This morning *my heart is like a singing bird whose nest is in a watered* . . . "

". . . Oh, shoot. I think you can speak to us all individually this time, over coffee, Angélique," Heseltine cut in. I'm afraid we've run out of time.

"But I want everyone to share my joy unspeakable and full of glory!" She rattled her beads with irritation.

"Angélique, I think everybody can share your joy unspeakable one at a time in the foyer. *Quelle horreur!*"

"As you wish, Daniel but may I say that I'm hurt. I have finally achieved a lasting liaison and this is to be celebrated, surely? May I remind you that my recent decision to return once more and to stay with this church is very much still in the balance and may be reconsidered at any moment. He is a gentleman . . ."

"Quite so, quite so. and I respect that attitude more than you may perhaps imagine but it's just that I need to speak to Morgan on a matter of some urgency, Angélique. However, you may be assured of my continuing, er, my continuing," Heseltine noticed Howard making for the exit. "Morgan! A word. Now."

"Yes, Daniel, is that the word you had in mind – *Now*?"

"A word in your ear in your flat, if you please."

"Fine. You'd better come on up then."

As Heseltine passed Darren and Pascal chatting, he said, in an ordinary conversational tone to Darren and pointing to Pascal, "He's an alcoholic."

Once up in the flat, Heseltine sat, uninvited, in the only armchair while Howard sat on his bed.

"Now, my displeasure," Heseltine began, "I have no intention ever of hiding, concealing or dissimulating. My discontent I will in no wise dissemble. Let me begin by stating my contention that this so–called *work* with the homeless is a blot on the life of the Fellowship and is bringing Bordeaux itself into disrepute all over, er, Bordeaux. *Quelle horreur."*

"Daniel, may I remind you that the Lord himself . . ."

"Listen, you, there's no need to bring religion into this . . ."

"That's rich! *Inasmuch as you did it to the least of these, you . . ."*

"You forget that I'm pretty skilled in batting round Bible verses myself, my fine young man, with your *exegesis* and your *hermeneutics. Come ye out from among them and be ye separate*, for one . . ."

"Wait, the context of that verse . . ."

"Context! I'm talking about the naked text not context." Heseltine shuddered. "Enough of your rhetorical ruses, your devices of Demosthenes. I'm talking pragmatism and practicalities not piety and prayer. Now, listen, young man, you know the city's bid to be European City of Food next year has been accepted?"

"I had heard that, as it happens. In fact, wasn't the bid accepted several years ago? I don't see what that has to do with . . ."

"The decision is in the archives, yes, but the event itself has crept up on us and now everyone knows the whole business is not going to be a victim of the cuts as we assumed, we need to pull out all the stops to rival Barcelona, Prague and even, who knows, the Abergavenny Food Festival itself."

"Abergavenny – *Now* I'm interested! Pray continue."

"I fully intend so to do. People will be coming from all over the world to sample not only the daytime delights of the main landmarks of Bordeaux but all the dubious and worldly pleasures which I am reliably informed are available hereabouts come sundown. But you'd know more about that than I would. *Quelle horreur!*"

"That's debatable. I saw you cruising round giving out tracts – or so you said – to the nightlife that once, don't forget."

"Right, I'm going to cut to the chase, do you understand?" A faint blush, to the widow's peak. "Nobody wants to stumble in the street over the rabble you seem to love and whom you positively encourage to come here. With their dogs and their drinks and their drugs."

"We are performing . . ." began Howard with a heroic effort of patience.

" . . . *a valuable service*. I've heard it before – *ad nauseum*. *Speaking truth to power, lighting a candle in the darkness*. *Quelle horreur!*"

"*Ad Nauseam*, actually. You've done your level best to shut us down but, listen, you have failed at that. The vote went my way if you remember. It was tight but it was right." Howard winced inwardly at his own sententious saying. "Listen, if you . . ."

"No, it's your turn to listen to me. Know, then, that there is a higher authority than God . . ."

"I beg your pardon?"

"No, that's not quite right, I'm sorry, but what I mean is that in matters of this sort, there is another authority whose voice carries weight even above even that of a church meeting and a simple vote of discernment."

"Which would be?"

"Only the City Council, that's whose voice. And you may well know that Madame de Pigalette, the Lady Mayoress, is also a member of Parliament and the chair of the departmental council, a prominent member of the wine-makers' federation and the secretary of the Chamber of Commerce to boot . . ."

"I know. A clear case of abuse of function, the *cumul des mandats.* So, that don't impress me much, Daniel."

"Madame de Pigalette is coming."

"What? Now?" Howard made a fluttering heart gesture, "Be still, my beating . . ."

"She's coming on Tuesday. She's coming with a small delegation to inspect the homeless breakfast on Tuesday and it so happens that she will come bearing this letter signed by my own hand recommending the closure of the work with the homeless once and for all. I intend to have it delivered to her by courier tomorrow at lunchtime at *La Rotonde* where she dines in conclave." Heseltine brandished yet another of the threatening official documents Howard was used to receiving pretty much weekly by now.

"You can't do that."

"I can and I shall. Wearing her various hats, Madame de Pigalette has voted herself pretty draconian powers I can tell you to beautify the city in good time for the European Year of Food and she will be coming here on Tuesday bearing her clipboard of judgement and of doom. Thank you and good day to you, Morgan. *Quelle horreur!*"

Pascal had been lurking halfway up the open staircase and he had to beat a hasty retreat as Heseltine flounced away and made a noisy exit into the street where he climbed into his midnight blue Jaguar. Slinking back up the stairs Pascal called up, undulating with concern, "Can he do that, Boss – you know, what I couldn't help but overhear – about the closure of the breckers?"

"I don't know, but I suppose we'll find out on Tuesday. Maybe we could put the dogs in kennels and hire morning suits and top hats for the guys? That sweatshirt of yours will have to go for a start. No? Well, it was just a thought."

"We'll come up with something, Boss. In the meantime, I'll get the lads to be on their best behaviour."

"Ha! That's what I'm afraid of."

6

It was a shoestring operation because there was no kitchen downstairs in the Roxy so all the coffee had to be made up in Howard's flat with two machines dripping away non–stop and carried downstairs in four great thermal jugs. The six folding tables and crockery were stacked in *Salle Une*, though, so they just had to be taken through into *Salle Deux* and set up for opening time at seven thirty. The freezer was in the projection room and the bread, milk and butter had been defrosted overnight and were ready to be brought through and put on the tables. Howard was glad of the extra couple of pairs of hands and along with Pascal, Emma and Darren were willing workers at this type of thing.

"What's it going to be like, Howard?" asked Darren with trepidation.

"Oh, there'll be quite a rush at the start. Maybe twenty of them – all men, plus the dogs – but then it'll become a bit more steady till ten. Then, we start trying to get the last few of them to think about leaving. Closing time is 10.30 but you often get a few of them hanging round till eleven. I manage to chase most of them away by offering a Bible reading with them. You have to make sure there's no one hiding in the bog – there has been known to be bit of drug misuse in there."

"What do you want us to do?" asked Emma.

"Not much. You can just hang round, talk to them, bring them more coffee. It's not too bad, actually and it'll do wonders for your French – as long as you don't say too many of the things you hear in polite company. It's all a matter of register, as the French say and this is gutter language."

"That Angélique said she'd come along and help, didn't she?" asked Darren. "An extra pair of hands."

"Ha! You've got a lot to learn about church life Darren. You can always get plenty of volunteers but you can never get enough people to turn up."

At about seven twenty, Bunty arrived, parked up outside the *Aigle d'Argent* and came in with an officious clatter. Veronique was just behind her. Sally leaned up the stairs and called out, "I'm here, chaps, panic over."

"Great! Just come up and give us a hand with some of this coffee, please, Sally," Howard tentatively suggested.

"No chance! I didn't come here to do menial tasks; you'll have us delivering leaflets next. If you want me, I'll be outside chatting with the guys."

"Menial tasks indeed! I've got two degrees and I still have to do these menial tasks as you call them," complained Howard.

"Why don't you have a little think about what you've just said for a moment and ask yourself why, Howard?" And with that, Bunty was gone and the door slammed behind her.

"I'll give you a hand, Howard."

"Thanks, Veronique. Right, five minutes and counting, Dynamix. Jam on every table? Don't forget the sugar – that's the most important thing after the coffee itself."

"Can I have a cup?" asked Emma, shaking.

"You can have as much as much as you want when you're not up and down those stairs. I suppose we'd might as well open up now – it's all ready and waiting."

Howard threw the double doors wide and as usual instead of an eager rush of happy people there was a crocodile of weary young men who trudged through and threw their bags in the corner of *Salle Deux*. As well as the twenty–odd *Sans Domicile Fixes – the SDFs:* those of no fixed abode – there were five or six Alsatian mongrels who settled under the tables, happy to be inside in the warm. Some serious smoking began and soon the air was thick.

"All right, Paulo," began Howard, "Gimme some skin, ma bro. Real cool, cats! Get your guts around some of this nosh, man..."

"Howard," Bunty strode up, "just stop it, will you? You're making a spectacle of yourself: why don't you just talk normally, you fool?"

Veronique tried to intervene, "Oh, Sally! Howard was just..."

"*Getting down with the kids? Groovy, man*! For a grown–up person, you're pathetic, you know, Howard," Sally was distracted. "Hey, if it isn't Paquito Lopez!"

"Sally, The Queen of the Vines! Long time, no see, honey lamb. What brings you to Bordeaux this time?"

"I'm working for . . . I mean, I'm *with* him. I'm killing time for a few months before I go up to Uni. after the Bahamas. I was in Thailand but they couldn't accommodate my radical ideas and my bushy–tailed dynamism."

"What are you going to study?"

"I'm reading French, Maths and Law at Oxford."

"Oxford! Why do you need to go to Uni at all?" Paquito was genuinely mystified. "I mean, Howard's French is pretty good but next to yours well, frankly, it pales. There's something unusual about his accent you can't quite put your finger on but, as for you, you're more like one of us."

"Muchas Gracias, Señor: sé que tengo un ligero acento, pero he conseguido recoger un buen montón de canales españoles en el camino, no creo que lo hago muy mal teniendo en cuenta. No es tan bueno como mi francés, por supuesto, pero entonces usted no esperaría que, ¿verdad?"

"All right, there's no need to show off," laughed Paquito.

"If you've got it . . ."

". . . why not flaunt it? I suppose you're right."

"Anyway, the answer to your question is that I need to put the French in some kind of framework, hence the Law and Maths. There'll probably be a business application at the end of it all – in fact, there already is, in a smallish way – a line in cosmetics down this way that nets me a few thousand. Above all, I hope to emerge as an even more fully–rounded personality than I am already."

"Excuse me," cut in Howard, "but do you mind telling me how you two know each other?"

"With pleasure, for Paquito is like a third grandfather to me. It's a bit complicated but my paternal grandfather, Pa Fanshaw we called him, was involved in the Spanish Civil War and had something to do with Paquito's father and some of his associates."

"In the International Brigade, was he – *Homage to Catalonia* and all that?"

"No, he was on the other side."

"Oh well."

"Yes, he was running guns in and out of Cadiz for the winners. You see, quite a lot of the family's prosperity dates back to that time. It involved Swiss bank accounts of course but it didn't pay to be too scrupulous in those days – it so rarely does if you look at the record. So, ultimately he worked under the Generalissimo."

"Franco?"

"No, he was paid very well for it, as a matter of fact."

"No, I meant . . ."

"I know quite well what you meant, thank you, Howard. It was a simple pun – a play on words, you see, nvolving the French. I'll explain it to you later, if you like. Come to think of it, maybe you could join Emmi and Dazz for a daily lesson with me when I'll go into some of the grammatical intricacies and cultural reference points."

"I need to get on now thanks, Sally. All right, Paolo? All right, Gino?"

"Actually, Howard, I was wondering if you could front me ten euros?" asked Paquito.

"You know we don't give money, Paquito."

"Actually, it's not for the red stuff this time, it's for a tube of ointment for this." Paquito rolled up his right trouser leg to reveal a weeping ulcer on his calf.

"Ouch! It doesn't seem to be getting any better does it? Look, I've still got some of that stuff left over after the last time it flared up so why don't you let me clean it up and dress it for you?"

"I don't want to put you to any trouble."

"That's what I'm here for. In fact, that's all I'm good for, apparently," said Howard in a rueful voice. "Darren! Could you go up into the flat, please and in the cabinet by the sink in the kitchen you'll find a tube of ointment and some sterile dressings and some bandages. Can you bring them down for me please? Oh, Emma, could you go up as well and get a bowl of hot water, a flannel and a towel, please?"

"I don't know why you bother," said Paquito. "I'm going to lose this leg anyway one of these days. You should see the varicose veins further up – like great thick ropes right up to my groin, they are. I can still do most things I want to but there's quite a bit of pain when they come to the surface and the itching . . ."

"Too much detail."

"Hey, more coffee over here," called Paulo.

"Sally, could you take care of that, please?"

"Can't you see I'm talking to Paulo, Howard? He was just filling me in one or two health and safety issues he's concerned about. Is it true that you let Gino replace a fuse with tin foil when the power was still on?"

"He said when he was nobbut a nipper he used to be a pretty ace sparks and . . ."

"Just say *electrician*, why don't you. All this ancient slang with that stupid accent doesn't give you any more credibility, you know. *Jeepers, you fellas!* Anyway, you'd better go and get that coffee or Paulo is going to cut up rough."

"Right, Sally."

Howard climbed the stairs to the flat with a thermal jug and the next batch of coffee was already through. Emma and Darren already had the things ready for Paquito's leg but they seemed hesitant about going back down.

"What's up, Dynamix?"

"Can we stay up here?" asked Emma. "We can't understand a single word anyone says and it smells awful down there."

"And I'm petrified that all that smoke is going to set off my asthma," said Darren with a little cough.

"Come on, this is how you improve your French. In fact, this is how I started, helping out in a soup kitchen in Lille, many moons ago, even before I went to college. And, as for your chest, you've brought your inhalers, haven't you, Darren?"

"Dogs are a trigger as well as the smoke."

"Snap. I've got a touch of asthma, as well. Just go outside for a few minutes, I you feel an attack coming on. The other thing is to make sure you keep going with the brown puffer and then keep the blue one with you and you should be all right."

"But Sally said . . ."

"But Sally said, nothing. The way I see it, what we're doing is worth it for its own sake. Come on – *Once more unto the breach, dear friends, once more.*"

"What?"

"Oh, nothing."

"About time, too," said Paulo as Emma poured the coffee into the jugs. "I was about to come up with *this*." He drew a nine inch kitchen knife out of his rucksack. "Or set Pallax on you," he gestured to his mangy Alsatian under the table which pricked up its ears and growled at the mention of its name.

"Put that thing away, please, Paulo," said Howard.

Paolo took no notice. "Hey, Howard. You know you said something the other day about *turning the other cheek* or something?"

"Yes, you mustn't fight violence with violence. Why?" Howard was delighted – this was a rare opportunity.

"Because I'm going to come at you with this right now."

"Why would you want to do that?"

"Because you're rich . . ."

"I'm not rich . . ."

"You are. You've got a lot of things I haven't got a hope of – a car, a flat . . ."

"If you can call Cornflower a car. Anyway, you could have a flat as well if you'd just . . ."

"Not with Pallax, I couldn't . . ."

"Get rid of the flipping dog, then!"

"See what I mean? Right, I'm going to come at you with this. Are you going to turn the other cheek? I'm interested to see if what you say and what you do stack up."

"Oh, I don't know what I'd do. Obviously." Howard was exasperated and turned away. "Just put the thing away, will you? I've got to see to Paquito's leg – unless you want to do it."

"No chance. I could cut it off with this and then he wouldn't have any more bother with it. Anyway, you'd better get on with that. See that, Sally," Paolo was jeering, "pooing himself, he was and now he's kneeling on the floor wiping away a dosser's pus."

"I know – some people are all talk, aren't they? As for me, I have a black belt third dan in judo and represented Surrey in the British Championships last year, coming fourth and *highly commended* when faced with some more experienced ladies in their twenties. It was in a dreadful place called Newport. Don't you come from there yourself, Howard?"

Howard looked up. "Cardiff, actually. We don't think much of Newport ourselves, as it happens. In my opinion they've ruined the city centre over and over again even in the years I've been going there. Where did you learn your judo?"

"At school. You see, Brabourne Acres is an all–girls' school and they take our safety very seriously, so all the pupils have to take part, even the swots, or the *grunts* as we *naturals* call them. We don't describe judo as self–*defence* for nothing, you know. There's no aggression involved at all, you see. One uses one's opponent's own strength against him or her. You should consider going in for it if you're going to insist on putting yourself in situations like this where you're clearly out of your depth, Howard. There's no need to talk about turning the other cheek if you can disarm your assailant, you see."

"Is that any better, Paquito?"

"That's soothing that is, Howard," Paquito purred.

"It doesn't happen very often, though. The attacks, I mean. Just once a bloke decided to teach me a lesson when I kicked his dog. I didn't realise a guy's dog is sacred but I took the punishment like a man and I never did it again."

"There you are, you see. It might not be a frequent occurrence but you must agree it does happen. I have an example. I'd like to share with you as an admonition, Howard. Once, in Delhi, I disarmed two moped thieves who had run off with a friend's clutch bag with her passport and all her knick-knacks in it. It so happens, that I know the city tolerably well, so I was able to cut through a street market at a brisk jog and head them off. Then, I egged them on to come at me and they were unfortunate enough to take the bait. One of them I threw off balance with a sweeping leg movement and the other I dumped over my back like this, you see? Then, I picked up the bag and walked calmly past them while whistling an air of Purcell's. The poor muggers just lay there for a while but when they got up, they actually applauded me so I gave a little bow. I wrote it up for the *Telegraph* Saturday travel section. They seem to like what I do a little more than the *Huffington Post* where they don't publish my stuff anywhere near as much as I'd like."

7

By midday, it was time to start thinking about packing up. When Howard announced that there was going to be a Bible reading, nearly all the men got their things together, gulped a last coffee and made for the corridor. In the end, only Pascal, Howard, Paquito, Paulo and the Dynamic Teens remained. Howard had devised a leaflet – a folded sheet of A4 he called, *A walk through the New Testament in thirty days* and whatever the date was he followed it. Today it was Paul writing about the ideal of love in 1 Corinthians 13 so he read through it in a spiteful murmur and said a bitter little prayer.

"At least that one's easy to understand, Howard," said Paulo.

"I suppose."

"The hard thing is doing it, isn't it, Boss?"

"At least we get plenty of opportunities to try it out here," said Howard ruefully.

"Is that it, then? You're not discouraged are you, Howard?"

"Not at all, Paolo – this is how I am most of the time these days. See you tomorrow. Don't forget, the delegation is going to be here from the Council so put in a word with the others, okay? Then, there's the film on Saturday evening, don't forget. *The Biding* Place – you like that one. There'll be coffee there, too."

"Sure thing, Howard."

"Now, Dynamix, seeing that it's your first time on the breakfasts, I thought we could go and get a sandwich in our local *brasserie* over there and have a bit of a de-brief. I know from experience that this can be a bit of a strange environment at first."

"Oh, Howard," put in Bunty, "I'm afraid I can't really manage that today. You see, I have a sleeping business interest down here that I need to bring up to speed over lunch with Daniel and some others – it's a new brand of coffee scrub – so you'll have to excuse me. At the moment we're trying to find a way of adding ground up grape pips into it without the fragments getting stuck in people's pores. We need a specifically Bordeaux slant on the product while keeping it entirely free to produce, you see. The mark-up is simply colossal. Later on I'm thinking of making a killing on a face mask called something like *Pipznskins*. Anyway, if you need me, I'll be in *La Rotonde* in a booth. You know, the place on the *Quinconces* with all the Michelin stars. Yum yum."

"What about this evening? Could you join us then? Please? For dinner? Drinks?"

"I'm afraid this evening I'm to go to an early music concert at St Luke's with some student friends. Angélique is coming along too with her beau. You see, the soprano Sufficiency Hill-Treworgan is in town along with Ashley Hoyt-Burton from Boston, Mass. and the *Fustian Ensemble*. I'm simply unable to resist a bumptious little countertenor in Buxtehude, you see." Bunty registered Howard's incomprehension. "Buxtehude – the composer. An earlier contemporary of Bach. J.S. Bach, another composer . . . of music."

"The *Aigle d'Argent* it is, then, chaps," said Howard. "You coming in with us, Pascal? I'm sorry, but this is all going to be in English, if you don't mind."

"That's fine by me, Boss. It's about time I made a start on the language of Shakespeare, anyway."

"Didn't you do any English at school?"

"I can read and count – in French – what more do you want?"

Howard locked up and as Bunty made her way up into the commercial area of the city, he and the Dynamix wandered over to the *Aigle*. Even though in the night and at the weekend it was transformed with glitz and pounding music into a nightclub, in the chill of a late autumn Monday morning, the ground floor was just a bistro like any other. As usual it was empty before the lunch hour so they chose a table near the window, Emma and Darren with their heads in their hands and Howard slumped back with fatigue. Leaning forward again, he massaged his sore knees.

"Hi, Howard. How'd you get on?" asked the barman.

"Not bad, Alain. A typical Monday morning, really. When the winter bites it gets a bit more challenging but for the moment, nothing to report. I got threatened with a knife but I think it was probably a joke."

Alain tossed his head and tutted. "Paolo, I expect. Anything in the rumour they're trying to close you down because of the European City of Food thing next year?"

"There is talk of it but to be honest as long as we keep the dogs in the building rather than out the front of the Roxy and tell the guys not to hang about in the street smoking, I can't really see much of a problem."

"You can tell them from me it doesn't bother us in here. If anything we might get one or two extra customers if any of the guys are in the money but as you can see, there's not much passing trade in the morning." Alain gestured to the empty room. "So, who are your new friends?"

"Oh yes, sorry, this is Emma and this is Darren. They're here to help our for a few months so they'll be living with me over in the Roxy."

"I'm vegan," said Emma.

"Very good. I'm Alain – welcome to Bordeaux. In that case, this one's on the house, so what'll it be?"

"That's very kind of you." Howard consulted with Emma and Darren. "A hot chocolate, a black tea and a *café calva*, please. Oh, and a beer for Pascal. A *Seize*."

"A *1664* – Some things never change. Coming right up." Alain began the coffee procedure.

"Oh, Alain, some sandwiches in your own time as well, please. One cheese, one just dry bread for Emma and two ham and cheese – I'll pay for those, of course."

"I know you will."

"How about coming to see the film on Saturday night, Alain?" Howard thought it was tie to show Emma and Darren how to slip an invitation to church into the conversation without causing offence.

"How can I? I've got this place to take care of. What's it about?"

"It's called *The Biding Place* and it's all about a Belgian carpenter in a Nazi concentration camp in Poland – it's a Christian film, obviously but, actually, this one has quite high production values. They got a proper actor and everything. Can I leave some of these on some of the tables?"

Howard showed one of the thousand A5 flyers he'd photocopied and cut up the previous day but Alain recoiled in horror because it showed a great black swastika blotting out a map of Europe above details of the Roxy's location and the time of the film.

Alain turned away and busied himself polishing a glass. "You *are* joking, of course aren't you, Howard? It looks as if you're setting up a new party to the right of the *Front National* or something."

"It's just illustrating the film. Striking isn't it? I'm quite proud of this flyer – you can't ignore it. The film itself has got a positive message about forgiveness – couldn't you just let me . . ."

"The answer is no." Alain turned his back.

Howard was discouraged but he'd already set the afternoon aside for doing a few hundred letterboxes so nothing had changed in reality. He returned to Emma and Darren.

"Okay, guys, I thought you did very well this morning and you didn't have any meltdowns so that was good. Normally, Pascal and I are charging up and down those stairs like mad fools but today we had a chance to have a sensible chat with the guys. Sorry about that incident with the knife but it's an ongoing discussion we're having about how far people are prepared to go in support of their ideals."

"Who *are* these people, anyway?" asked Darren with a guffaw of disgust.

"Yes, how have they ended up like this?" put in Emma.

"You mustn't generalise but there's usually a fair amount of alcohol involved. Plus, sometimes relationships have broken down. Often a broken home. Unemployment, obviously. They gravitate to all the big cities, especially in the south where the winter climate is so much more clement, sorry, nice . . . " Howard launched into the speech of introduction he always used on these occasions – it was like a recitation by now because he had delivered it scores of times from the front and over coffee in British churches.

"But where do they, like, get the money for their lifestyle, Howard?"

"I'm glad you asked me that, Emma." This was always the first question. "It's a bit of a vicious circle really because they all get this lump sum of money once a month, like a dole cheque. It's called the R.M.I. – the *Revenu Minimum d'Insertion* – and theoretically they are supposed to use it to try to get their feet on the ground. Really, though, they have this enormous binge for however long it lasts. They book a hotel room sometimes, even. Then, the rest of the time, they beg. Alcohol is a bigtime addiction – well, you saw that. That's why it's pointless to tell people not to give money to beggars. They've got to have alcohol until they really decide to turn their lives around. You're not going to stop them by not giving. Or by starving them, for that matter. Hence the breakfasts."

Alain brought the drinks on a tray. "Enjoy!" he said.

"Shan't!" replied Howard and they both laughed at their private joke.

"Where do they all live? Have they got flats?" continued Emma.

"I'm glad you asked me that, Emma." The recitation again. "Not usually. Some of them are in hostels: the ones without dogs can do that. Some of them are moving between friends' houses, what do you call it – there's a word, isn't there?"

"You mean, sofa–surfing?"

"That's the one – they do sofa–surfing. If they're sleeping rough, some of them have got regular spots that are a bit warm or they manage to blag their way into a hallway. The ones who come to us tend to be the worst, though, and a lot of them are in underground car parks. Bottom floor, behind pillars, out of sight – that kind of thing. The dogs are a huge handicap but it's their only chance to have a relationship where they are in charge. That's how I rationalise it. Plus the companionship, of course. It's every man for himself on the streets."

"Isn't that a bit sexist?" asked Emma.

"If you like. They *are* practically all men, though. But, it's every man or woman for her or himself."

"For themselves," Darren put in.

"I was shocked once near the beginning. One of the first guys I came across died in hospital – Jacques Humbert, his name was – but because he'd been out of circulation for a month or two. When I told them about it, all the others had already forgotten his name. I couldn't believe it. But it wasn't callous, particularly, just that they all live hand to mouth. A friend of mine wrote a song about that called *Writ in Water*. That's a quote from Keats – *Here lies one whose name was writ in water*. He wanted it to be put on his tombstone."

"Keats? So, Paquito and Pascal. Are they *SDFs* as well?"

"John Keats, the poet – You now, *Season of mists and mellow fruitfulness . . . My name is Ozymandias, king of kings . . .* It depends how you define *SDF*, I suppose. In my book, Paquito is an *SDF* The thing is with him, though, is that he was the first guy I met through Pascal. So, he's latched onto us and he's kind of semi–detached now and as long as he keeps it quiet from the others, we let him sleep behind the cash desk, as you know, and I suppose you could say that he's kind of on his way to starting to think about getting off the streets now."

"How'd you mean?" Darren cupped his hands around his drink and Howard downed his *calvados* in one go and put a sugar lump on his teaspoon and touched the surface of his espresso. Howard watched the coffee creep through the grains – a satisfaction that never seemed to grow old.

"Well, Just because he's spending so much time with us, he can get his mail addressed to the Roxy and the next step, really, is for us to try and find him a flat somewhere because then he could apply for the housing allowance."

"Why doesn't he go ahead with it?" asked Emma.

Howard crunched on the sugar. "A lot of it depends on the landlord. Some of them are surprisingly kind. In the very early days of email I went through the *Compuserve* directory for

Bordeaux, if you can believe there ever was such a thing, and asked upfront if anyone had a flat they weren't using. I got a response and the guy was in there for nearly a year! Actually, with Paquito we're talking to a developer who's knocking down a building soon but not straight away. It looks as if he might be happy for Paquito to stay in one of those flats for the time being. The problem there, though, is it could be for as much as a couple of years or only a month or two. Then he'd be back to square one. *Compuserve*! I expect you can just about remember floppy discs? When I had my first computer, it was an Atari and you used to buy them individually in the supermarket at the electrical counter! By the way, how old do you think Paquito is?"

"Maybe sixty–five," ventured Emma.

"Forty–eight," said Howard. He always loved that part of the conversation and revelled in Emma and Darren's genuine shock.

"What about *him*, is he homeless?" asked Darren, gesturing towards Pascal who jumped.

"Do you mind if we talk about you for a minute, Pascal?"

"Not at all. You go ahead, Boss. It saves me going into it," replied Pascal but his shoulders began working and his lips to purse.

"No, Pascal's not an *SDF* At least, not now. He *has* been, and he's been inside as well."

"What for?" Emma shrank back involuntarily.

"It's okay," Howard laughed, "he's not violent or anything. When he was younger, there was a lot of drugs involved as well as the alcohol, but prescription drugs, mainly. There were a few suicide attempts, one with a shotgun. So, he got involved in some break-ins – even stole from his mother. In fact, that was the one that put him inside because he was living in a squat in Paris at the time and she turned him in. They weren't close, so he even had to break in to her place. He confessed to all the other burglaries to get a clean slate. In some ways, that was the best thing that happened to him."

"How'd you mean?" Darren was intrigued now.

"He'd just met Julie and she followed him down to Toulouse to the prison at Muret. When he came out, he'd got our kind of religion inside – you know, the right sort – and they both went to live in a community in the Pyrenees, a sort of halfway house that gave them both a bit of structure. There are quite a few of those down there – it's very sparsely populated in the *Ariège* department and all kinds of things go on in those valleys, all kinds of experimental groups off grid. This is six or seven years back, at a rough guess."

"So why have they ended up in Bordeaux?"

"They both wanted to *confront their demons* as they put it. The way they tell it, all the bad things happened in the city so they needed to see if there was anything to their faith by coming back to the same setting, I suppose. They've ended up in a tough district – *Le Bousquet* – on the twenty-third floor of twenty-seven in an *HLM* and the lifts are often out of order but it's a place of their own. A lot of gangs."

"*HLM?*"

"*Hebergement a loyer modéré* – a lot of *HLM*s are council housing but not all. There's a famous song by Renaud about them." Howard sang, "*Ce qu'il est blême, mon HLM* Everybody knows it."

Both Emma and Darren looked blank.

"It's quite an old song now, I suppose, from the 70s or the 80s. *Blême* means – what does it mean? It means pale or sickly here, I suppose. So, *My HLM is sickly.* He was talking about Lille. A city in the north. Of France."

"I'm glad there's been a happy ending?" said Emma, sipping on her tea.

"Ha! It's not exactly that – not just yet – but we are working on it. He still drinks a lot and sometimes she throws him out. Their kids are a bit wild – Rebecca and Jacob, Becka and Jake. When that happens he dosses down in *Salle Deux* but he makes sure he does it discreetly so half the time I don't know how things stand between them, to be honest. They're not exactly on the rocks but it's not the happiest marriage I've seen either. But, then, whose is, eh? Tell me that."

Emma was quiet. "My parents split up when I was ten," she said. "Will we meet Julie?"

"I'm sorry about that. Julie? Probably not. She goes to the Pentecostals on a Sunday and when she's not there, she's cleaning for some of the people in the actual houses in *Le Bousquet*. They've got a more stable thing going than we have over at the Penties and she thinks it's better for the kids to have the benefit of that. It's a bit authoritarian but some people like that over here because it's what they're used to if they've come out of the Catholic church. There are no other kids in our place, anyway, as you know. We did have one family but there was a fight after the service one Sunday and they left."

"And Pascal? Why doesn't he go to the Penties as well?" asked Darren.

"He thinks we've got a better chance to help the *SDFs* here in the city centre than the Penties do out in the suburbs in their plush new building. He's not wrong, in my humble. In fact, he's thinking of trying to train as a kind of social worker for people on the streets – *un educateur de rue.* I can't help thinking he needs to be a bit more stable himself, though. Right, come on, those leaflets aren't going to deliver themselves."

"Have we got to do it?" asked Emma, "Sally says it's a menial task and we shouldn't let you exploit us."

"Exploit you? I'm hardly doing that. I'm going to be doing it with you for a start. Plus, it's a good way of discovering the area and sometimes you get into good conversations. I quite like boring, repetitive jobs, anyway, so I do menial tasks myself. Once, somebody said to me *You're wasting your time.* I thought about it and said, *Okay, but at least it's my own time I'm wasting.*"

8

After about twenty minutes of circular negative conversation between the beds, Darren cried himself to sleep and Howard lay awake for a good while with the World Service on long wave under his pillow, going through the events of the last couple of days. He had to find a way to make the *Dynamix* gel as a team in spite of Bunty's semi–detached attitude and the lack of confidence of Emma and Darren. He'd have to try to neutralise her criticism of their French for a start because at the moment they were still trying to back out of any situation where conversation would be required, gravitating tinstead owards people who could speak even a few words of English.

      Howard heard Paquito come in noisily just as the news started at two a.m. and he must have drifted off soon after that because the next thing he knew it was six forty-five and time for it all to start again. His dreams had been full of courtroom scenes where he was somehow the defence lawyer and the defendant at the same time and had to justify his actions for crimes no one would specify. He reached for his glass of water to clear his head but knocked it to the floor where it smashed. Darren stirred and groaned.

It was the noise of the road sweeper grinding by in the *Rue Jean Jaurès* that had woken him and, glancing through the window, he could see there were already five or six guys hanging around in front of the doors, smoking. Howard wished they wouldn't do that because of the poor image it gave of the Roxy in the area – he was always having to put up with comments about it from those residents still trying to hold on to a more respectable image of the quarter. In fact, it was this feeling that had led him to decide to allow the homeless people to light up inside the building and bring their dogs inside as well. Ironically, he now had the problem of them stinking the place out but it still didn't stop them hanging around outside as well. After a quick shower and shave, he started making the first batch of coffee, siphoning off the first cup for himself. He shuddered, because being straight out of the filter it was the strongest of the day. At seven, Howard roused Darren and went downstairs to rouse Emma, past Paquito who was snoring like a pig being slaughtered in a zinc bath. He placed a tray with a croissant and some coffee on the ground outside the door to *Salle Une*. Of course, he could eat the croissant himself later.

At the far end of *Salle Deux*, Howard could hear knocking at the emergency exit so he went down and let in Pascal.

"Colder today, Boss. *Winter draws on.*"

"The old ones are the best. *It's over the wall.*"

"What is?"

"*The other side.* Just go up and wake Darren, will you? I'll make a start on some of these tables."

"That reminds me, Boss, we'll should join the food bank. People were very generous the other day at *Prisunic* and we're flush but it's only November and we'll probably need more before the end of the winter."

Howard remembered how many meetings with the supermarket manager it had taken to organise the last collection, even though in the end the locals had come up trumps and the freezer was full and the cartons of milk piled high in the projection room, so he agreed. "I reckon the food bank is a great idea, Pascal. It's quite close to where you live, isn't it."

"Yes, the warehouse is huge and they've even got a cold room in there. It's a good idea but there are quite a few hoops you need to jump through: I think we need a couple of letters from social workers and there's an interview, plus we need to be able to collect the stuff. Do you think we could go with the Salvation Army, Boss? They've got a van."

"That's an idea. All right, I'll ask Captain Ruffet when I see him – or, actually, Cornflower would be fine for the amount of stuff we need because we're not exactly a huge operation, are we? In the meantime, here's ten euros if you need to pop out and get anything at any point. For the guys, I mean."

"There's plenty of everything for today, but I'll have the ten euros anyway, Boss. "Hey, Darren, rise and shine!" he yelled up the stairs but, as a matter of fact, Darren was already on his way down, coughing – a little theatrically, Howard thought.

"Have we got to do this every single day, Howard?" Darren was yawning and rubbing his eyes, too.

"Not at all, just Mondays, Tuesdays and Fridays at the moment, though we may expand now we have your extra pairs of hands. After all, the guys need to eat every day, don't they? The Salvation Army do breakfast every morning, so why shouldn't we? And they start their mornings with an actual service with songs, a sermon and everything and if you don't show up at that, you don't get in at all."

At this, Bunty arrived. " Everything in order? Good, carry on, chaps. Look, I stopped off on the way and got these." She took out a little cardboard box from a paper bag she was carrying.

"What's that?" asked Howard.

"This is a deck of tarot cards for later."

"What have you got those for?" asked Darren with concern.

"Isn't that rather obvious, Dazz? You see, it was so boring for the guys yesterday that I promised some of them I'd get a little something to distract them and these things fit the bill admirably, I'll warrant."

"But, you can't start telling . . ." began Howard, but it was too later because Bunty was already back through the doors again and mingling with the group outside which had by this time swelled to around fifteen.

"She's a popular character," said Darren, "I wish I could be more like her."

"Right, Emma's here. Morning, Emma. Five minute warning, please."

"Howard, have we got to do this every day without fail?"

"Ask Darren, Emma – we've just had that conversation. Come on, here are the other two jugs, get the coffee down and we'll make a start, shall we? Got your blue inhaler, Darren?" Darren patted his jacket and nodded.

Straight away, the rigmarole began again with much fetching and carrying. If anything, it was even more busy than the previous day because there were two men Howard had never seen before, although Bunty seemed to know them well and was deep in conversation with them and Paulo at a table just in front of the screen. They were intent on something on the table, Howard could see from a distance.

About twenty minutes in, Emma and Darren came up in some agitation. "Howard, can we have a word with you in private, please?" asked Emma.

"Problem? Sure, just come up into the flat. Pascal, hold the fort for a second, will you? We're just going up for more coffee."

They were all in Howard's kitchen now and Darren and Emma were shifting nervously from foot to foot. "Howard, we don't know how to say this," began Emma. "But . . ."

"You don't know how to say what? Come on, out with it."

"It's just that, it's Sali. It's just that she's only *telling fortunes* down there. She's got those tarot cards out and now they're taking it in turns three at a time to get her to tell their fortunes."

"Are you positive?" Howard had been fairly sure that Sally wouldn't be quite so brazen about it but had feared something along these lines. All the same, he had to try to avoid a confrontation with Bunty. "You know Sally is a bit of a free spirit," Howard went on, "so what exactly do you expect me to do about it?"

"Myself and Emmi, we've already had a discussion," began Darren.

"Emma and I," corrected Howard.

"What? You weren't there. Anyway, if you don't put a stop to it right now, we're leaving. And we're going to go straight to Milton Keynes and we're going to tell Vicki and Catti about it, what's more." He gave a little defiant guffaw.

"You'll probably lose your job, Howard. Isn't that right, Dazz?" added Emma.

"Definitely. You know, like Ivor Morris did," said Darren. "They won't listen to you but they'll listen to us. After all, we're the church of the future – they keep saying it."

Howard could see they were in earnest, weighed up the probabilities and came to a decision, "All right, I'll do it. Come on, you two, back me up."

"Wait a minute, Howard," said Darren with a superstitious shudder, "Don't you realise there are occult powers involved in this? You can't do anything without spiritual protection. Can't you call a priest or something before you start?"

Howard was hurt. "Call a priest? Hey, may I remind you that we're nothing here in France if not Protestants and I do happen to be an ordained minister of the Lighthouse Agency, don't forget, but if it makes you feel any better, I'll think up a bit of mumbo jumbo. Come on, and bring the coffee with you or there'll be a riot and that really would be something to worry about."

"We'll stay here and cover you in a blanket of prayer," said Emma, still doubtful but taking a seat at the table. "Oh Lord, you just know that Howard is just a weak man with just no natural authority and just an unimpressive outward appearance and just with . . ."

"Oh, no you don't, Emma. You and Darren brought this up so the least you can do is back me up by actually being there. Come on."

Emma got up and crept down behind the others. Howard wasn't quite sure how to proceed as he stepped back into *Salle Deux* but, responding to a moment of inspiration, he crossed his index fingers in front of his face and brandished them as he strode down to Bunty's table, singing the chorus of, *Shine, Jesus, shine* at the top of his voice with Darren and Emma cowering behind him and humming along. *"And Let there be Light!* Oh, thou Honourable Sarah Ottiline Fanshaw, oh, thou Honourable Sarah Ottiline Fanshaw, I do hereby most earnestly adjure thee to renounce Satan and all his works! Oh, ye powers of darkness, that dwell in eternal night, I do command you to begone, begone. In the might, powerful, strong and, er, all-conquering name of . . ."

"Howard, what exactly are you doing?" asked Bunty calmly, gesturing to the cards laid out on the table, "can't you see I'm busy here with this?"

"I'm actually adjuring you to renounce Satan, Sally," answered Howard in a conversational tone.

"*Adjuring!* What kind of language is that? Adjuring me to renounce what for what? Isn't this all a bit medieval?"

"I'm adjuring you to renounce the gross sin of divination." Bunty looked blank. "You know, with those tarot cards. Which I intend to consign to the deepest pit of hell. As soon as I've finished having a good look at them."

"Oh, I see what you mean," Bunty laughed, "your inexperience knows no bounds, does it Howard? However did you accede to the role? Don't you know that here in France, tarot is merely a card game? I suppose it's a mistake that's easily made, but the 78 card deck is so much more satisfying than our own 52 card one because it's that much harder to memorise the fall of the cards as the game goes on, you see. I caused a sensation at Brabourne Acres when I introduced the game and I pretty soon succeeded in establishing a league. You can easily guess who came out on top when all was said and done."

"But I thought . . . That is, Emma and Darren were thinking . . . So. we thought. "

"Ah, I see what's been going on – you've all jumped to a conclusion. But, the use of the tarot deck for fortune telling is a comparatively recent development, you see. The game itself goes back at least to the fifteenth century, you know. Now, if you'll just excuse me, I'm about to complete a trick."

"A trick! A trick!" guffawed Darren, "there you go again – Magick!"

"A trick at cards, Dazz – honestly!"

"Do you mind if I watch? You must show me how to play, one of these days." Howard wanted to keep the peace if he could.

"If you like. It must be quite an education for you to have me here in Bordeaux."

"It's certainly giving me a new perspective. Actually, I need to make an announcement, so you'll have to stop playing for a moment anyway, I'm sorry."

Howard jumped up onto the platform and clapped his hands for quiet. There was a murmur of resentment in the room but eventually it was calm enough for Howard to speak, although an undertow of angry muttering went on.

"Thanks, guys. Now, as you may know, Bordeaux has been named European City of Food next year and it's a really big deal for the city. I know it's unlikely to affect you directly very much for obvious reasons but it does apply to us as an organisation here at the Roxy. I've got to tell you that it so happens that not everybody is delighted for us to be running these breakfasts and there's a move to close us down." Gino whistled between his fingers and Paolo was heard to boo. "Anyway, this morning there's going to be a bit of a delegation of civic dignitaries coming round to have a look at what we do here. I know probably Paquito and Paulo have mentioned that we'd like you to be on your best behaviour this morning when they come round but I thought I'd make it a bit more official, hence the speech. Any questions?"

There was a silence and then Gino asked, "What can we do any different? We're not causing any trouble – you can see we're just sitting here."

"I don't know, actually. I suppose no big knives would be a good start. Yes, I am looking at you, Paolo. Also, if you could avoid smoking out the front of the building, I suppose that would help. Keep the dogs out of sight in here, maybe?"

"Don't you think that's a bit patronising?" objected Paulo.

"Patronising, me? I hate . . ."

"We've all heard it. It wasn't funny the first time or any other time," jeered Paquito.

"Oh, sorry. Anyway, as you were, then . . . only better, in some way," Howard concluded.

As he jumped off the platform, Howard noticed Rev. Brian Filcher come striding in. He hurled his briefcase onto one of the occupied tables, forcing the men seated round it to recoil. Filcher was the minister of the First French Free Methodist church in the affluent suburb of Latresne. He was tall and broad and wore a dog collar under a two thousand euro dark suit. Howard went up and shook hands.

"Hello, Brian, how's tricks?" he asked cheerfully in English. Their paths didn't often cross but Howard was a regular attender at the Bordeaux Ministers' Fellowship of which Filcher was the President, so they had exchanged words a few times. Howard loved going to watch the more powerful ministers bickering and he was such a fixture that he had even been asked to help take up the offering in a large rally organised by the combined churches. As usual, the event had ended with a violent incident where one of the pastors had been beaten up by disgruntled former members.

"I'm sorry, I don't understand," replied Brian, in French.

"What are you on about? I seem to remember you're from Rochdale aren't you?"

"I am from *Roshdall een Gretter Monshester* but I've been in France for so long, I've practically completely forgotten how to speak English now. All of thirty-five years in January, it'll be."

This was in French, too, so in the end Howard had to give in and reply in kind. "But, Brian, your wife is British as well. You're not trying to tell me you speak French at home, are you? *Chéri* and all that malarkey?"

"Sure. French is the loving tongue so I get plenty of practice if you get my meaning. If you were as committed to ministry in France as Caroline and I both are, no doubt you'd do the same."

"Maybe, except I'm not married." Howard wasn't going to stand for this and nearly said so but he decided to attack on another front: "Actually, I have to admit that you're right, Brian. We have an expression in English, *When in Rom, do as ze Roman, 'e do.* Let me see, this quaint saying means that if you are living abroad you should try to fit in with the locals by acting in the same way that they do – adopt local customs and so on. I must say, English has a lot of pictureque sayings like that. You should try relearning it, some day. It's become quite the world language now, I'm told."

"There's no need to be sarcastic, Morgan. I no longer have an English sense of humour either but I could see more or less what you were getting at there and it lacked respect due to my person, if you ask me." Filcher drew himself up to his full height, glowering.

"A French sense of humour! You prefer to see people throwing custard pies around these days, do you?" Howard tried but failed to remove the sarcasm from his tone. "Anyway, what brings you round here slumming it, Brian? Sit down. Coffee?" Howard was already seated at a table and invited the older man to take a chair beside him.

"No thanks, I have already breakfasted and I prefer to stand," replied Filcher before, for no apparent reason flinging himself to the ground and doing twenty press–ups before putting one foot on a chair and his hands on his hips. "I've still got it. Not bad for sixty-four, I think you'll agree. I should explain that I'm part of the delegation this morning. They wanted to invite a senior member of the Protestant community so, naturally, the lot fell on me as chaplain to the City Council."

"Very good. So the others are on their way?"

"No doubt. I came on ahead because I wanted to form my own view on exactly what it is you do here." Filcher sniffed the air and looked round censoriously. "Not a very modern set–up, is it? Not really fit for purpose, one might say. Those electrics there," he pointed to the fuse box in the corner, "those don't conform to EN–60065. Fire extinguishers are inadequate for this use and that's just a start. If we decided to do something like this at the Free Methodists – not that we would – we'd do it properly, I think it's fair to say. We have a number of doctors and social workers who could advise as well as all the proper contractors in full membership."

"We do the best with the resources we have, actually, Brian," said Howard proudly.

"Well, I don't suppose I could do what you do with these wretched men, Morgan – if, God forbid, I had to try – but, then again, I don't suppose you could do what I do, could you?"

"How'd you mean?" Howard was mystified. "Aren't we basically in the same game?"

"Hardly. What I meant is that you probably wouldn't be able to run a successful operation like ours at Latresne. My role is more like that of a company director than anything else. I often describe it like this: I'm senior management with an extensive staff of fellow professionals and more than three hundred people under me running the different departments of what is, by any standards, a vast enterprise with many smaller dependent church plants in all areas of the city and even out in the sticks."

Howard wasn't going to stand for that. "As a matter of fact, back in Wales, I was youth minister in a place where we had more than five hundred . . ." Howard made as if to get up from his chair but Filcher prevented him with a hand on his shoulder.

"The way I see it, Morgan, you run an operation that resembles a little village post office whereas I am in charge of a large chain of department stores like your John Lewis in Britain or your Debenhams." Filcher thrust out his crotch, forcing Howard to sit back in his chair. "Or, to change the metaphor, you have charge of a little beaten–up old Citroen 2CV while I, as I do in fact, drive an impressive Mercedes with all the latest features. You are a frail light aircraft hopping from airfield to airfield carrying cargo of little value – shiny trinkets and gewgaws for the natives – while I am a transatlantic jumbo jet transporting the elite to important destinations and with the hold filled with many a precious commodity alongside the crates of bullion."

"A large, torpedo–shaped object, in fact."

"Exactly. This plays out in many other areas, too. Take your sermons, for example. I'm told you use a somewhat colloquial style when you preach. For my part, I could never get away with anything like that. My sermons are literary creations – what we French people call *textes*. There's a certain depth and gravitas to what I do that you simply don't need here, Morgan."

"You think that? Actually . . . "

"Certainly, I *do* think that but I feel I have to encourage you to persevere. If you do, you too may have an international ministry like mine one day. As you may know, I am often in Quebec and even in the States, speaking at large conferences about the spectacular church growth I have achieved here. I always speak, I might add, through an interpreter. Were I you, I should be inclined to recommend a move of the church bodily from the city centre to the suburbs where one finds a better class of Christian without having to bother much with the problems of the inner-city."

"Were I you?"

"I should be inclined . . ."

"Yes, I caught that bit, thanks."

"In fact, I have been having some serious discussions along similar lines with Daniel de Moulinet and with his most charming helpmeet Madame de Moulinet."

"You know Daniel and Suzon?"

"I do. In fact, just between ourselves, I have been involved in offering them considerable incitements and enticements to leave this operation and throw in their lot with us in Latresne. Daniel particularly is, shall we say, not uninterested in the proposition. Either that or another plan would be to make your place a satellite of ours by your handing control to our board. Ample resources would begin to flow your way – I can guarantee that. Money, not people. Naturally."

"So, you've been trying to poach our members?" Howard was outraged, "that's not ethical."

"Not as such, of course, but I have merely been pointing out some of the advantages which might accrue to Daniel and Suzon from a change of, how shall I put this, a change of churchmanship. We already offer a home to several people of your own denominational persuasion who have come to Bordeaux for work, have done their research beforehand and have come directly to us without even considering a courtesy visit to your little operation." This was a revelation: Howard had often wondered why the annual round of promotions and postings never resulted in any new attenders for the Roxy.

"Morgan, I have it in mind to offer you a treat." Filcher took Howard's arm and brought him to his feet.

"What is it, an internship at Latresne?"

"No, I have it in mind to let you sit in my car, so that you can imagine what it must be like to live the life I lead, if only for a moment. Come on, I'll direct you but you are to keep your eyes closed so that you can take in the wonder of it at one glance." Filcher was clearly going to brook no refusal, so Howard found himself outside in the cold again and being directed towards the *Aigle d'Argent* until in the end he received the order to open his eyes.

"There she is – a Mercedes Maybach S600. Jump in and luxuriate."

"How can I – aren't you going to unlock it?"

There was a heavy clunk from the car. "I can not only unlock it, but even start it from a distance. Look." The motor purred into life and Howard prepared to get into the front passenger seat. "Unfortunately, there's no time for a spin before Madame de Pigalette arrives but you can get the idea: 12–way adjustable front seats with massage facility. Get in."

As Howard sat, the leather upholstery began to touch him intimately and sensuously. "Could I have the window open, please?" Howard asked.

"Certainly."

"I was talking to the car, actually, Brian. Anyway, enough of this. As long as a car gets me from A to B, that's enough for me," Howard wrongly thought he had managed to keep the envy out of his tone.

"I hear that comment a number of times a day, Morgan, but somehow it so rarely convinces." Some glossy leaflets in one of the more prominent glove compartments caught Filcher's eye. "I intend to leave some of our church publicity with you, Morgan. You might just scatter it around. After all, as you said, we're not in competition as such."

Howard could see that on the front of the colour brochure was a picture of a tremendous facility with happy people milling round while in small roundels were dull images of some of Bordeaux's other churches, including the Roxy, all crossed out with a printed X. Inside, the screed began, *When you think of the church, you inevitably think about cold buildings, outdated rituals, ineffectual social action and irrelevant services. We on the other hand . . .*

"Thanks, Brian. I'll make sure I scatter them round, like you said. Oh, maybe I could give you some of these in exchange?" Howard fished out a dozen creased flyers for *The Biding Place* from an inside pocket and handed them to Filcher.

"What's this?' asked Filcher with distaste and holding them at arms length.

"Just some flyers for a film we're putting on this Saturday, Brian. *The Biding Place*."

"No, no. I can see what they are. I meant the paper." Filcher was rubbing one of the invitations between finger and thumb. "But this is ordinary 70 gram photocopier paper isn't it?"

"I suppose – I've never really thought about it that much."

"We have a 90 gram policy, I'm afraid, so we can't take these. By the way, did nobody tell you that in French, unlike in English, there's a gap between text and an exclamation mark or a question mark – like this ?"

"Is there? No one told us that in Uni. Are you sure it really matters that much?"

"Precision is everything in this job, Morgan; it earns one respect through fear. You'll learn that or fail here. By the way, I heard you use the word *mecenat* at the ministers' meeting the other day. You'll find it's *mécenat*." Filcher strode back towards the Roxy.

As Howard climbed out of the Mercedes, he noticed that his fists were clenched in his pockets and he decided to avoid further confrontation by stalking back into the flat to pick up a coffee before the delegation arrived. As it happened, though, he was only able to have a couple of sips before Daniel de Moulinet came in downstairs with an elegantly dressed woman.

"Brian, are you well?" Daniel shook hands with Filcher but Howard he ignored. "Now Madame de Pigalette, as you can see, this is a quite untenable situation and I think it would be wise if we were to proceed directly to the ratification . . ." Daniel was showing her his letter.

"Excuse me, de Moulinet but didn't you say we were to meet the pastor here this morning?"

"Oh, I'm terribly sorry, Madame. Yes, here he is – Morgan. Howard Morgan." He pointed at Howard with distaste. "Morgan, may I present Madame de Pigalette, Member of Parliament, lady mayoress of Bordeaux, President of the Regional Council and so on and so forth. The Reverend Doctor Brian Filcher, you know, of course."

"They call me Anne–Sophie and I'm delighted to meet you, Monsieur Morgan," began Madame de Pigalette with some warmth, "I've been hearing some very impressive reports about how you . . ."

Unfortunately, Howard was still furious after his exchange with Brian Filcher and he had come to the conclusion during his disturbed night that attack was the best form of defence so he jumped in with both feet.

"Right, de Piglet or whatever it is you're called, I've got to tell you straight away that we are not going to put up with you coming in here and throwing your weight around like a . . ."

Pascal was at Howard's side, "Boss, cool it! Can't you see . . ." he began with concern.

"No, no. I'm going to have my say now. I've done enough listening and kowtowing this morning and you're going to listen to me. You've decided to close us down but I'm not going to go down without a fight."

"But, Monsieur Morgan, on the contrary, I'm going . . ."

"Look at the three of you. It's just a stitch up. Just like the time you shipped all the homeless people out of the city centre during the finals of the Europa Tournament that time. That was a disgrace. You look down on these people because of the way they . . ."

"Boss, boss, she's trying to tell you . . ."

"*European City of Food*, indeed," Howard's voice was dripping with sarcasm, "Look at these poor guys sitting here. They're just grateful if they get a couple of *biscottes* and jam and a cup of . . ."

"Monsieur Morgan, I'm in no way responsible for what my predecessor may or may not have done during the Europa Cup. I'm merely trying to tell you that I . . ."

"And I'm *merely* trying to tell *you* that if you think you can come in here and gang up on us and we're not going to stand up for our rights, you've got another thing coming."

Howard was blazing with rage. "Go on, look round. Poke your silk sow's nose in where it's not wanted. Look round and sneer but if you need me, I'm going to be up in my flat." And he stalked off again, banging the door to his quarters and stomping up the wooden staircase.

"De Moulinet," Howard could just hear Madame de Pigalette turn to Heseltine, "I can honestly say that I've never been so insulted in all my life except during the wine-watering scandal back in . . ."

"Job done," Howard muttered to himself with satisfaction.

Pascal was after him in a shot, "Now look what you've done, Boss. Get back down there and apologise."

"Apologise? For what? I only told *truth* . . ."

" . . . *to power*. That's a bit old now – I've heard it a thousand times. Couldn't you tell she was on your side?"

"How do you mean?"

"She was being polite and she was getting ready to give you a compliment. She might have given you grant or suggested some better premises or something?"

"I won't be bought off like that, Pascal. All I want to do is l*ight a candle* . . ."

". . . *in the darkness*. I know. Ditto. Same old same old. Get back down there and you can keep on doing that, maybe. It might not be too late." Pascal was begging.

Howard had stopped shaking by now and as he ran through the events of the last few minutes it began to dawn on him that maybe Pascal was right. He poured another coffee, drank it off and saw the whole picture. He made for the door, with a sheepish grin of apology to Pascal.

By the time he was in *Salle Deux* again the delegation had been completed by another man – it was Martin Fontenau the trouser tycoon of *Fontenau Bags* fame – and they were all seated round one of the tables so Howard made as if to join them.

"Not so fast, Morgan" said Brian Filcher with a sneer. "I think Anne–Marie has a few concluding remarks to make, so you can just stand there and listen." Howard spread his hands in a gesture of contrition. "No, no, it's too late for that. We've already made our decision."

"Monsieur Morgan," began Madame de Pigalette, "I came here this morning quite well–disposed to what you have been trying to do in the centre. As you know, the problem of homelessness is one we take very seriously here in Bordeaux and any of our partners who show a willingness to alleviate this scourge can count on us to . . ."

"Madame de Pigalette . . . Anne-Marie . . . "

". . . can count on us to help shoulder the burden if they play ball with us. But don't you dare *Anne–Marie* me. Instead, I've come here, and you have subjected me to a tirade of abuse and false accusations the likes of which I've rarely heard even in Parliament. It is our decision that today's session is to be your last until after the European City of Food events next year, on whose conclusion we shall carry out another visit of the premises, focusing on conformity to the current regulations and a further decision will be made."

"Madame de Pigalette, may I . . ."

"The decision is final," declared Heseltine, "*Quelle horreur!*"

"This morning, I brought the power of closure prepared by our lawyer Monsieur Dobachi. I must say I was quite prepared to impose my veto upon the order, in spite of the fierce opposition of these gentlemen," Madame de Pigalette indicated the other members of the delegation, "but, as it stands, I hereby sign it in triplicate, thus, thus and thus, and I apply the municipal seal here, thus and thus and thus."

Howard studied the document and was relieved to see that it only applied to the opening hours of the homeless breakfasts and not to all the activities of the church. He thought he could see a loophole. "Apparently, Madame, this document does not prevent us from re-opening for breakfast on the days not specified by your Monsieur Dobachi."

"Study it at your leisure, Monsieur Morgan, and you will discover that it is in fact not so. Now, if you will excuse us, we have a series of wine tastings beginning at ten-thirty at the *chateau de Moulinet.*"

"Wait a minute," Howard waved the document in Madame de Pigalette's face with a gesture of triumph, "Dobachi is an anagram of *Ichabod* – that's so obviously a made-up name. You're having me on."

Madame de Pigalette looked closely at the power of closure, "Ha! So it is – *Ichabod* – *The glory has departed,*" she laughed, "how very apposite! I assure you, however, that the name is a genuine one and the suspension of service is no less real and binding. Health and safety regulations may sometimes be interpreted in a flexible manner but in the right circumstances, they are a powerful weapon indeed. Gentlemen? All rise."

As the delegation left, the conversation among the homeless men resumed and Howard could hear that most of it was a grumbling undertow connected with the flow of coffee which had been interrupted for nearly twenty minutes by now, so Howard asked Emma and Darren to fetch some refills as he made his way to the platform once more.

"Gentlemen! And so, you see," he began in a passionate voice, "the iron fist has spoken and has trodden us underfoot. We are all, are we not, equally victims of a faceless bureaucracy? For my part, I'm humiliated, sorry, I am frustrated in my efforts to bring a ray of sunshine into your sea of misfortunes. For your part, you are forced to suffer all this because of a minor indiscretion which I may or may not have . . ."

"Suffer? We don't suffer because of this," called out Paulo with a cruel laugh.

"How's that? I thought we provided a valuable service. Out, brothers, out . . ."

"Out! Out we go from here," Paolo went on, "that's right, because we don't want hassle from Madame de Pigalette but there are plenty of other places, you know. The Salvation Army round the corner and across the square, for one. The only disadvantage is the captain doesn't let us smoke in there and the dogs have to stay in a separate room. But that's nothing really. We don't mind sitting through the service either because it's in the warm. We don't sing, mind. So, this is convenient, the Roxy, but there are plenty of other options."

"Nonetheless, I call on you all now a to stand up for the forces of, of right and free assembly," shouted Howard. "We're not going to be told what to do by a city that washes its hands of us, as soon as it's convenient, are we? We are not! It's time to light a candle in the darkness and speak truth to power! As your great compatriot Robespierre once said to Danton, *Georges,* he said, *Georges. Yes, Maximilien, or may I call you Max? replied Danton, an enigmatic smile playing about his robust features . . ."*

"You're a fool, Howard," said Bunty with a laugh. "A likeable fool, some say, but a fool nonetheless. I think of you as a *Candide* – an eternal victim of events. What you do in here isn't all that unimpreeive, actually – a bit amateurish but it does the trick. Even you can see you've really blown it this time, surely? Can't you get it through your thick skull that none of these guys is ever going to risk a conflict with the City Hall or, dare I say it, with the Police just to make you feel a little better about yourself?" She turned to the room. "That's right, isn't it, guys? He's blown it, hasn't he? Just when he was doing so well." There was a loud murmur of assent and already most of them were gathering their things together and making for the door.

"Guys, wait. The Bible reading is all about the Whore of Babylon today. You know how much you like that one. How about it, Paquito? I expect you'll stay."

"I'll give it a whirl," said Paquito, scratching his bad leg with savage vigour but in the end, apart from Pascal and the Dynamix, he was the only one who stayed as the others trudged towards the Salvation Army citadel, so Howard decided to give the reading a miss just this once.

As he left, Paquito turned to Howard and said, "You know what Sally said just now?"

"Which bit are you thinking of?"

"When she said none of us would stand up for you. I'm not sure she's right about that."

"Ha, thanks a bunch! Group meeting, in my kitchen, Dynamix," Howard called out and he stomped up the stairs with Emma, Darren and Bunty to reassemble around the table.

Howard picked his French dictionary off the shelf and looked up *mecenat*. It turned out there was no accent. Filcher was always doing that to the junior English speaking guys. He was a bit of an Alain, in that respect – a bar steward.

"Right, gather round, chaps," began Howard.

"That's right. Gather around you the tattered remnants of your authority, Howard. We're all ears."

"There's no need to take that tone, Sally. You saw I was outnumbered back there and I just lost it for a moment."

"For a moment! Why don't you just say you lost it? You remind me of a beak we used to rag at Brabourne Acres because of her weakness for a little drinkypoo."

"Now that's over, what are we going to do with our time, Howard?" asked Emma, with obvious relief.

"Have a lie–in, for a start," replied Bunty. "I've been getting up at five thirty, doing half an hour of piano – scales and arpeggios mainly – going for a five kilometre run in the vines and then doing my New Testament Greek, all in order to be here by seven, you see – and that's with my foot down to the floor in Minerva."

"Do we have to tell Vicki and Catti about what's happened?" asked Darren with a guffaw of mingled concern and relief.

"Above all not," said Howard, "In the next couple of days I'll write a newsletter on all our behalf all about a well-earned break and a warm new contact with leading local politicians and they can send it out to the churches in a week or two. They'll lap it up. We have to keep the funds rolling in, don't forget, and you can't do that by talking about setbacks. That much I *have* learned. I tell you what, though, there's always this." Howard took out of his pocket five or six dog-eared invitations for *The Biding Place*. "I'll run off a few thousand more of these . . . "

". . . on a clapped-out old *Banda* machine, it looks like."

"Sally! I'll have you know these are photocopied, four-up. It may only be 70 gram paper but, still. I'll run them off and, Darren, you can put them through the guillotine – you're good at that and it's a real gift – and then we're all set to go out and not only do the letterboxes again but even give them to people in the street. Engage them in conversation. *Compel them to come in.* Come on, pull together why won't you?"

"Ha! I'll not be doing that," scoffed Bunty.

"I think you'll find you are, though, Sally."

"What? Give out leaflets with a swastika plastered all over them? No chance. Have you any idea of how things stand in the political landscape here, Howard? Do you even stop to think for a moment? The last thing the French want is to be reminded of the Nazis. Many of them have a less than glorious past, having backed the wrong horse, you see. Even Pa Fanshaw would have felt the same if Franco had lost in Spain."

"Sally, in this context, the swastika is above all a potent symbol of oppression with a remarkably wide reference. These leaflets will have a considerable impact on all who see them. I fully expect a strong reaction and I shall ride it out." Howard bristled with pride.

"Exactly. I couldn't have put it better myself except for the bit about riding it out. In brief, I'll have no part in it. If you need me, I shall be taking care of pressing matters appertaining to my toiletry range. We decided on a name in *La Rotonde*: it's to be *Shatto – Vintage Claret and Coffee scrub by de Moulinet et Fanshaw.* Oh, Dazz and Emmi, we shall be looking for a couple of entry-level sales reps when we get back from here ." She tapped the side of her nose, "Even you, Howard might get an interview because we have in mind many a menial task. Networking, you see. Good morning, all." Sally's tread in the staircase was light and carefree.

"Darren, get that guillotine out ready or heads will roll."

9

A couple of hours later, Howard, Pascal and the Dynamix had arrived at the street market at the foot of the *Pey Berland* tower and there were plenty of people round. They each held a large heap of the flyers – the top few were already beginning to curl in the light wind but it looked as if the rain would hold off for long enough for them to make some inroads on the pile.

Darren was hanging back and asked with a little guffaw, "Could we not have one more coffee, before we start, Howard? It's been nearly half an hour since the last one."

"Nonsense. We'll have a break when we're earned it in about twenty minutes, Darren and we can put our heads together and compare notes about how it's been going. You know, plan our next move." Darren and Emma still looked doubtful. "Look, tell you what, I'll do the first one or two and you can see how to set about it. Here's the spiel I've put together: *Good morning, I represent the Roxy Christian Centre, rue Jean Jaurès. We're showing this exciting and thought–provoking film on Saturday. I hope you can come. Free entry and light refreshments available. Libre P.A.F."* Emma and Darren wer stumped."*Libre*

Participation aux Frais – a collection but with no obligation to contribute."

"How about, *Good morning. A film. Goodbye?* Is that close enough?" asked Emma.

"It's a start. It's only the bare bones but you can expand on that as you get more confident. Anyway, just look at the way I do it. You'll soon get the hang of it and you'll be begging me to let you go out by yourselves at all hours. Watch and learn."

Howard went up to an elderly lady with a basket on wheels who was chatting at a fruit stall. "Good morning, *Madame*," he began, offering a flyer. " I represent the Roxy Christian Centre . . ."

The reaction was dramatic. The woman stared at the paper, tracing the crooked cross with a trembling forefinger, snatched it from Howard, tore it once, then twice, threw the pieces to the ground and spat on them. "That's what I think of that and that's what I think of you and people like you. I didn't go through . . ."

"No, you don't understand, it's just a . . ."

"Just a? I *understand* better than you could ever know. My brother was just three years old when the Nazis came to the village and we'd all heard about what happened at Oradour when they . . ."

"No, it's just a film that's about . . ."

"I don't care if it's a twenty volume set of encyclopaedias. Don't you think we suffered enough under the Nazis without having to put up with a film . . . ?"

"I didn't say it wasn't a good film . . ."

The lady sized Howard up as if for a blow, even from her small stature. "You . . . prat. Now, if you'll excuse me, I have some shopping to do." She turned her back and even the stallholder tossed her head.

"*Madame,* If you'd like me to help you carry your shopping home?" She ignored this.

Howard returned to the others. Emma had blanched and Darren was shaking while Pascal was doubled up with laughter. "There you are, that's all there is to it," said Howard, "but I've been thinking it may not be the best use of our time, after all. Now, maybe we could start by having a coffee, then we can do a few hundred letterboxes: there are some quite big blocks of flats near here so you can get a lot done in a short time if you can get into the hallway. Pascal is good at that, aren't you, Pascal?"

"Leave it to me, Boss."

"If you run out of letterboxes, the next best thing is to put them underneath people's windscreen wipers. In fact, a row of those looks quite striking. Make sure there's no one sitting in the car, though." Howard demonstrated how that was done with a row of three cars but the fourth was occupied so he just turned to the team and said, "You see? Piece of cake."

10

"Shall we push the boat out and show it in *Salle Une* just this once, Boss? It always looks so much better on the big screen – there's a better sound system in there as well." Pascal was eager, shifting from foot to foot and undulating wildly. Howard was half inclined to give in to his enthusiasm.

"Hmm, I'm not sure. There's you and me but you'll be in here with the projector, there's the the Dynamix – or Emma and Darren at least because Bunty might still think of something better to do. Paquito loves a film, of course." Howard was counting on his fingers. "The Heseltines will be there. That warm contact from the fruit stall at the market definitely gave me the impression she'd make an effort and turn out. Some of the guys – the weather's not great but let's be optimistic and say four. Yeah, maybe we're probably looking at *Salle Deux* as usual to be honest, sorry."

It was the evening of the film, with just under an hour to go and Howard and Pascal were in the projection room making the last few preparations. They had already got the canisters with the two reels of *The Biding Place* out and had been debating which projector to load with the Donald Duck short they were showing first.

"Darren, come up in here and we'll show you how to thread the film through. That's a useful skill for the workplace."

"It's all video and, actually, online online these days, Howard," said Darren, climbing with trepidation up the steel ladder and putting his head round the heavy door.

"You never know when you might need to do this, Darren. Don't forget there are plenty of churches that will never get a sniff of the most recent equipment. I still use a slide projector myself when I'm going round the churches."

"Through here, round here, up there, through here, and down there," explained Pascal, showing remarkable dexterity. "Now, we're ready to go live, Darren." The ancient projector whirred into life in a convincingly smooth way because Pascal had spent some time that afternoon, oiling this and that and refreshing his mind with the handbook. "Those numbers you can see on the screen are what we focus with. Like this. Nice and sharp, see. It's crucial not to stop the film with the light still on or it burns through straight away. So, off with the light – this button here – and we're ready to go."

"Opening time or *doors* as we call it in twenty minutes. " Howard rubbed his hands together. "There's just time for a coffee, Darren – would you do the honours, please?"

"Why is it always me?" Darren made as if to settle down one the other side of the projector to Pascal.

"It's a compliment – you make the best coffee of all of us, so bring it down on a tray, will you, and we can drink a toast to the success of *The Biding Place.* It never fails to make a big effect. You'll see."

By the time they had finished the coffee it was time to open the doors and Howard and Pascal stood outside and scanned both ends of the street.

"Look, Boss – Hollywood Boulevard," said Pascal as Daniel and Suzon de Moulinet drew up directly outside in their Jaguar, parking where the oil drums had been a few minutes earlier. "Is that really a feather boa Suzon has got on? Sequinned dress in the foyer lights. Nice."

"Blue blazer, brass buttons. Alain Delon! Good evening, Monsieur and Madame de Moulinet. Hi, Véro. I should have rolled out a red carpet. Why didn't I think of that?"

"Save that for Sally," said Véronique, laughing. She rarely went out in the evening, so this was a special occasion for her and she was determined to make the most of it. She had put on a little black dress and, on the whole, it wasn't too bad, Howard thought.

"Where is Sally, anyway?"

"She's looking round for Paquito in Minerva, I think. Oh, there she is now."

Paquito got out of the passenger seat and Bunty took his arm, satirically, "And, arriving with one of Bordeaux's leading homeless men is the Honourable Sally Fanshaw, entrepreneur, muso, socialite and wit," said Howard.

"Actually, I have to give you an accolade for once, Howard, this does look passably impressive and almost as goo as the real thing. I've just seen Paolo and Jean–Pierre making their way here, but there was a bit of a disturbance round the corner behind the *Aigle d'Argent* so I had to take a short detour via the river." She gestured down towards the expressway.

"A disturbance?"

"Yes, two groups of people with banners were having a bit of a barney, you see. I couldn't quite make out what it was all about."

"Probably a hen night, I imagine. Anyway, come through here – we're using *Salle Deux* tonight and the music is already on. No necking, mind."

The *Rue Jean Jaurès* was already becoming animated even though it was still quite early and Howard paused to sense the night scene just coming to life. He was always thrilled to be part of it but just as he turned to go back inside, he stopped to listen more intently to a detail in the soundscape. It was an unfamiliar sound to Howard's ears but unmistakably a rumour of chanting coming closer from somewhere behind the club opposite.

"What are they saying, Boss?" asked Pascal.

Howard shrugged his shoulders. "Don't know. Sounds like *Brown with old ashes.* Come on, it's nearly time to get going. This is when my Dad would always get us a choc ice."

"*Brown with old ashes?* They're shouting the names of the bride and groom, I expect, Boss."

"Maybe. Anyway, let's check the Heseltines are comfortable. Madame Joris, if you would care to walk this way? You too, Paolo." Howard turned to Pascal with a self-satisfied smirk. "There you are – I told you so. There'll be a dozen of us at after all."

"Eleven, Boss."

"That's what I said – a dozen. Howard counted on his fingers. Anyway, there *are* twelve."

Howard escorted the latest arrivals to *Salle Deux* and it was satisfying to see that the room didn't look empty at all. "No kissing in the back row, please," called Howard in a cheery voice.

"You've already said that or similar. Any ice creams available?" asked Sally.

"Just enjoy the music. Its Didier Deschiens – who has actually performed here, don't forget," said Howard, "in *Salle Une*, what's more."

As Howard made his way back to the entrance for a last look up and down the street in case of any late arrivals, he noticed that the chanting had got noticeably louder and was now coming from a little nearer – just down the road by now. By now, it was even possible to make out the words quite clearly: not, *Brown with old ashes* at all but, *Down with all fascists*.

"Early evening. Funny time for a demo, Boss," said Pascal with a puzzled tone.

"Some stragglers from something down town this afternoon, I expect. Hang on, listen." Howard cupped one ear. "There's some more chanting coming from down there in the other direction. What are that lot saying? It sounds like, *Keep pants for the trench?*"

Pascal strained to hear. "What kind of advice is that? A gardeners' demo? It's not, it's, *Keep France for the French*, Boss. Whew! I hope they don't meet up with this other lot or there'll be fireworks. Still, not our problem."

"That's right: not our problem. One for Madame de Pigalette and the City Council, if anything."

At that, just as Pascal and Howard turned to go inside, the two groups came into view – there were about thirty or forty in each column – and at the same moment, they caught sight of each other. The chanting died away on either side for a moment as they took stock of the situation, but then started up again with renewed vigour as the rival demonstrations began to converge.

"Ha ha! You could almost think they've come for the film," laughed Howard.

"That's what I'm afraid of, Boss."

"What?"

"Remember that flyer, Boss? *A powerful piece of communication*, you said?"

"Right, Pascal," said Howard as light dawned. "We're using *Salle Une* after all. Get Darren and Emma to move everybody across and you get busy. Put Donald Duck in the other projector. I'll stay out here and keep the peace. Focus. Focus."

"Focus! Are you trying to tell me my job? That's what the numbers are for. I'll get the oil can. It should be basically okay from the last time we showed *The Bible and the Zipgun*, though, Boss."

By this time the two demos had arrived in front of the Roxy and an uneasy calm broken by one or two taunts had ensued as they sized each other up. Howard decided to seize the moment and clapped his hands,

"Welcome, ladies and gentlemen, to the *Roxy Christian Centre* and to the latest in our series of very popular film nights. As you can see, the building dates from the art deco period and has many of the original fittings. We have a real treat in store this evening as before *The Biding Place* we have a vintage Donald Duck cartoon. A feast for all you nostalgia buffs out there. So without, any further ado . . ."

"*France for the French*," called an uncertain voice from the crowd.

"*Down with all fascists?*" suggested another.

"Before we begin," went on Howard, "may I remind you that, as well as being a cinema, the Roxy is a place of Christian worship. The Lighthouse Agency, founded in 1887 as the . . ."

"Death to the Catholic Church!"

"Joan of Arc! Joan of Arc!"

" . . . We are Protestants, actually. If anybody is interested in the Reformation or even just the sixteenth century, really, I have a course I can run about it – the Wars of Religion? So, see me afterwards because it's quite a big part of our identity, so may I ask that due decorum be observed when you get inside and . . ."

They were already on their way in, the two groups mingling, jostling and arguing amongst themselves.

" . . . there will be a freewill offering to cover . . ."

"Out of the way, mate."

" . . . to cover, er, any, er, depredations . . . So, at the time of the Reformation, in the sixteenth century many groups of Christians of our type, disillusioned with . . ." Howard gave up because everyone had now moved inside.

*

Salle Une was more than half full by 7.30, the rival factions separated by the central aisle. Howard considered another speech but in the end decided the best way of making sure there was no trouble was by starting the film, so he went out and gave the prearranged signal to Pascal by reaching up and tapping on the projection room door with a broom. He could make out a muffled call of assent from Pascal inside, so returned to his post next to Heseltine at the end of a row.

"Well done, Morgan. Your efforts have paid off for once."

"Yes, it's going to be a night to remember, Daniel." Howard crossed his fingers and clutched the collection plate to his chest, turning his attention to the screen.

The cartoon was all about an attempt by developers to demolish Donald Duck's house to make way for a modern office block. His struggle was against a bright yellow bulldozer the animators had turned into a human personality with an angry face and a contorting body. Before too long, Howard could tell that the audience had taken sides with what was going on on the screen. At each new incident of destruction by the machine or of resistance by Donald, there was cheering and booing on all sides. Slogans began to be called out and taken up by groups in different parts of the room – *Support the little man* and *Capital! Capital!* were the most prominent.

"Morgan. Put a stop to this," Hissed Daniel, "They're spoiling the film for me. Go and point a torch in somebody's face or pace up and down with a tray of ices. That's how they did it in the old days."

"I can't do that. There are too many people involved," replied Howard. "We're just going to have to tough it out and rely on the power of cinema to tell the story and draw them in."

"Make Pascal turn the sound up, then. *Quelle horreur!*"

"Don't you think that'll only make it worse?"

"It's worth trying. Just do it. The power of cinema needs to be both seen and heard to have a fair chance of casting its spell on the people."

Howard went out, placed the ladder, climbed up and hammered on the door of the projection room with his fist.

"What is it, Boss? It's going well – as far as I can tell, they're loving it so far!"

"Turn it up – we've got to try to drown out the chanting. This is getting dangerous and *The Biding Place* hasn't even started yet." Howard could hear a patter like rain on a sports car roof from *Salle Une*. "People are starting to throw things at the fu . . . the funny film."

"Yes, I squinted through. They're screwing up the flyers for *The Biding Place* and throwing those – I knew you shouldn't have put one on each seat. Okay, Boss, here goes with the sound. Get back in there: there's a great bit coming up. Donald drives a steam roller over the bulldozer's scoop and it comes out looking like a duck's beak. Go on – you don't want to miss it."

Howard was just in time to witness the reaction to the scene. The music was deafening now but did nothing to subdue the chanting as the place erupted. It was just like Saturday morning pictures in Splott, thought Howard. How had they coped with the uproar back then? A raffle. If only the church covenant didn't rule out games of chance. Howard noticed that Bunty was at the front with her back to the screen, conducting with a pencil as a baton a chant of *Progress! Progress!* A moment later she had jumped across the aisle and was leading *Resist! Resist!* The cartoon had come to an end by now but the pandemonium went on, if anything even louder than before.

Heseltine was on his feet, outraged. "There's to be no intermission. Put on *The Biding Place* straight away, Morgan," he yelled as Howard rushed by to tell Pascal do just that. Even though she want given to revealing her feelings, even Suzon looked mildly concerned.

Howard was once again up the ladder, "Pascal, as quick as you can," he yelled, "*The Biding Place.* I've had an idea. Can you run it at double speed?"

"This projector won't do that, Boss. Anyway, we'd never be able to show our faces again – that would turn the whole evening into an utter farce."

"Fair comment."

As soon as Howard got back into *Salle Une* the certificate for *The Biding Place* was on the screen and soon after, the credits began. Unfortunately, they were underscored by a menacing orchestration of *Deutchland, Deutchland Uber Alles*. Roughly half the room joined in, singing to *la* while the other half rose and prepared to storm across the aisle.

Howard got up and made for the front, ready to make another speech but then something unpleasant began to happen to his eyes – they began to itch and water as he started to cough. Heseltine had obviously been affected in the same way and within moments there was panic in the room as the disturbance became general.

"Gas! Gas!" yelled Howard. "Everybody out! Out! In an orderly manner, please. Out! Darren, the emergency door."

"Where? How do I open it?"

"There, by the screen, where it says *Sortie*," Howard was spluttering, "There's a bar you push. Some of you others, through here," Howard shouted, trying to prop open the double doors leading to the corridor. Pascal was by his side, down from the projection room yelling, "You shouldn't shout *Gas! Gas!* You should be shouting, *Unknown toxic substance! Unknown toxic substance!* You'll cause a panic."

Howard was momentarily swept back against the wall by the rush but it only took a minute for the room to empty and then Howard and Pascal were able to grope their way towards the main exit. Howard's eyes were swollen to a slit and his face was burning. Outside was a milling crowd of close to a hundred people looking subdued and rubbing their faces although there were one or two brawls on the periphery and plenty of shouting. Then, Howard heard police sirens at either end of the road and the main body of people began to evaporate, some into the Saturday evening melee of the *Aigle d'Argent* and others down side streets and alleys still narrower than the *Rue Jean Jaurès*.

As two police cars came to a halt outside the Roxy from opposite directions, sirens going, another policeman arrived on foot. *"Bonsoir, bonsoir – qu'est-ce qui se passe ici, alors?"*

"What did he say?" sked Darren, who was clinging to Howard, weeping and guffawing by turn.

"He said, *Hello, hello – what's going on here, then?*" Howard turned to the policeman. "Nothing, officer. Everything is under control, thanks. We were just showing a film about the Nazis and two opposing political demonstrations turned up. It was nothing. There was a bit of argy–bargy but, hey, it wasn't exactly *La Bataille d'Hernani!*" Howard gave a little laugh before blowing his nose.

"*La Bataille d'Hernani?*"

"You know – the premiere of the play *Hernani* by Hugo. There was a lot of shouting and fighting in the theatre between rival groups of critics."

The policeman was writing in a notebook and mumbling, "Suspect: a man by the name of Hugo. Fighting within the precincts of the cinema. Has this *Hugo* a surname, sir?"

"No, anyway this happened a long time ago, years as a matter of fact."

The policeman went on writing. "A historic case, then. On the run is he, this Hugo character?"

"No, you don't understand," said Howard with a touch of exasperation in his tone.

"Excuse me, sir but if you're going to get aggressive I'm going to have to arrest you. That's what we do – we run them in. We run them in. We show them we're the bold . . ."

Howard could barely see or breathe now but somehow he dredged the information from the depths of his memory, "Look, *Hernani* was a play by Victor Hugo – a writer. He introduced certain stylistic innovations into his work and on the night of the first performance of this play there were two rival gangs who interrupted the show and there was fighting and so on. One of the factions was led by a flamboyant person called Gautier, another writer."

"So it's this Gaultier character we're looking for, is it? You're not making sense, you know."

"This happened in, let's see, 1830." Howard was coughing and retching into a corner of his jacket, "I was just saying there was a disturbance in our cinema this evening but it wasn't really worthy of being compared with what happened on the evening of the first performance of the theatre play *Hernani* by the writer Victor Hugo in the year of our Lord 1830, an event attended by many famous people including the poet, critic, novelist and dramatist, Théophile Gautier. That's my story and I'm sticking to it. There's a young woman here somewhere called Sally Fanshaw who will confirm all that and probably recite excerpts from the play as well, if you like or do the whole thing in mime."

Howard looked round for corroboration from Bunty but she was nowhere to be seen. Daniel, Suzon and Véronique were comforting one another over by the Jaguar. Pascal was wandering around picking at his face and swigging some *Evian* from a litre bottle. Emma was crouched on the kerb, bewildered and being comforted by Darren, but of Bunty there was no sign.

"Wait, there's someone missing," said Howard, looking round, counting and comparing. "I think It's Sally – yes, it is. I'll have to go back in there and see if she's collapsed or something. I think it must have been mace they used or some similar substance. Pascal, put some water on this handkerchief, will you?"

"You're supposed to pee on it, I think, Boss. Here, give it to me, I'll get in that doorway and do it."

"Water will be fine thanks, Pascal. I'll take my chances."

Pascal soaked the handkerchief, Howard covered his mouth and nose and went back in past the cash desk. In fact, whatever substance had been used had dissipated quite a bit by now so Howard's eyes were not affected any more than they had been before. He flicked each light on as he went by and he could quickly make out that no one had remained in *Salle Une* or made their way into *Salle Deux* for refuge. Howard pushed first into the Gents toilet then the Ladies, calling out for Bunty but there was no reply even though he slammed open the door of each cubicle.

"You don't need that hankie now, Boss. Just don't touch anything because if you do that and then touch your eyes, you'll start it all over again." Pascal was by his side, breathing freely. "This is a total mystery. She's vanished without trace. Sally! Sally!"

"These villains, Gaultier and Hugo, do they have a history of desperate behaviour?"

"Oh you're still here. I thought you'd closed the case and gone away. Look, in 1830, there was . . ."

The policeman began writing again, "1830. So, at six thirty in the evening, Theophile Gaultier and Hugo Victor . . ."

"Excuse me, officer," Howard was indignant, "but we have a missing person here."

"So she's turned up? That's good. I'm glad to have been of assistance but I'd might as well leave. Goodnight, sir."

"No, no. A person has gone missing in this case and we are still looking for her. We're in here looking, because this is where she was last seen."

The policeman snapped his notebook shut. "No, it's beyond me. I think if you're agreeable, sir I'd best withdraw and file my report. I thank you for your time. Good evening, all."

"Do you know what I think, Boss? You saw that she was doing a kind of cheerleader thing during Donald Duck?"

"Yes, I did notice that, as it happens, Pascal."

"Well, my theory is that she already knew some of those people there tonight and she's made good her escape with them. They're probably sitting in a café somewhere having a good laugh about all this at our expense."

"You may well be right. Either that or doing a TV interview or writing something about this for *Le Figaro* or *Le Monde Diplomatique*. I expect she'll turn up sooner or later. Let's all have a coffee and sleep on it."

"*Quelle Horreur!*" Heseltine was there now, indignant. "That's nowhere good enough, Morgan. As you can see, the police are involved and we have already gone over your head and declared it a missing person case. Statements will need to be made, fingerprints need to be taken; witnesses need to be heard, people like you need to waken and bring your best mind to the case and make some advance in enquiries. The evidence needs to be . . . "

"Stop making lists. Stop, look and listen," cried Howard, putting a finger to where he assumed his blubber lips still were and straining his ears, "can you hear that?"

"Can I hear what, Morgan? You really are quite impossible in these situations of crisis. I well remember the time we had that other farcical incident the night of the Didier Deschiens concert when you somehow failed to see that the offering plate had been rifled and . . ."

"Daniel! Stop talking and listen. Sorry. No disrespect intended but it's just that I thought I heard Sally's voice . . ." He strained his ears.

"Hello!"

"Be quiet, Morgan! I just heard something that sounded like a voice – can you hear it?"

"Stop taking, Daniel."

"Hello! Can anybody hear me?" It was muffled and distant, but it was unmistakeably Bunty's voice.

"Sally?" Howard put his head round the door of *Salle Une* then *Salle Deux*, searching everywhere, between the rows, behind the piano, through the emergency door. "Sally, where are you?"

Howard ran into Pascal as he came out of *Salle Deux*. "It's coming from up there, Boss – I think it's coming from up in the projection room."

"Don't be ridiculous – how could she get up there without being noticed? But do you know . . . I think it is. Quick, let's get the ladder and the key and get up there."

"There's no sign of the ladder, Boss," said Pascal, running his hand under the carpet where the key was normally hidden. "Believe it or not, the key has gone too, but I know I put it back there earlier on."

"She must be hiding from us. But why on earth would she do that? She must be ashamed of what she did during the film . . . No, on reflection I suppose that's not very likely. Sally! If you can hear me, give me a sign," shouted Howard, "one knock for yes . . . This is silly, Pascal, get me a table and a chair. I'll stand on them and see if I can reach up."

"You can try, Boss but it'll still leave you a good way short. Maybe if you stood on a chair on a table and then I got on your shoulders?"

"What do you think this is – Laurel and Hardy?"

"Hello! Can anybody hear me?"

"Right," Howard made an impatient gesture, "silence, you lot. Yes, Sally, we can just about make out what you're saying," yelled Howard.

"Get me out." The voice was still muffled and indistinct.

"I know it's been a rout, Sally, but you didn't exactly cover yourself in glory, you know with those antics during the cartoon."

"I said get me out, you fool! And, no, I don't want anybody to read me a story – not even *The Lion, the Witch and the Wardrobe* which I adore. I'm nearly eighteen years of age."

"We're going to do our best. We *are* keeping cool, by the way."

"I heard that remark about your doing your best all right and I must aver that's precisely what I'm afraid of."

"Oh, thanks a bunch!"

"I know you're out to lunch. I've known that since the first day. But what plans do you have to get me out of here?"

"Get you a glass of beer? Why would you want a beer now? Listen, Sally, How did you get in there in the first place?"

"My birthplace? Why in the name of all we hold holy do you feel you need to know that? St. Joseph's Banstead, if you really must know. It's a BUPA. establishment, naturally."

Howard turned to the others, "This is ridiculous. This stupid conversation could go on for ever and we'd still be no further forward."

"What we need is a kind of intercom or something," said Pascal, undulating from the waist, by far the most expansive version of his tic.

"Okay, we could probably sort something like that out in the morning, even on a Sunday but in the meantime, how are we going to communicate? You can see there's not even enough room under the door to pass a note through."

"Boss, I'll tell you what we could do. We could go into *Salle Deux* and talk through the place where the beam comes through. The one in *Salle Deux* is a bit less high up in the wall. You really could get to that by standing on a table."

"Brilliant."

In a moment, they were back in *Salle Deux*, inspecting the set up. Unfortunately, they could see straight away that the films were projected through thick safety glass . Howard thought that this could probably be removed with a hammer and screwdriver but he was disappointed to realise that, in strict accordance with Sod's Law, the tool box was kept in the projection room. He was pacing by now.

"Darren! Come here a minute, please."

"Howard?" Darren coughed and then took a hefty puff on his blue inhaler, then another.

"Just run across to the *Aigle d'Argent* and ask Alain if he's got a hammer and a screwdriver, will you?"

"I haven't got the vocabulary." Darren was petrified. "Howard, you'll set me off again if you stress me out and you don't want to see that. Why can't you send one of the French people? Couldn't you send Pascal?"

"Pascal is busy keeping this table steady, look. Anyway, that's a ridiculous evasion about the vocabulary: I know they didn't have screwdrivers back in Molière's day but . . ."

"Actually, you'd probably have to check with Sally before making a rash statement like that . . ."

"You're stalling, Darren. Hammer is *Marteau* – masculine noun so, *un marteau. A* screwdriver is *un tournevis.*"

"If I say that to Alain won't he think I'm trying to order a drink?"

"No, because they probably call the cocktail a *screwdriver* the same as in English." Howard was losing his patience as he rocked unstaedily on the table "Again, we'd probably have to ask Sally to confirm or deny that. I tell you what, Darren," he added with heavy sarcasm, "you don't half realise how useful she is to have around once she's gone – who needs Google."

"Right, I'll go but can you give me a sentence to say, Howard?"

"Okay. Go up to Alain and say, *Eh, là, mec file-moi un marteau et un tournevis, merde.*"

"*Hey, La Mècque, fille m'en bateau est une tournade de merde.* I think I'll stick to something more simple, actually. What was it? *Un bateau et une tournade, s'il vous plait, monsieur?* How does that sound?"

"Darren, be more decisive and just go, please. We need to make some headway here. Can't you see we're getting nowhere at this rate?" Howard didn't know how much more of this he could take.

"Right. I'll be more decisive and just go, I think. Is it okay if I take Emma with me? She can do the asking and I'll carry the things." With that, Darren and Emma were gone and Howard tried to peer through the glass. He could just make out some shapes moving around inside but the width of the passage was limited: the projector lens blocked most of his view and, in any case, the glass was quite dirty on the inside and everything looked distorted. There may even have been two thicknesses of glass between him and Bunty, Howard thought. He knocked hard on the glass a few times but there was no response so he gave up. It hurt his knuckles, anyway.

A few minutes later, Alain himself arrived carrying a blue steel tool box. "I heard about your trouble but I couldn't really make out what these young people were asking for. They seemed to be miming screwing something in, so I offered them one of the guest rooms at first but then they started singing *Bob the Builder* and the penny dropped. What are you trying to do?"

"Thank goodness you're here. Somebody's locked in the projection room behind this glass and we need to be able to communicate to find out what the situation is and work out what we can do."

"Why don't you just go in through the door, Howard? That's the simplest solution, I reckon."

"That's not an option unfortunately. The projection room is built like a bank vault. That's logical, I suppose. The projectors were probably worth a fortune in old money when they built the place."

"So, whoever it is has locked themselves in," explained Alain. "Anyway, let's make a start." He climbed up onto the table beside Howard. "I can see your problem. This is safety glass. What you need is a hammer and a screwdriver to break the seal around it. See?"

"Brilliant, Leonardo."

"So, hand them up, Pascal, and I'll make a start."

After a few minutes of knocking and prising, Alain had managed to remove the thick pane in one piece but he was faced with another sheet of glass of just the same thickness but far more difficult to reach. "They really wanted it completely soundproof back in the day, didn't they? Does the Roxy go back to the days of silent movies, do you think?"

"Only in terms of some of the behaviour that goes on here, Alain. No, I think it was built to cash in on the talkies, actually. We're looking at the early thirties."

"That checks out. Look at these walls, they are reinforced concrete, not blocks." Alain leaned into the confined space and resumed the hammering, emerging again with a second intact pane of glass with some shreds of the rubber seal still attached.

Howard peered inside again and even though the light from within was dim, this time he could make out Sally sitting with her back to him but there appeared to be someone else lumbering round in the background. "Sally, thank goodness you're all right. We'll have you out of there in no time now but who's that in there with you?"

"It's Paquito, Howard. And you won't put an end to this situation as easily as you think, for I'm being held in captivity against my will, you see. Paquito has Paulo's big knife in here with him, although he promises he won't have recourse to it and I do tend to believe him since we do go back such a long way together."

"What? Paquito, come here this instant."

"Shan't."

"So, what's the story, Sally?"

"I was having a whale of a time, Howard, as you may recall – simply marvellous. I happen to have committed to memory know all the words to all the verses of *Deutchland, Deutchland Uber Alles* and I was singing them out, too. I was hoping they'd play the *Horst Wessel Lied* at some point in the film so that I could join in with that, as well. Naturally, I am no fascist although leaning somewhat to the right of a classic Centrist position on most issues, but my studies of history and my time in Germany have given me a certain insight into demagogues and populist . . . "

"Then the balloon went up. And?"

"Yes. And in case you're wondering, it *was* mace. They will have used a deal of it. I'd had some training in that type of attack because I happened to be in Japan when there was a ricin scare – not the main one you probably remember but a later one. There's still quite a deal of anxiety connected to the issue, you see. So, I simply applied the techniques of evasion I'd been taught and I was out of the room quite soon while all of the rest of you were floundering around aimlessly."

"Where does Paquito come into this, then?"

"Now, Paquito, it seems, had been ruminating upon a plan all along. You see, he's rather upset by this closure of the homeless breakfasts Madame de Pigalette has decided to enforce by decree. He wasn't responsible for what happened with the mace – that was an anti–fascist called Dani Bohn–Kensit whom I know of old, but Paquito *had* planned to cause a panic by crying *fire,* so he was standing close to the door awaiting his moment, you see. Them, you most unwisely cried, *Gas!*"

"Paquito! What's this all about?"

"She's right. They're not closing you down. I'll see to that. Anyway, somebody threw that stuff into the room and I saw people plunging around and I thought, *this is my chance.* I didn't plan any of this but Pascal locked up the room, came down the ladder and got involved with the people down there after replacing the key, so I took my time. I got the key . . ."

"From under the mat, yes . . ."

"I climbed up the ladder. Hard work with my leg. Step by step. And I lay low in here for a bit while you were all panicking and running round . . ."

"Now this is where I reappear in the tale once again," cut in Bunty, "you see, being an experienced survivalist does impose certain responsibilities on one. So, when I heard a plaintive voice from up here calling piteously (although, in the event, with a heart of deceit) for help, I didn't hesitate – no, not for a moment. Not I! I climbed up hand over hand, two rungs at a time, and came in here without a moment's thought to do what I could to alleviate the distress of the person who had been calling, whoever it might turn out to have been."

"Of course, I didn't know it'd be Sally," put in Paquito, "but I thought she was as good as anyone to make my point and maybe better than most because of all her connections. For instance, Pascal wouldn't have given me any bargaining power at all. Or you yourself, for that matter – no cachet. *Sally, on the other hand*, said I to myself, *Sally is a person of some consequence in Bordeaux*. So I said to Sally, once she was in here . . ."

"So Paquito said to me, *You're a hostage, Sally. This is a kidnap situation.* He pulled up the ladder, double locked the door and concealed the key, ahem, about his person. In a rather intimate place, you see. And, behold, this is how we are situated."

Howard was puzzled and asked in English. "Why didn't you use your judo to overpower him, Sally? In fact, why don't you use it now even at this late stage?"

Sally's tone was more scornful even than usual. "Howard, as so often, you misunderstand. First, because judo is an art of self–defence and ill–suited to a setting where aggression would be called for. Second, because this is a jolly confined space and it would be rather hard to use the momentum of one's opponent against him in a place like this, don't you you see? In any case, would it surprise you to learn, Howard, that I am inclined to be somewhat well–disposed towards Paquito's protest? Obviously, I would much prefer not to have been embroiled in your toils in my current capacity as a captive but I'm sure there will be a resolution on favourable terms."

Howard was seized by an inspiration. "Tell me, Sally, did they have screwdrivers in Molière's day?"

"Certainly," replied Sally, without missing a beat, "this useful instrument was first mentioned in a document known as the *Housebook of Wolfegg Castle* which the overwhelming majority of scholars agrees dates from the end of the fifteenth century. Oddly enough, this technology is one of the rare fields which the Chinese do not appear to have explored before the Europeans. Of course, it would be wrong to imagine that every household possessed a screwdriver in Molière's Paris because other forms of fixation were far more prevalent in domestic use than the screw which is rather difficult of manufacture and in practice tended in his time to be confined to some military and early industrial settings. However, the mere mention of a screwdriver in a Molière drama or indeed in any seventeenth century text, although rather incongruous, would be far from anachronistic."

"Could you give us an example?"

"I was coming to that. Now, even you remember, of course, the fantastical list of Harpagon's possessions given by La Fleche?" Sally gave a little rosy–cheeked laugh at the mere memory of this example of the dramatist's whimsy.

"In *The Miser?*"

"That's right, Howard – in *L'Avare*, once again. Full marks for that, though I somehow doubt if your acquaintance with the dramatist goes much further than that. Now, given the bizarre nature of this inventory one could easily interpolate the mention of screwdrivers into that speech and elicit no comment, you see. Like this, let me see (this is just a brief extract from a much longer speech, by the way): *Plus, un luth de Bologne, garni de toutes ses cordes, ou peu s'en faut. Plus, un trou-madame, et un damier, avec un jeu de l'oie renouvelé des Grecs, fort propres à passer le temps lorsque l'on n'a que faire. Plus, un jeu de tournevis de fabrication allemande prest à démonter tout sauf un meuble suedois. Plus, une peau d'un lézard, de trois pieds et demi, remplie de foin; curiosité agréable, pour pendre au plancher d'une chambre. Le tout, ci-dessus mentionné, valant loyalement plus de quatre mille cinq cents livres, et rabaissé à la valeur de mille écus, par la discrétion du prêteur.* You see?" exclaimed Bunty with a triumphant tone. "That reference to a set of screwdrivers fits in quite unobtrusively and there is even a little topical joke I threw in – that's sometimes necessary in a modern production of a classic drama and that kind of touch rarely fails to raise a small laugh if the audience is sufficiently *au fait* with the text. Anyway, why the sudden interest in early-modern tooling? Surely that's a subject for a monograph? I can tell you straight away you're not bright enough to write one of those. Nor do you have the staying power to endure the longueurs of a doctorate."

"No reason. Thanks. I see what you mean about the longueurs, though. What was a *trou-madame* anyway, Sally?"

"That was a game – a kind of bagatelle, you see – the context alone should tell you that but there's a footnote in most school editions: I'm surprised you didn't notice it when you studied it. I noticed *L'Avare* was on your meagre shelf."

"I'll check when I get back up to my flat." Howard blushed because his only books were from his 'A' level and university days. He called further into the room, "Hey, Paquito, can you hear me? how long are you going to carry on with this ridiculous pantomime?"

"I'm in it for the long haul, Howard. I'm outraged – after all, the Roxy has been good to me and I'm not going to let the City Council take away an important facility for no reason. I'm surprised at you rolling over so easily, to be honest."

"Quelle horreur!" Heseltine was by the table and shouting up now, "that's Lopez isn't it? Now you listen here, Paco Lopez, or whatever your name is. The Council decision has been duly signalled, signed and sealed; endorsed, initialled and authorised. You are all held to conform to what it says on pain of sanctions severe, stern and stringent."

"That's you, Daniel de Moulinet, isn't it with your venal verbosity verbalised vocally? You listen to me you, you blazered buffoon. You may be used to being in charge here at the Roxy, but I hold all the cards this time. Sally's in sympathy. The freezer is full of butter, bread and some frozen sweetcorn and there are about fifty cartons of milk, so we're not going to go hungry whatever happens here."

"Don't be a fool. No one can survive on bread and butter, milk and niblets," Heseltine exploded with scorn.

"We'll see about that, Monsieur de Moulinet: you have a stand-off on your hands. And I'll be blowed if it isn't your move."

11

"Daniel, we can hardly deny them that!" Howard was outraged at the suggestion.

"Why not? If we give in to them on this, they can hold out indefinitely but if we withhold it, surrender will ensue in pretty short order, I tell you, Morgan."

"We're talking about a simple humanitarian gesture here, Daniel. An empty milk carton may well be sufficient for one, er, *use* but not for the other, er, bodily function."

"You speak for yourself, Morgan, but I, for my part, am unwilling to consider lowering myself to this level. They must be held to account for their actions. They must realise the consequences of the course of action they have so rashly espoused."

It was a council of war in Howard's flat on day two of the occupation, and now the issue of waste disposal had arisen. As if to focus the discussion Pascal came in with the little red bucket from under the kitchen sink and placed it in the centre of the kitchen table.

"Boss, this is crunch time. Do I hand this in to them or don't I? I've just been in to check and it'll just about fit along the side of the projector if I squeeze it a bit."

"We're at an impasse, Pascal. Here I am, saying we ought to do the decent thing and let them have it but Daniel here thinks that this is our trump card and we should tell them to hold it in or give up. What do you think?"

Pascal thought for a moment and then began, "Boss, I think we should be careful about leaving ourselves open to a charge of . . ."

". . . cruel and inhumane punishment. That's exactly what I've been saying to Daniel but he won't listen. I mean, if it turns into a dirty protest, just imagine . . ."

". . . what it would be like to clean it up afterwards. And guess who'd be doing it, Boss. *Some are born great . . .*"

"Actually, I was thinking more about the bad publicity. If it ever got out that we were denying a basic human right that was in our power to give or withhold, our name would be, our name would be . . ."

"Your name already is mud, Morgan. I've seen to that. We are talking about the management of a situation which will reflect pretty badly on you throughout your career, lengthy or brief; otherwise glorious or filled with the opprobrium you so signally deserve." De Moulinet swept the red bucket to the floor with an imperious gesture.

"And it helps us how, exactly, to leave Sally and Paquito to wallow in their own filth, Daniel?" Howard picked up the bucket and put it back on the table. "I hardly think Paquito is going to give in because of something as trivial as that. We're talking about somebody who's been living rough for upwards of twenty years, don't forget."

"You can already smell the stench from here, practically," pointed out Pascal, holding his nose.

"There's no need to exaggerate. Look, I say we take a vote on it and we abide by that" suggested Howard.

"Don't forget that my vote counts double. I bankroll this operation: there's no reason why I should be railroaded into supporting a *pis aller*. *Quelle horreur!*"

"Now you come to mention it, why should anyone's vote count for more than anyone else's, Daniel? Don't forget this is a setup where we . . ."

". . . I know, I've heard it before, Very well, but at the very least we should have a church meeting with a vote on it, Morgan."

"A church meeting? About a stupid bucket? Don't be absurd!" Howard remembered a church meeting in Cardiff about moving a piano across the front of a chapel and said with a rueful grin, "Oh, actually, I suppose we've all been there, haven't we? The situation is more urgent that that, though, and it won't wait for a church meeting to be convened. Come on, a show of hands." The result was as Howard had expected. "There we are – I thought so. Put the bucket through, Pascal. And put a couple of rolls of toilet paper in the bucket, too."

"So, you're giving not only compassion but comfortable solace, too. Don't forget that democracy gave us Barabbas. I warn you that the Lighthouse Agency will be hearing about this, Morgan. A bucket will be the cause of your downfall.

When you tour the churches that final time, whispers will be heard: *there he goes; the fool fell over a bucket, you know."*

The downstairs door opened and a light step was heard on the staircase leading up to Howard's flat. There was a knock at the door and Véronique craned her neck around the door. In a diffident voice she enquired, "Have you seen my stool? It's black."

"How dare you?" exploded Heseltine, "how dare you come barging in here with such an impertinent and disgusting enquiry? Wash your mouth out, my girl. And if you need any medical advice, there's a pharmacy . . . "

"I think Véronique has come for my piano lesson actually, Daniel. Yes, Véro, it's here." Howard indicated a piano stool by the television. "I had to bring it up because we wouldn't have had enough chairs otherwise. I'll be down straight away and I'll bring it with me. In fact, I think we've finished here, haven't we? Pascal, you bring the bucket and put it through."

Once they were in *Salle Deux* and seated at the piano, Véronique asked, "How far have we got in Quoniam and Nemirovski, Howard? We're about half way through, aren't we?"

"We're on page 66: *White Rabbit.* I'm finding it quite difficult to manage the little shift in the right hand for the chord near the end."

"Right, let's work on that. Sit down. You can have the stool. I'll sit on this."

"Paquito! Bucket coming through," shouted Pascal at the back of the room. "I'm having to bend it a bit. There we are. Let me know when you want me to fetch it back out. Don't leave it too long or all the stuff is going to slop over the rim when I compress it."

There was a muffled reply from within.

"Please tell me you're not going to stay in here for the whole lesson, Pascal? I do like a bit of privacy on these occasions when I bare my musical soul."

"No, Boss. Duty calls. I need to do a bit of shopping for Julie and the kids but I'll be back as soon as I can. Maybe this evening. How are you going to occupy Emmi and Dazz?"

"I'll think of something but I'll let them sleep on what's happened." Howard turned back to the piano. "Right, I'm just going to play this through if that's okay, Véro? Ladies and gentlemen, *White Rabbit*," Howard declared, flexing his fingers and then cracking his knuckles.

"Actually, I thought we might start with a couple of scales, Howard, if that's all right with you? I mean, you say if you really want to play the piece instead."

There was an exasperated yell from the projection room. "Be more decisive, Véronique, for goodness sake. You can't just ask him what he want to do. You're to impose your will as an educator. Have the vision of a true pedagogue."

"All right, Sally. Thank you. Scales, Howard." Véronique spoke in a determined voice. "C major." Howard stumbled through the right hand by itself.

"That was very good, Howard. Now try the left hand . . . Please."

"No, it wasn't very good at all," came Bunty's voice again, "it wasn't smooth and evenly played by any stretch of the imagination. You could clearly hear the fingers going over on the way back down, you see. Again, Howard."

"Yes, Sally." Howard played the scale again, more smoothly this time.

"That was much better – for a beginner. Now that you've done it properly once you should do it again another twenty times. Go on." Howard began but stumbled. "Again!" He managed twice more properly but then broke down on the third attempt. "Right, twenty more. Go on: repetition is all part of learning the piano. Remember, all the great composers and pianists have passed this way."

"Sally," Howard called up, "who's giving this lesson – you or Véronique?"

"I'll not answer that, Howard. Keep playing. I can hear that you're dropping your shoulder, too. Sit up straight. Straight back, forearms at a right angle with the keyboard. Correct hand position. Play more on the tips. I rely on you to see to that, Véronique. Again!"

"This is ridiculous, Véro," whispered Howard. "What can I do?"

"Nothing. Sally doesn't like it if anyone questions her authority – and she really is an excellent teacher of even very advanced students."

"I didn't sign up for this, though. Right – I've had a brainwave. Change places and you play something, Véro."

Veronique began something that sounded Spanish and under the cover of the music Howard crept to the back of the room and approached the gap in the wall leading to the projection room from the side. Leaning down, he picked up one of the two pieces of safety glass resting against the wall. He found it was quite easy to prop it up leaning it on the lens of the projector.

"Who's that and what are you doing? It's you isn't it, Howard? Stop that immediately – I can't hear the piano properly any more, you see, and I was going to make some constructive remarks about Véronique's Granados. It's far too clunky for my liking, you see, and there was a *fermata* which came and went without any finesse . . ." Howard ignored Sally, picked up the other pane of glass and wedged it in place an inch or two in front of the other before returning to the piano.

"That was very nice. Spanish. Now, then, Véro, where were we? I think that's enough scales for one day, don't you? Let's get on with *White Rabbit.*"

"Actually, Howard, I tend to agree with Sally. That scale wasn't really all that smooth and even so, if it's all the same to you, I think I'd like you to play it again, please."

"Not twenty times, surely?"

"No, but let's say five. It really will do you good in the long term, you see. I mean, it really will do you good in the long term."

"Ha! You noticed."

"Just play the scale. Please."

Howard played it five more times and it really did become more smooth and controlled so he switched to the left hand and that was fairly quickly up to the same standard, more or less.

"Now, we can begin with *White Rabbit,* Howard. I'm not going to ask you to play it all the way through though."

"Don't you trust me? Why not?"

"It's like this: most people think that to make a piece better you just have to play it over and over again. Actually, you need to put right any problems first, so let's get that chord you mentioned sorted out before we go on." They turned to page 46 of the children's primer.

"That reminds me of something my old teacher in Splott used to say. Miss Horler her name was. I only had lessons for about a year when I was about seven – five shillings each they were; Mam used to give me two half–crowns wrapped in a hankie. In every single lesson she'd say, *Howard, why do we practise?* I had to reply, *To get better, Miss Horler* and she'd say, *No, Howard. We practise to get rid of surprises. Only then do we get better.*"

"She was a wise teacher. So, that chord – take a run at it from bar thirteen, here."

12

"Hello, I wonder if I might speak to a certain Mr. Howard Morgan, pastor of the Eglise Evangélique de Bordeaux Centre, please?" The voice was suave and reassuring and it spoke in English with a faint but unmistakable twang of Estuary about it.

"Yes, speaking – what's it about, please?" Howard was guarded.

"Ah now, have no fear, we're off the record at the moment, Howard but I'm wondering would it be convenient for us to have a brief talk about – how shall I put this – about *recent developments*, please, sir? With a view to establishing a more permanent record of *these events* at the Roxy."

"I'm sorry but who are you exactly?"

"Oh, I'm sorry, I should have mentioned that straight away. The name's Stringer, Ted Stringer. I'm the Bordeaux man for Reuders – you know, the news agency. Strictly speaking I do cover the whole of the South of France but I live here in Bordeaux and I wear quite a few other hats in the media down here."

"Excuse me, but how did you get hold of my number? This is an outrageous invasion of privacy."

"Ah now, that'd be telling but I can confirm that it's one of your associates here. He's been known to feed me the odd story – I follow up and see if it's any good and if it is, I pay him in kind. *You scratch me, and I'll scratch your back.* I see him as a kind of underworld contact. He has gone off the boil a bit since he took up with your lot but there's still often something useable. As for the privacy aspect, if you can't hack it . . ."

"Pascal. This is Pascal you're talking about isn't it?"

Stringer laughed but he didn't deny it. "Ah now, I couldn't possibly comment on that, sir but if it wears a green sweatshirt, it probably wears a green sweatshirt, so to speak. *If the hat fits* . . . So, would it be convenient for me to drop in?"

Howard weighed his options and came to the conclusion it was probably better to try to stay in control of the story. "I suppose. How long will it take you to get here?"

"Ah now, it so happens that I'm in the *Aigle d'Argent* at the moment (another one of those, Alain, if you please). Of course, if you'd care to join me for a wee drop of brandy this could easily be arranged?"

"Brandy – It's only nine thirty!"

"It's not compulsory. *The wheels of commerce grind exceeding slow but they grind exceeding sure*. Will you join me or shall I come over? It's all one to me."

"I'll come to you, I suppose." Even though he thought he could see the benefit of some free publicity Howard was keen to keep Stringer off his own territory at least for the time being. In any case, a *café calva* was always more than welcome.

Howard left Emma and Darren sleeping sweetly. Since the homeless breakfasts had come to an end and since Bunty had been off the scene, they were noticeably more relaxed and seemed happy to stay in bed till lunchtime, watch a little television in Howard's flat and then get on with whatever business of the day Howard could invent. Around five in the afternoon they began thinking about a meal and winding down towards bedtime.

Howard hugged himself against the early winter cold and scurried across to the bar opposite."Morning, Alain. Colder now. I've had a call from a character called Edward Stringer – he says he's in here."

"Hi Howard. Ted? Yes, Ted's in the back there. Do you want a drink?"

"Just the usual please, Alain."

"Early start – make sure you don't try to keep up with Ted, mind. First of all, you'll start saying things you'll regret later on and then you'll wake up under the table."

"And regret it later on. Wise words – thanks."

"I'll bring it through."

Stringer was at a far table in the back room with a notebook and a large brandy in front of him. He had on a creased fawn suit with a plain brown tie unknotted round his neck. He was about thirty-five but already thinning on top with a sandy comb-over and had cut himself shaving that morning – a tiny square of paper adhered to his chin just below the jawline.

"You'll be Howard Morgan. Stringer – call me Ted."

"So, what is it you need to know, er, Ted?" Howard was on his guard so he didn't sit down just yet.

"Ah now, it's not quite as simple as that, Howard. You see, I know all the basic facts through my contact – *man takes girl hostage* – but what I'm after is what we in the print call an angle, Howard."

"What kind of angle – do you mean some kind of spin? Which paper do you work for anyway?" Howard was curt.

"Ah now, you misunderstand exactly what it is I do, Howard. I don't work for any one paper – not as such, although some *ad hoc* arrangements do come about *pro tem*. No, Reuders is an agency, so what I'm looking for is a way of – how shall I put this – *interpreting* this story not for any one paper or for all of the papers taken as a whole but for each paper taken individually, Howard."

"How do you mean?" Howard sat down, intrigued now.

"Well, Howard, for the *Telegraph*, obviously, we need look no further, Howard, than the Brabourne Acres and the Balliol College, Oxford aspect, Howard. May I call you Howard?

"That's fine, Ted."

"Sally is a natural blonde, I understand?" Stringer asked, making notes.

"Sort of. Dullish blonde but cut in a bob."

"Ah now, that's a pity because long blonde hair is the look we need for the *Telegraph* front page. There is a distant royal connection through the Spencers though, so maybe a stock photo of Princess Diana might be used over the story. That's the usual way round it . . . The other young lady, Emma, is she a natural blonde? No? Rather a *retiring violet*, I gather. But there's plenty to go on with there in terms of Sally's privileged background. You're Welsh, aren't you?" Howard nodded. "I thought I could pick it out. Do you get on with Sally?"

Howard bristled. "Perfectly, thank you."

Stringer scribbled something in his notebook, muttering, *"Some obvious tensions there. Taffy was a Welshman. Taffy was a crook . . ."*

"Now for the *Express* and the *Mail* we can run with the same slant for both – in fact they share the same feed for most stories, certainly ones of this nature. This man Lopez, he's a Spaniard isn't he?"

"Originally, yes – second generation, though."

"Good because that takes care of that particular feed. A nice little anti–Europe thing with an understated racism for these particular colleagues. The comments below the line will be a little more, er, explicit in their condemnation of Mr. Lopez, I should think, so the story will have served its purpose. I take it he's a skiver? *What is this life if, full of strife, we have no time to stop and stare?"*

"He doesn't work if that's what you mean, not unless you can call standing around with an old saucepan work." Howard checked himself. "Actually, that can be an ordeal in really hot weather. Or really cold weather. So, it's a job I wouldn't care to do myself. What about the *Sun* and the *Star*? Let me guess." Howard gave a sarcastic laugh.

"Ah now, you're right to have that reaction and naturally that's where you come in. I'll be quite open about this, Howard – what I'm looking for is sex in any of its myriad forms. Of course, if you've become involved with Sally – or indeed with Emma . . . or with Darren for that matter, then there's no need for you to say anything at all because I'll just find out in another way and you can't do anything about it. I'd be after you for comment, of course. But, if you can point me towards anything else going on, shall we say any *undercurrents*, Darren-Emma, Darren-Sally, Sally-Emma, any third parties – you get the picture – there could be an emolument for you. You can remain anonymous, of course."

"Well, Sally is stuck in there with Paquito Lopez, so . . ."

"Ah now, anything of that nature going on in there would, of course, be something of a jackpot, so to speak."

"I didn't mean to suggest that there's anything . . ."

"No? More's the pity. We're interested in swimwear as well. Most of the papers want that. Beach volleyball is very well regarded."

"Not *The Guardian,* surely? Or, the *Morning Star.*"

"Ah now, the latter does not subscribe to the premium service and as far as *The Manchester Paper* as we call it is concerned, what they are looking for above all is what we call a social aspect. We call it a B.H. In fact, there's no real reason why you shouldn't write this one yourself if you've a mind to. What makes a man fall as far as Lopez has done and so on and so forth. What society is doing to try to keep these people in a manageable box – legitimising actions like your own which are of no real value in themselves but which hide the problem while making people feel better about it."

Howard was interested. "I've seen the kind of thing. B.H. would be *bleeding heart?* And you think they might publish something I wrote along those lines?"

"Ah now, it would have to be online, of course. They are extremely content-hungry at the Manchester Paper. You might have to resign yourself to seeing it as one short article in a catch-all, or even as an illustrative example in an article by Polly Toynbee."

"So, *the Financial Times,*" Howard was quick to cut in, "let me guess. They want something about *Shatto*, the coffee scrub company and how Sally being out of circulation is likely to affect shares in cosmetics and even futures in coffee."

"Ah now, you're quite right, Howard and that's the angle all the pink pages will want, but I do have another contact down here to deal with that and I must say he does it superlatively well so I won't be calling on you for a contribution there."

"Blue blazer, brass buttons?"

"I couldn't have put it better myself, for all my training. I hope you don't think any the less of me for saying that gentleman reminds me a bit of that Michael Heseltine. Of course I have to pay him in readies for any stories he supplies but to be fair he does give me a case of *premier cru* every year so it's honours even. Now, I've been thinking even while we've been talking. May I count you in as one of my sleepers down here, Howard? If, for instance, you could let me in there to get an interview with Sally I could probably get you a warm write-up in *Sud-France.* You know, happening place, dynamic young minister. The Welsh angle. Rugby."

Howard was horrified, "I don't think that's appropriate at this stage. After all, we're less than a week into the siege . . ."

"Into the *Siege of the Roxy?*" Stringer jotted that down. "It has a ring about it. Yes, but this is about to hit the fan – it's going to be all over the press in the UK by the weekend and there's going to be a need for comment. I'm only with Reuders, don't forget, but I expect to pick up some commission work on this although I expect some of the rags will be sending their own people. There'll be film crews, no doubt. In fact, I'm coming along later today with a camera to do what we call a *five* for FR3 – another of my hats."

"FR3 – you know how to speak French, Ted?"

"Ah now, Howard, you've jumped to an unjustifiable conclusion there, I'm afraid. It so happens that I *am* French. My folks came out here from Basildon in the fifties – Pop was in military aviation (Dassault, the *Mirage* and all that) – so all my schooling was here. The *Lycee Montesquieu* then an *Ecole de journalisme* – E.J.T. in Toulouse. I did do a year on the *Oxford Mail* as a kind of finishing placement but apart from that, French. French, French all along the line. Naturally, I have both passports. *One man in his life plays many roles* as the Poet of Avon so astutely observed. Alain, Another round – the day is young! *Awake, for morning in the bowl of light has flung the stone which puts the moon to flight . . . something, something, something noose . . . the sultan's turret . . . no, that can't be right.* Hey, that rhymes *and* scans – I'm a poet and I didn't realise it!"

Howard rose to leave. "Listen, Ted, I'm going to make a getaway now but before I do, can I ask you a favour? You know, man to man."

"It depends what that favour is, Howard. I don't really work exactly on that basis though," Stringer had his pencil poised.

"I'm going to ask you straight out. Do you mind not involving Emma and Darren in this? They're young and impressionable and they're not very worldly wise, so they may easily say the wrong thing. You gentlemen of the Press are not known for . . ."

"Ah now, Howard. *The early worm* and all that. I'm afraid you're much too late there and you've missed the bird. The two young people in question have already been in touch with me through my other contact and they have given an extensive interview on the record. The young man with the green sweatshirt, I mean."

"Oh no! What have they told you?" Howard checked himself, "I mean, really? I wonder what they had to say for themselves?"

"They just gave me a little information on yourself. And they passed on to me some names and email addresses at," Stringer consulted his notebook, "at, at the *Lighthouse Agency* in Milton Keynes. That sounds like a nice setting – a village is it? Let's see: Vicky, Cathy, Susan. In fact, the office is my next port of call to fire off some messages to these folks." Stringer handed over a card. "These are my numbers. Don't forget, you scratch me and I'll scratch you back. *I think this is the beginning of a beautiful friendship.* One of my compatriots said that."

"I know the scene but it was Humphrey Bogart who said that, actually, Ted."

"No, that was *Play it again, Sam.*" Stringer got up and finished his brandy. "*Round up the usual suspects.*"

"*Here's looking at you, Ted.*"

13

"Howard, this is like, Catti speaking?"

"Oh, hello, Cathy. Let me just pop the toast up." Howard took the phone at full stretch into the kitchen. "What's the weather like in Milton Keynes? We're having a bit of a cold snap down here at the moment. It's still about seven or eight degrees, though. We're technically in the South of France, see."

"It's Catti? You listen to me, I'm not interested in the climate in Bordeaux. I've just had a Ted Stringer from Reuders on the line – I think it's some kind of ski resort?"

"Oh Yes? Are you sure you're not thinking of Klosters – Reuders is a news agency. Wait, let me butter this and put some Marmite on."

"Never mind about that. Why didn't you tell me about the situation down there with Sali?"

"What situation would that be?" Howard was playing for time. He screwed the lid back on the king size jar of Marmite and put it back in the fridge.

"I'm only talking about the kidnapping crisis."

"Oh, that? It's nothing really. I thought I'd put it in a bi–monthly prayer letter. I didn't really think it was that important to be honest so I didn't think it was worth bothering you with it."

"You didn't think it was that important? It's only going to be in all the papers over the weekend. There's only going to be like, a five minute slot on the Channel 4 news with a reporter called, let's see, Ted Stringer?"

"Yes, he's bilingual. So how much do you know about it, anyway?"

"I've had a long series of emails from Emmi and Dazz. I know poor Sali is being held hostage by a wild, bearded tramp with a knife and she can't practise the piano and it's all taking place on your watch, Howard."

"I suppose that's all true as far as it goes, but I can't do anything about it, can I? The Dynamix must have told you It's just a waiting game. Maybe the Council will reinstate the homeless breakfasts or maybe Lopez will just lose interest and let her go. They're living on bread and butter and milk and there's no alcohol so things are stable."

"That's not what Dazz and Emmi – the Ditsies, by the way – have told me. They said some creepy man called Pascal has been handing in half a bucket of red wine every two days?"

"That's nothing to do with me, Catti. That's between them and Pascal. It's only a small bucket."

"It's Catti?"

"I said *Catti*."

"Oh yes, you did didn't you?"

"It was a slip of the tongue, Cathy. Anyway, what do you expect me to do about it?"

"You're only, like, the pastor? You're only, like, the hands and feet of the Lord down there? If you can't do something, who else can? I'm coming down there right away to get like, boots on the ground."

"Oh, I shouldn't bother really. It's all under control – like I said, we have to wait it out, that's all."

"I'm actually on my way, Howard – it's all booked?"

Howard sat to attention. "So, it'll take you a couple of days, will it? TGV at fifteen forty, day after tomorrow, say," Howard checked on his calendar, "Saturday?"

"TGV – what's that? I'm flying – I'll be there this afternoon at fourteen ten at Bordeaux–Merignac it says here?"

"Ten past two? We're an hour ahead of you, don't forget, so I've barely got time to get out there. I'll do my best, but . . ."

"Howard, the limo is getting a deep clean and a valet as we speak. Get there and sort out some accommodation, will you?"

"Certainly, that's easy: you can sleep with Emma in the Roxy. I'll sort out another camp bed for you – I think one of our members has got something along those lines." Howard thought he could just factor in a drive to the *chateau de Moulinet* to pick something up.

"A camp bed! Listen, Howard: there's a Holiday Inn at a place called Pessac? You are to book me in there. It's like, £96 for a double it says here?"

"A double – don't tell me you're bringing Vicky, too?"

"No, but I do like to have a bit of space in a crisis on the field. Will you sort a hire car as well – a mid-range saloon? Oh, and I'm going to need an interpreter?"

"That's all right – I'm confident I can do any translation you need doing, within reason."

"A *professional* interpreter, Howard? Sali would be well able to do it but she's tied up at the moment, isn't she?"

"I don't think she is tied up, actually. She *is* otherwise engaged but there's no actual rope or blindfolds or anything involved as far as I know."

"You know what I mean? So, a top interpreter – there's a list in the tourist office usually."

"Check. Do you need anything else?"

I don't think so? Oh, I tell a lie. What's the weather like down there at the moment? I need to know what to pack – you know, just for a little light tourism I want to do when I'm not being a missionary stateswoman striding the world stage?"

"I told you: it's quite cold for the season but this is the South of France, so you'd probably think of it as very comfortable. Eight or nine degrees. So, just a couple of nights shall I book?"

"Howard, book an open–ended stay will you! I need to be there for the duration. In fact, come to think of it, you'd better make it a suite. Let's see – those are, like, £343 a night, it says here?"

"Isn't that a bit excessive, Cathy? After all, this is the punters' money we're talking about. You said that yourself when we were chatting about Ivor Morris."

"The punters! The punters don't need to find out, do they? We just put it in the accounts under *evangelism* and the punters lap it up and send even more. Anyway, if you care about it that much you can just sort the situation out and I'll be on my way as soon as Sali walks free. Actually, I need to go to Brazil after this so get me an open ticket to Rio as well will you? The *Favelous Timers* have finally turned up running an English tea room at Copacabana wherever that is?"

"*Her name was Lola, she was a showgirl . . .*"

"No, their names are Becki, Jezz and Angi?"

"You know – Manilow."

"No, he's definitly not one of them."

"Barry Manilow is a singer."

"They're all singers these day, aren't they? At least, they think they are. Well, I suppose we all think we are. Virtually everybody who applies for the Ditsies bursts through the door at the interview going, *I've got the X Factor.* Anyway, I'll see you this afternoon at fourteen ten? And, Howard, I've got one thing to say to you."

"Yes, what is it?"

"Do all those things? Milton Keynes? Hmm?"

14

"I was expecting a much better welcome than this, Howard. After all, I've just spent forty minutes at the carousel retrieving these?" Cathy indicated the three large ill-assorted suitcases that Howard had just heaved onto a trolley. "In Kinshasa there was a children's choir and even in Naples there were balloons. As it is, you've just turned up with *him*?" She gestured to Pascal who was waiting and undulating, gazing in wonder at the great cylinder of lime and canary printed African fabric before him, letting his eyes wander upwards past the coral cupid's bow to the shaved back and sides and little pineapple tuft of bleached hair. "What a creep! What does he think he's looking at? Tell him to keep his hands to himself, will you?"

"I think he's in awe of you, Catti – you see, he's never seen, er, a missionary stateswoman striding the globe before and as for the welcome, you're none the less welcome for that, er, Catti, I can assure you of it." Howard wasn't going to risk any awkwardness in view of his difficult situation and given that he was face to face with his line manager, so it was going to be *Catti* for however long she stayed.

"You'd better just take me to my car, Howard. Then, I'd like you to take me on a tasting tour of some of the leading vineyards – there's still plenty of time before I meet the church tonight, isn't there? Oh, and I need to chat with Sali at some point, of course."

"Actually, Catti, I haven't hired the car here at the airport. It's waiting for you at the hotel in Pessac. Maybe if I just took you there I could show you round the city while it's still light and . . ."

"Howard, I'd set my heart on those vineyards," Cathy wagged her finger, "so if you'd just like to phone up and cancel the hire car and get me another here?" Cathy sounded as if she'd brook no refusal.

"But, I've paid a non-returnable deposit!"

"Which will be reimbursed from the central evangelism fund, of course?"

"But, what about the punters' money?"

"The punters will be delighted, Howard. This is going to be like, such a big story. Granted it's not a tsunami or an earthquake but a hostage crisis is the next best thing barring a nice war and an evacuation?"

"Oh, Catti, I'm terribly sorry but I completely forgot – all the vineyards are closed for the day. After all, it's . . . what day is it?"

"Wednesday."

"Wednesday: that's right. Museums, art galleries . . . vineyards – they all close on a Wednesday in France." Howard mentally crossed his fingers. "Boy, that's quite a blow. We'll have to drive into the centre of Bordeaux in my car but you have my word: I'll put you in good hands for the tour of the vineyards first thing tomorrow morning – I know a woman called Véronique who'll be happy to oblige. Come on, if we hurry we'll still be within the hour to get out of the car park."

"Send this Pascal on ahead. I'd like to hear your account of what's been going on because so far I've been relying on Emmi and Dazz and it seems a bit garbled."

"Fine – Pascal, here are the keys. We'll catch up with you in a minute."

"So, it's all been going so well with the Ditsies. Everybody pulling their weight – very harmonious, a real all–body ministry. Dazz and Emmi revelling in the mastery that Sally brings to each task, enjoying sitting at her feet drinking in her wisdom and experience. Then, a spiritual war breaks out in the heavenly places. Many hearts are opened to the gospel at a classic Christian film but the Enemy of Souls is always on the lookout for a way to disrupt the work. He puts it into the mind of one of those attending to throw a noxious substance around in the room and under cover of this, Sally finds herself a captive for the Lord. We are to step into the breach and uphold with mighty prayer . . . "

"Spare me the jargon, Howard. You screwed up on the film, some thugs turned up because of badly targeted publicity and Sally's holed up with like, a dirty old man. Is that right? I'd managed to gather that much from the Ditsies."

"In a nutshell. Here we are. Jump in the front and Pascal can sit in the back with the luggage."

"You don't honestly think I'm going to travel in this old thing after getting used to the limo do you, Howard?" Cathy kicked one of Cornflower's front tyres and swivelled the left headlamp all the way round. "The back door doesn't even match the rest of the bodywork."

"Actually, Catti, that's a stylistic feature and I've hired this especially for you. You see, I was thinking that if we take some photos of you in one of these picturesque old cars, they are virtually guaranteed to appear on leading Christian blogs and may even make it into the national dailies when the story breaks and people are looking for developments."

"In that case, let's get started! Where should I stand to get the full effect?"

"How about here in the front, waving the starting handle? I take it, you have a camera with you?"

"I use my phone. Here."

"Great. Pascal, get out here and take some photos with this, please. Catti with Cornflower. Catti with me. Catti with me and Cornflower."

"Sure, Boss. Do you want a box or something to stand on next to the lady?"

"No, maybe she could sit on Cornflower's bonnet for some of the shots."

"What's this Cornflower you keep on mentioning."

"It's the name of the car."

"I thought you said it was a hire vehicle?"

"It is, but they're very endearing, aren't they? I couldn't resist a nickname. Now, if you'll just get in, Catti, I'll have you at Pessac in no time and you can rest up before the church meeting. I couldn't get you the suite so I've got you two interconnecting doubles for the same money."

"That's better than nothing, I suppose. Will I be able to get a drink?"

"Yes, there's a mini–bar. In fact, there are two mini-bars."

"Ooh, aren't I the lucky one?" Cathy began her gasping, panting laugh and Howard had to hum to shut it out. It happened to be *Rule Britannia.*

15

"I declare this pretty important meeting open," declared Heseltine. "The lines are drawn, the troops deployed; the time of testing now has come. And we who gather in this holy place must summon up the will to win or else desert in calumny the field."

"Maybe we should begin with a Bible reading, Daniel," put in Howard from de Moulinet's side. In fact, I think it would be a good gesture if we asked Catti here to bring it as a sign of solidarity." Howard leaned over to Cathy who was also sitting on the platform and whispered something in English, bypassing Reg, the interpreter whose details he had found in a curling list on a noticeboard at the city hall.

"A Bible – why on earth would I have brought a Bible? There wasn't any room for luxuries what with all my outfits," Cathy hissed. "I tell you what, I could do a greeting in Thai? In fact, I could do a greeting in any of the languages our people work in. Anyway, maybe one of the Ditsies might have a Bible?"

At that, a voice could be heard issuing from the hole in the wall leading to the projection room, "It so happens that one has much of the New Testament and Psalms by heart, you chaps. What kind of reading did you have in mind, Howard?" asked Sally. "Something nugatory, I'll warrant!"

"I don't know really, Sally. It *is* a church meeting, though, so it does need to be uncontroversial. I suppose something about captivity? It could be quite brief."

"Right you are. Here's Psalm 126 in the King James Version. It's free of copyright, you see:

When the LORD turned again the captivity of Zion, we were like them that dream. Then was our mouth filled with laughter, and our tongue with singing: then said they among the heathen, The LORD hath done great things for them. The LORD hath done great things for us; whereof *we are glad. Turn again our captivity, O LORD, as the streams in the south. They that sow in tears shall reap in joy. He that goeth forth and weepeth, bearing precious seed, shall doubtless come again with rejoicing, bringing his sheaves with him.*"

"She's marvellous, isn't she?" whispered Cathy, "I really must catch up with her later on in the trip."

"Quite remarkable," replied Howard, grinding his teeth, "she's not going anywhere in a hurry."

"Now, before we reflect on those words, just a verse from the apostle Paul.," continued Bunty, "We remember, don't we, that Paul was in prison himself when he wrote that stirring exhortation to the church in Philippi: *Rejoice in the Lord always. Again I will say it, rejoice.* How often in our Christian lives do we find ourselves in a similar situation in a captivity made up not of bricks and mortar but of chains of our own making – what the poet Blake called *mind-forged manacles* although in this case he was referring to . . ."

"Actually, we weren't after a sermon as such thanks, Sally," called Howard. "In fact, I'm terribly sorry but we're going to have to put up the safety glass because we can't run the risk of having Paquito listening in on our planning. Pascal, could you do the honours? And, Ted, this is under exclusion of the Press so, if you'd like to withdraw, please?"

"Ah now, Howard, it's against the law to try to exclude someone from an act of Christian worship, Howard."

"Ah now, Ted, it's not an act of Christian worship. This is a church meeting – quite a different animal, you see. I mean, quite a different animal. Pascal, see the gentleman out, please. Oh, Ted, before you go – you haven't bugged the room have you?"

"Ah now, Howard, I can neither confirm nor deny that a type A listening device has or has not been installed by a technician known or not known to me within the precincts of this or any other building."

"If it's like that you'd might as well stay, then."

Howard turned to the meeting. As well as the platform party made up of Howard and Heseltine, Cathy and Reg the interpreter there were only Pascal and Ted, Emma and Darren, Suzon, Véronique and old Madame Joris present. Even this meagre turnout made the meeting quorate by a large margin because only Angélique of the current church members was absent – she had told everyone she was weak from secret fasting about the situation.

"Now, to recap, our predicament is as follows," began Howard, as Reg bent to his task, whispering in Cathy's ear. "They have an indefinite supply of food in the freezer in there –

probably enough to last them a couple of months or more if they eke it out. Paquito has the key concealed about his person and at the moment Sally is broadly in sympathy with the aims of the siege. She has, however, expressed some discontent about the conditions of her imprisonment because of the many sanitation issues. Now, I'm open to any suggestions from the floor about how we should proceed."

"Why can't we just throw some more of that mace stuff in there to flush them out?" asked Pascal. He made the appropriate throwing and coughing movements by way of illustration.

"Out of the question," said Heseltine to murmurs of agreement from all the others. "That would be cruel and unusual . . ."

"Punishment." Everyone finished the sentence.

"I rather think," began Suzon in a velvety undertone, "that if we were to cut off the power to the freezer, by removing the fuse to the projection room, for instance, that the bread and butter might then begin to defrost and in a week or so even to begin to go off or at least begin to be rather disagreeable."

"I see your point, Suzon," replied Howard, "but I think we'd still be morally bound to feed them in there. It's not a very good look to be caught trying to starve them out." He glanced over at Ted who nodded his approval.

"What about if we turned the heating right up in there," asked Old Madame Joris, "as once in the burning fiery furnace was done for the Israelite children, Shadrach, Meshach and Abednego? The Lord would know who was his and great would be the declaration thereof. We might even witness a third marching about in there – one like unto a Son of Man."

"There may be something in that, Madame Joris," said Howard. In fact, Pascal will you just go and tinker with the heating and we can start that plan straight away? We don't know if it would be effective, though, do we? Or on what timescale. So we do need some other suggestions."

Véronique had her hand up now, which was rare in a church setting. Heseltine loudly rebuked her, "Put your hand down, Véro. Can't you see we're having an important discussion here? *Quelle horreur!* If only Sally herself were able to bring a full contribution to the forum we'd easily have a solution straight away."

"Actually, Dad, it's something along those lines I was going to suggest," began Véronique with diffidence, "you see, I can't help thinking that our best bet is to try to change Sally's mind and get her to start working on our behalf in there." Full of confusion, she sat back down.

"What a perfectly ludicrous idea, Véronique," stormed Heseltine, "she's adamant and not at all for turning. A face of flint she turns to all who seek to influence her exacting mind. Come on, you others, let's have some more serious suggestions."

"Actually," began Howard, "Véronique's suggestion may well have some merit. "It seems to me that If Sally does have a failing," there was a gasp from the room, so Howard tried to back-pedal, "and I'm not suggesting for a moment that she does, but if she did have a failing, if she were to have a failing – I'm just flying a kite here – it would be that she does like to be in charge. Which is, in and of itself, a strength, of course." There was a sigh of relief and even a ripple of applause.

Cathy had received the translation from the interpreter and stood over Howard, saying, directly in English, "You are treading on very thin ice, Howard. I suggest you retract that remark about some kind of failing in Sally. This is a Fanshaw we are talking about. Remember what happened to Ivor Morris."

"It wasn't meant to be a criticism, Catti. I'm as much in admiration of her as you are yourself, if not more so. All I was saying is that Sally is a very strong–willed individual and that, really, I think our best bet is to put her in charge of the situation in there. You know, begin to see it more as her holding Lopez hostage and not the other way round, if you like. I think you can see that if she could be perceived to be making a stand, there might be considerable moral authority in that."

"Yes," said Pascal, "even Madame de Pigalette would find it hard to stand up against someone of Sally's calibre who was making a point about social justice. Plus, don't forget Madame de Pigalette was really on our side at the beginning. It's only because of Howard's stupidity that . . ."

"All right, we get the picture, Pascal," Howard cut in, "so, it's up to someone to try to get Sally to take authority. I think the key to all this is just that. The key. If she can only somehow get Paquito to hand over the key to the projection room then we can present the stand-off as a challenge to the closure not by a deadbeat but by a principled young campaigner. Then, maybe we can kill two birds with one stone

– end the siege and get the homeless breakfasts back on track . . . So, who's up for it?"

"You can count me out of that, Morgan." began Heseltine. "What's more, I wholly and categorically insist that Véronique and Suzon have nothing to do with it either."

"I can't help but think this is best coming from you, Howard," put in Suzon, "After all if you can pose as the mastermind in all this then it can't help but cement you in your position."

"I suppose so. Anyway, it's too late to do anything more this evening so let's all just commit the situation to God. Maybe you'd like to do that for us, Daniel?"

"Certainly I would. Let us pray. *Lord, thou seest what a horrific hash Morgan has made of this sad situation. May rapid retribution fall fast upon his haughty head. Oh, and help Sally in there. Amen.*"

"Thank you, Daniel. The meeting is closed."

With that, Ted Stringer came up and addressed Cathy, "These French, eh? You never know what they'll get up to next. I was wondering if you and Howard would like to come for a drink in the bar opposite – off the record. We could sup a fine vintage and we could bring the interpreter, too. I know Reg of old."

"Who is this, Howard? Maybe you could introduce us?" Cathy looked Stringer up and down with obvious appreciation and Stringer in his turn checked his comb–over.

"This is Ted Stringer, Cathy – a gentleman of the press. Remember you were talking about the guy from Reuders and Channel 4?"

"The press – well, lead on! I take it they do serve fine wines over there – I have like, an expense account, you see, so I don't mind if I do? You can take the gel out of *Sarf* London but you . . ."

As they all pushed through the glass doors into the crowded street, Howard saw the trap but it was already too late. A spatter of flashes blinded him and he found that Ted was pushing a microphone into his face and that Stringer had brought a couple of camera teams with him. Howard turned in confusion and made as if to rush back into the Roxy but Heseltine grabbed him by the arm and forced him back into the glare of the TV lights where he tried to cover his face.

"No you don't. You'll face the music this time, Morgan."

"Good evening, this is Ted Stringer, reporting live with an exclusive for FR3 from what is already being called the *Siege of the Roxy*. A dedicated and saintly young English worker with the homeless has been taken hostage by one of those appalling men she sought to help – the ones we all fear and whom you see in gangs waiting with ferocious, slavering dogs around cashpoints. With me is Howard Morgan, the young, callow and inexperienced minister of the church which meets here. He it is who placed the Honourable Sally Fanshaw, musician and coffee scrub magnate – *Shatto* is her signature brand and I have a pack here with me and excellent it is – in close proximity with the booze-crazed knifeman Paquito Lopez – a sly, swarthy, sinister Spaniard – who now holds her captive. Mmm, does that *Shatto* smell good! Monsieur Morgan, how does it feel to be responsible for the biggest crisis for the Protestant community in Bordeaux since the sixteenth century Wars of Religion?"

"Wait a minute, surely the Second World War was a far bigger crisis, not to mention the Revolution and even the crisis of 1905?"

"Are you trying to deny that you are responsible, Morgan?"

"Well I . . . *responsible* is a strange word to use when I didn't actually do anything to . . ."

"Our viewers can clearly see that the truth often hurts, Morgan. What plans do you have for bringing this catastrophic situation – a situation entirely of your own making – to an end in the best possible conditions? Can you salvage anything from what I can only call a debacle?"

"We've just had a meeting where . . ."

"A meeting!" Ted scoffed, "Talk. More talk and still more talk? So this is all the church has to offer nowadays in response to one of the most pressing social needs of our times? Let me pose that very question to my next guest. I have with me the Reverend Doctor Brian Filcher, who leads the Protestant ministers' fellowship here in Bordeaux. Brian, it's great to see you again and thank you for coming along in your splendid robes this evening. Now, this . . ." Ted consulted his clipboard, "this, *Morgan* character is not acting under your authority, is he?"

Filcher gave a little laugh of contempt, "Not at all, Ted. My views are often sought by other leaders but never binding. The churches involved in the ministers' fellowship are independent and free to act according to their own understanding of the holy gospel. In this case, it has ended badly – a well–meaning but amateurish approach so often does, doesn't it, Ted? In fact, I warned Morgan only last week about the dangers of the work he has recklessly undertaken and I was part of a delegation here under Madame de Pigalette which made the decision to put a stop to it – it now appears, sadly, too late."

"Your own church is out in the suburbs at Latresne isn't it, Brian? Fine modern premises and a ready smile on the face of every parishioner, if I remember? The finest coffee in town! Many influential members from all walks of life. Ten thirty on a Sunday morning. Bus route eighteen and ample parking."

"Ha ha. It's not *my* church, Ted: it belongs to God, you know! I may say, though, that if we at Latresne were to take on what is arguably the biggest scourge of contemporary French society, that of homelessness – and may I say that we are by no means indifferent to this need, making as we do the biggest contribution both monetary and in kind to the food bank of any church in Bordeaux this winter – we would do so only with the most stringent of safeguards in place. This *Siege of the Roxy* is all too predictable and appears to me to be the result of foolhardy bravado rather than of praiseworthy and responsible Christian concern."

"You make an overwhelmingly powerful case, Dr Filcher. I wonder if you can think of an example of more responsible Christian social action, off the top of your head?"

"It's interesting you should ask that, Ted because I immediately think of the initiative I undertook a few years back when I came to the decision to open one of our buildings – the gymnasium – to stranded motorists in the hardest winter in living memory."

"Yes, I remember that. You were remarkable. And we have some film of it that we can see now."

As they ran the film in Paris, Howard squared up to Stringer, even grasping him by the collar. "You've set me up, you, you, you . . ."

"Not now, Howard, this clip is only thirty seconds long. In fact it's coming to an end in five, four, three . . ." Stringer straightened his tie. "Thank you, Reverend Doctor Filcher – and what an heroic action that was – your *Legion d'Honneur* was well–deserved. May I be allowed to say that you've hardly aged at all. As you can see, I was just a young reporter with all my hair at the time." a winsome, self-deprecating chuckle.

Stringer turned to face the second camera and walked up to Cathy. "Also here with me at the scene of the *Siege of the Roxy* is Ms. Catherine Spedding, Howard Morgan's line manager at the Lighthouse Agency, an organisation that exists to put people in dangerous settings throughout the world," Stringer had switched with no effort to English. "Ms. Spedding has been flown in at enormous expense from the leafy village of Milton Keynes to support the helpless victim, Sally Fanshaw. But it's about another matter I'd like to quiz you, Ms. Spedding."

Reg the interpreter had been talking into a separate microphone all the time, clearly making a simultaneous translation on the air.

"I hate having to put you on the spot like this on live national TV," continued Stringer, "but an undercover reporter for Channel 4 news in the UK has discovered one of your workers, Ivor Morris, living in squalid conditions in a North London homeless shelter, having been unceremoniously sacked by the Lighthouse Agency from his work in Thailand. What do you have to say by way of response to this shocking allegation? Is yours a credible organisation, or do you recklessly deploy your pawns in perilous situations so that the funds keep rolling in?"

"Good evening, Ted, and good evening also to your viewers. Thank you for the opportunity to set the record straight on that one. I'm delighted to say that Ivor Morris is one of our most valued workers and is currently preparing for a tour of the churches which is widely anticipated to be a fond farewell to a fine fellow who has in the past been shortlisted by the Palace for one of the highest honours of the Realm. Indeed, there is a persistent rumour that a knighthood may be offered if and when the monarch steps down and there is an Abdication Honours List, Ivor – or *the Soul of the Lighthouse,* as we all call him in Milton Keynes – has been in Thailand for thirty–four years come next February 18th. This makes him the second–longest serving worker of the forty–seven currently supported by the Lighthouse Agency in ten countries and on three continents. Ivor's embrace of the ascetic life in solidarity with his fine work with the Thai orphans is well–known and much emulated though never equalled in the intensity of its discipline. Brother Morris – who has an excellent sense of humour and collects first–day covers – models himself on Gandhi, on Albert Schweitzer – that great French Protestant missionary to Lambarene in Gabon and . . ." Cathy wiped away a tear, "on Mother Theresa herself. How like Ivor it is to bow out of his work by taking in this way the lowest place in a spirit of humility! I'm sorry, I can't go on, I'm overcome."

"What about Morgan, this hapless blunderer? Does he have the support of the Agency?"

Cathy was brisk, "We are doing all we can to resolve this situation. Thank you and goodnight, Mr.. Stringer."

"This is Ted Stringer for FR3 news, here in Bordeaux. Goodnight . . . and . . . Channel 4 news, Ted Stringer. And . . . cut."

"Thanks a bunch, Ted," Howard was livid, "I take it this, this little stitch–up is going out live in the UK as well?"

"Ah now, Howard, you may have noticed a little plug for a Channel 4 story back there? The etiquette is for them to go on the story early evening – we're an hour ahead of them here, of course – and then you can expect the BBC and ITV to lead with it at ten and it'll be on the news cycle for a day or two or longer if the story gets worse – or *better* as we call it. Anyway, it's out there now. The roles have been allotted, you might say, and we'll be expecting you to play yours to the hilt."

"Why didn't you, like, tell me about this, Howard?" Cathy was down Howard's throat. "I could have thought a bit more carefully about what I was like, going to say? As it was I had to regurgitate an old press release? Anyway, where's that bar. I need a drink after that – I was literally flying by the seat of my pants?"

"That was a pretty good interview, Catti – I can see why they made you Press Officer. I think offering us a drink was just Ted's way of getting us outside, though."

"Nonsense – there's a bar just over there. Will you be joining us, Ted? You too, Reg?" Cathy winked at Howard, "You've got to keep the press sweet."

"Actually, all this has left a nasty taste in my mouth, Cathy. I'll just let you get on with it and catch up with you later on if it's all the same to you. Don't forget, you really need to have a word with Sally at some point – you've come all this way and it would be a pity to miss that."

"All right, all right, there's no need to nag: it's on my to-do list. Right, you know my room numbers. If by any chance I'm not there, you can leave a message at the desk." Cathy went across to the *Aigle d'Argent* with Reg on one arm and Ted on the other.

Howard wandered back into the Roxy where he met Véronique running the vacuum over the corridor. She switched off, came over and leaned on the cash desk. "I thought you came over very well, Howard. You managed to get some good points across."

"You don't really think that, Véro – you're just trying to make me feel better about making a fool of myself."

"Somebody's got to try. You should take care of yourself a bit more. You're always beating yourself up. None of this is really your fault. Anyway, you always say there's no such thing as . . ."

". . . bad publicity. I know there's not meant to be but there is now. I'll never recover from this."

"You've just got to keep going. Come on, I'll give you another piano lesson if you like. *White Rabbit* is really starting to come together."

"Maybe a bit later on. First of all I've got to try to persuade Sally to take charge of the situation. That's what the meeting decided, don't forget, so it's down to me to take it forward."

"Shall I come with you? She may not respect me as a musician but she does like me."

"Best not. I think I'm going to have to do this in English to make sure Paquito doesn't understand what's going on. *Once more unto the breach* . . ."

"*. . . dear friends, once more.* Shakespeare Henri the fift-th. That's hard to say."

"Well spotted. I'll let you know how I get on."

Howard made his way into *Salle Deux* and jumped up on the table – Pascal had consolidated the dodgy folding mechanism with some lengths of string so it was more or less safe now. He took the first pane of glass out and laid it carefully at his feet. As he moved the second, the hot and fetid stench from the projection room hit him in the face and he had to choke back a desire to throw up on the spot. There was sweat in it and urine and faecal matter but also the result of days of futile attempts to mask the worst of the odours – they had been putting through toiletries in knotted plastic bags in the buckets of wine for a couple of days now. There was another element of the reek: several days' worth of rancid alcohol filtered through the diseased body of Paquito.

"Sally. Sally." Howard didn't know why he was whispering but it seemed the right thing to do and almost a matter of common decency. He heard a whimpering and then a sob. "Sally, is that you?" A surprisingly slender hand appeared, reaching out along the side of the projector into the gap. It was testing, tapping, searching for contact yet Howard held back.

He found it was hard for him to ignore the resentment that had built up since the Dynamix had arrived. He had to let go of it.

"Howard? Please . . . Please get me out. This has become intolerable to me. It was fine for a couple of days but there seems to be no end to this. Where's Catti – I heard her at the start of the meeting but since then, nothing. I'm having a little wobbly, you see."

"Hey, Sally, this isn't like you. You can do this." Howard took the trembling hand and brought it into the light. He could see that it was pallid under the grime. He squeezed it, unable to think of anything better to do or say.

"Come on, Howard, you're in charge, aren't you? You can do something about this, if anybody can. You know that Paquito likes you. In fact, he's only doing this because he believes in what you do at the Roxy and he says he won't back down unless you make some kind of commitment, some decision to keep going with the homeless work in spite of the worst Madame de Pigalette and the others can contrive to do."

"This one has got me stumped, Sally. I don't understand, though – you were so upbeat about the whole siege idea earlier on today. Only this afternoon you were going on about reciting your Molière and your Virgil and running through some of the Beethoven piano symphonies in your head."

"I know. I almost managed to convince myself but there's no end in sight, is there? I wish you could just spend an hour in here to find out what it's like. You'd soon see how I'm situated."

"I'd take your place in a flash, Sally." Howard was surprised to discover that he really meant what he was saying. "What's it like? Apart from the smell, I mean?"

"Basic. I've managed to rig up a bit of a curtain with some screen canvas I found, so I've a modicum of privacy when I require it but it's so perishing hot in here the milk has gone all lukewarm. It reminds me of the Boat Race one year. We were at Chiswick station and Nanny had failed to put the lid on the cool box correctly. Perfectly revolting. Daddy gave her such a rocket."

There was a flash of spirit there, but it was guttering and frail. Howard had to fan it into flame. "There you are, Sally. You can still do it. Have you talked to Paquito about some kind of compromise? That's worth a try, isn't it? Maybe you could do that in Spanish – the mother tongue and all that."

"Paquito? He's as happy as a pig in . . . A pig in a puddle. I tell you, Paquito is living the dream. He's as snug as a bug in a rug – why wouldn't he be? He has all the wine he can drink on a plate – well, in a bucket. The diet is a bit samey but he's not complaining about that – the alcohol is the main thing for him . . . you see."

"Do you think we should stop putting the wine through, then?"

"Please don't do that, Howard," Bunty was urgent and her grip on Howard's hand tightened, "he sleeps with that wretched knife under his spare blankets – you know, his pillow – and I think if you took the wine away he might turn nasty and attack me whilst I'm off my guard." Sally squeezed Howard's hand – quite hard, with a concert pianist's strength.

He winced slightly as the bones cracked, "All the Judo in the world is of no use to one if one is asleep and there's a knife involved."

"Point taken. Sorry, I see what you mean."

"It's all right – I can take some gallows humour. I'm British, remember."

"That's right – you can hack it. Sorry, you can easily cope with it."

"Yes, I'll have a good stab at it, Howard."

"That's more like it. *Stiffen the sinews . . .*"

"*. . . summon up the blood.*"

"You see, just remember the Black Hole of Calcutta."

"What's astrophysics got to do with it, Howard? I've had enough of that field of knowledge listening to Paquito hawking into his handkerchief."

"Actually, I think it was an event in India in, um, let me see . . . the end of the nineteenth century sometime."

"You seem to be conflating – you appear to be thinking of the Boxer Rebellion that blew up in China around 1900. The incident of the Black Hole of Calcutta, on the other hand took place In 1756, the year of Mozart's birth. I was only joshing, you see. Anyway, out of 164 held, 143 died in the Black Hole of Calcutta, so thanks for nothing!"

"Thank goodness there are only two of you in there, then. I suppose the statistics are still quite unfavourable, though."

"Yes, just over 87 percent of us would die."

"Look, you know we had a church meeting earlier on to discuss this whole business, don't you?"

"Yes, I did the Bible reading if you remember."

"I'll spare you an account of what happened afterwards when we put the glass back up – although, predictably enough, it involved humiliation for me. Anyway, at the meeting we all agreed that the best plan of action is to try and make sure you're in charge in there. You know, shift the balance of power in your favour."

"So how are we going to do that?"

"Right, let's go," began Howard, "now, Mr. P . . ."

"Mr. P?"

"P.A.Q.U.I . . ."

"Oh, right, yes, Mr. P."

"Mr. P has the means of egress concealed in an intimate emplacement about his ample corporation."

"Yes he's got the key hidden . . ."

"Shh. Speak in a scholarly way, Sally. This a farce to be recondite with. Really dress it up – you're good at that. It seems to me that we are under a clamant obligation to essay a concealment of motivation from Mr. P by means of extensive linguistic obfuscation."

"I respond in the affirmative to your importunate prescription. Could we not essay in the Latin tongue?"

"Not at all, Sally, French, Spanish, Latin, Portuguese are all more or less the same tongue in varying degrees of transmogrification, as you know. *Clavis, clef, clave, chiave.* They are all basically the same – the word *key* in the Romance languages. Why, there is even *Cheie* in Rumanian. In fact I wonder if *key* is related, because . . ."

"Howard! It isn't cognate but in any case, you are defeating the object now. Your elementary etymological philology – if you will pardon the partial and arguably debatable tautology (which I have just with humorous intent redoubled) – is simply exposing me to greater peril. Just speak fluent scholarly, for goodness sake. That's the key to all this."

"Don't say that word! You mean the fundamental resolution depends on our suppression of this semantic field. Right, Sally, listen. The means of egress in a compact metallic form named after an North American Ivy League place of learning . . ."

"Harvard, Princeton, Cornell . . . Yale!"

"Yes, the means of egress is concealed in an intimate anatomical place. Your salvific outcome lies in a subterfuge, in a sally – ha! – a sally, *manu militari* into the darkest places of anatomy in order to establish physical mastery of said means."

"Howard, are you mooting the placement of one or the other of my manual appendages in the frontal plane of Mr. P's lower wearing apparel? You jest!"

"I just what?"

"No, you do mistake me, sir – you are endeavouring a witticism. We did do dissection at Brabourne Acres but only of the amphibian and then of the female rodent. It's a leading girls' school, you see."

"Stop!" This was Paquito, roaring and angry in a way Howard had never heard before. There was some banging and clattering, too. "What do you take me for? I got the gist of all that. You're after the key aren't you? Well, you're getting hold of that key over my dead body."

"What a disgusting thought," said Howard.

At this there was a clinking sound. "There you are. The key, the key, the key. It's my most treasured possession right now apart from this kitchen knife." There was a clunking sound as of a much heavier object being placed on a table. Clink, clunk – the objects were being moved around, picked up and put down again.

"Paquito – no!" Sally was yelling now, "no – you'll regret this for the rest of your life . . ."

"Sally, I've been driven to it and I can't see any other way out of this than by what I'm about to do. I promise you this is going to hurt you more than it hurts me. No, that's not right. Sorry, I mean this is going to hurt me far more than it hurts you." Paquito was sobbing.

"Paquito, please put that thing down." Sally's voice was quieter now but still tense. She seemed to be trying with all her might to impose her will. "Give it to me. Come on, Paquito you know you want to."

Howard was frozen to the spot, listening to the scene being played out before him but powerless to intervene. He was unable even to speak. His hands gripped the sides of the gap into the projection room as he forced his head as far forward as he could but without being able to see any more clearly because of the canvas curtain.

"Right, I'm going to do it now. There's no point in waiting any longer. Prepare yourself, Sally."

"No! Don't. Paquito, you're frightening me. Please put that down – I'm actually pleading with you now."

"I'm afraid it's too late for that, Sally – here goes. On the count of three. Three, two, one . . ."

"Aargh – now look what you've done! No! No! It's dripping everywhere."

"Sally!" screamed Howard. Should I call an ambulance? Sally, please speak to me!" Howard was beside himself, tugging at the projector, trying to force it aside, to see more clearly.

"Howard, what on earth is the matter with you? I'm quite all right but this does change the situation somewhat radically, I must admit."

"He stabbed you, didn't he? I heard you telling him to put the knife down and then . . ."

"No, Howard. You've got the wrong end of the stick yet again. I told him to put the *carton of milk* down."

"What's the carton of milk got to do with a psychopathic attack?"

"A psychopathic attack? There never was any psychopathic attack – that was all in your crazy skull, mister. It *is* an emergency, though. You see, Paquito has only gone and swallowed the key. The milk was to help him gulp it down, you see, and, blow me down, it's gone everywhere."

16

"What do you suggest, Catti? We've all been racking our brains since the start of this but I suppose a fresh mind might come up with something different even this far along."

Howard was in the *Aigle d'Argent* with Pascal and the Dynamix. They had been up half the night in Howard's kitchen, covering again and again the same ground and had now reconvened with Cathy Spedding for a working breakfast. Once again a knot of people with banners had assembled outside the Roxy and already there were interviews taking place and pictures being taken, although Ted Stringer was nowhere in sight. Through the window, Howard could see that Paolo was pushing himself forward into shot with his placard crudely painted with the slogan, *Give me breakfast or give me death.*

"Woah, there – let me get my head together, Howard." Cathy was bleary-eyed. "Reg and Ted showed me around some of the night spots and it was quite a threesome, I can tell you. Those boys can handle a fine claret all right. It's Alain, isn't it?" Cathy gestured towards the barman who was busy putting the boiled eggs on the stand. "Alain, more coffee here please – he does understand that, doesn't he? I can't function without that. Milky. *Garçon, olé! Olé!"*

"Keep the croissants coming as well, please, Alain."

"Sure thing, Howard," Alain glanced over to Cathy whose place setting and some of whose frontage was already covered with crumbs and coffee stains, "and some more serviettes." He gestured over to the Roxy, "This is quite a situation, Howard. I don't see how the authorities can keep on treating it with a light touch much longer."   Howard shrugged – there seemed to be no way forward.

"So, looking at it again," began Cathy, "it's almost like a classic locked room puzzle, isn't it? I used to read a lot of Agatha Christie and so on at one time before Bridget Jones came out and I switched to chick-lit on all my long haul flights."

"These are *books* we're talking about are they?" asked Emma as Darren guffawed as if to distance himself from a difficult topic, leaning back in his chair.

"That's right," said Howard, "but it's not really a locked room mystery as such is it? One of *those* normally involves the murder of someone who is apparently alone in an inaccessible place and finds themselves dead – well, somebody else finds them dead. Fortunately we're not in that situation."

"Not yet, Boss."

"Thanks for that, Pascal. You see, you understand far more than you think you do but just keep out of it for a moment will you? This is a purely English literary device we're talking about."

"That's not true at all . . ."

"All I'm saying is the locked room mystery as a type of story..."

"You mean a genre... "

"... as a *type of story* might suggest a way out of this." Cathy gulped her milky coffee from the bowl and gestured for yet another jug.

"What, you mean a poisonous snake that looks like a hatband?" There were blank looks all round. "You know," Howard went on, "like in the Sherlock Holmes story, *The Speckled Band*. Holmes was a detective, Darren – in an old book. He worked out that a poisonous snake had been trained to slither through a ventilation shaft and down a bell rope before killing the victim. A lot of those stories have to do with an animal – like the ape in *The Murders in the Rue Morgue*. By Poe. The writer, Edgar Allan Poe. Other than that, there are a lot of mistaken identity plot devices and we know exactly who's in there so I'm not sure that helps at all."

"I was thinking more of a secret passage," Cathy spoke with her mouth full, scattering crumbs, "there's no skylight or anything in there?" she mumbled.

"Sorry?"

"Pardon me, there's no skylight or anything in there, is there?"

Outside, more people had arrived and some chanting had started although Howard couldn't make out what it was about. It sounded like, *My pig has a snout*. What was more worrying was the sight of Paolo talking to the newly-arrived Ted Stringer who was taking notes.

"No, there's no skylight. Funnily enough, there *is* a ventilation shaft but first of all we haven't got a poisonous snake; second we couldn't train it just to bite Paquito and in any case Sally would still be in there when it was all over so it wouldn't help us at all. The shaft is far too narrow and tortuous even for somebody of Emma's build to climb through so Sally certainly couldn't hope to get out that way even if she's a fully qualified contortionist. Don't say it . . ."

"What about getting in through the two, what do you call thems?"

"Auditoria. From *Salle Une* and *Salle Deux*? I think if one or both of the projectors wasn't there it'd be possible to climb in or out through the gaps quite easily but that kind of rescue attempt would involve both of them in there cooperating to unbolt the things from the floor and shift them back. The bolts are going to have seized up, anyway."

The chanting had grown in intensity by now because as Howard looked out he could see there were at least a hundred people in the impromptu demonstration. It was clear as well that they were chanting, *De Pigalette out.*

"How about just forcing the door from the outside? What are they chanting out there?" asked Cathy?

Darren and Emma both sighed. "We've thought of that," they said together.

"Oh, just something about local politics. Ted's there look, Cathy – he's obsessive about that kind of thing and he's always doing some *vox pop* or other. As to forcing the door, that's the most obvious solution, I grant you and goodness knows we've all been thinking about it from day one," explained Howard, "but if you took a really good look at it, say if you climbed up the ladder..."

"No thanks"

Howard glanced at Cathy's Junoesque form. "No, but if you did you'd see it'd be a really big job even with special equipment and the fire brigade or something in attendance. The door, not you climbing the ladder," Howard felt he had to clarify, "It's a genuine security door with several locking points – it's a real strongroom."

Cathy tutted. "You mean it's a *really strong room*, Howard."

"I meant what I said. The trouble is, when they come to demolish the whole place it'll probably still be standing up there in the middle of the rubble – a hut on a pillar of reinforced concrete."

"With Sally not still in there, hopefully. Alain, more coffee!"

"You are right, it is indeed to be hoped that Sally would not be still in there."

"And this Paquito Lopez still has that big knife, don't forget. He might not take too kindly to an attempt to break in. Somebody with nothing to lose is likely to be reckless."

"Do you know, I'm unlikely to forget that, thanks, Cathy."

"Oh well, we seem to have covered the ground. Don't worry, we'll think of something. What time's lunch round here, Howard?"

"Cathy, it's not even ten o'clock yet!"

"But I've heard you have a really long lunch break here in France. That's right isn't it, Howard? I could fancy some oysters or a large seafood platter. I'm drooling at the thought."

"Yes, that is true, but the extra time tends to be tagged on at the end of the meal, not at the beginning and certainly not straight after breakfast."

"I've heard they have such a thing as an aperitif, though. What's the earliest I could start thinking about having one of those?"

"Oh, all right, you win. Whisky, Port . . ."

"I thought I'd try one of these aniseed drinks they go on about. *Pernod* is one of those, isn't it? People say it's like that *ouzo* the missionaries in Albania go in for."

"Yes, but *Ricard* is the nicest of the lot in my opinion. Alain, a couple of *Ricards*, please. Nuts."

"At this time of the morning? You can say . . ."

"Don't you dare. Oh, and a *Seize* for Pascal here. He's been very patient. More lemonade, you two?"

"There are limits to how much lemonade you can drink, Howard. I'm still nursing this," said Darren, pointing to his glass. "This is my fourth *Pschitt* so far."

Alain brought the drinks across. "Enjoy!"

"Shan't!"

"Thanks, Boss. Hey, it's really building up out there. I don't know how much longer Madame de Pigalette can just stand back from it and not intervene." Pascal began undulating.

"What do you mean by that? You think she might be thinking of water cannon? The C.R.S? It's been a peaceful demo so far."

"I know, but it doesn't reflect well on the city does it? Plus, there's a rumour that *Les Restaurants du Coeur* are going to run a television advert based on what's going on down here and featuring Paolo."

Howard looked doubtful. "*Les restos du coeur,* eh? I'm all in favour of that but when you talk about a rumour, do you mean an actual rumour or is that hard information? It was a bit of a shock to find out you're in Ted Stringer's pocket."

"Oh, all right, Boss. You're quite right – the film is in the can. It's called *Breakfast or Death; Why make them choose?* It'll be going out over Christmas as part of their big appeal even if this is resolved by then. They've put Paolo front and centre in it and they're calling this a landmark case."

"Ha! I notice they didn't ask me to be in it. Or you for that matter."

"They did ask me, Boss," Pascal was sheepish, "but I didn't want to make the situation any more embarrassing for the church than it already is, so I'm just in it as Paolo's sidekick – I've got a few lines as *pathetic washout two.* I'm sitting on the floor shaking a tin and I say, *Cold Christian charity? Pah! What's that worth to a man like me?* Later on I say, *Howard Morgan? Pah! Just a heartless publicity seeker out of his depth.* Anyway, I expect they'll make a documentary about you later on when the dust settles. *The Roxy Siege: One year on.* You know the kind of thing."

Outside, Paolo was getting more animated now. In fact, he had climbed up onto a white van with his Alsatian and was addressing the crowd through a loud hailer although it was impossible to make out what he was saying from inside the

Aigle d'Argent. His speech was going down well and was regularly punctuated with loud cheering and more chants of *De Pigalette out.*

"Oh, hello, come to apologise have you?" asked Howard as Ted came in and joined them.

"Ah now, it's quite all right, Howard. I made it up with your line manager here over some cocoa of a dark red variety last night. As a matter of fact, as a form of recompense and a gesture of good standing we're thinking of putting you and Paolo on a televised debate against Brian Filcher and Daniel de Moulinet."

"Oh, yes, what's the motion? *Should we bring back the guillotine for treasonous ministers?*"

"Ah now, there's a thought! It's an idea that's in the early stages of development as yet but it's a definite possibility if this goes on, say, a month longer. We were thinking of making it a bilingual Eurovision thing and getting a Dimbleby to chair it along with Jean–Fier Poucault. Not one of the main Dimblebys – a cousin from the younger generation, maybe. The theme would actually be something like, *Naive Charity: are there any limits?* That kind of thing."

"We'd jump at that, wouldn't you, Howard?" put in Cathy. "Will you join us in an aperitif, Ted?"

"An aperitif at ten? Hardly! I will have a *drink*, though. Alain, a double gin on ice, please. And another one of whatever these are having."

"Coming up, Ted."

"How's that story developing, Alain?" Ted, tapped his nose to indicate discretion.

"Hey, Alain, that's not fair," said Howard, "you should respect me as a regular customer and not brief against me."

"Ah now, Howard, you've misunderstood again. *Rumour has a thousand mouths,* as they say. I have many contacts all over Bordeaux and there are many stories in all kinds of stages of, ahem, gestation. This one concerns a wine scandal, so it's got nothing to do with the *Siege of the Roxy* at all although brass buttons and a blue blazer are likely to feature at some point even if we are not yet sure in what capacity. It's unlikely to break for another two or three years in any case – a real slow smoulder. Alain, this is good: I'll have some of this!"

"Coming up, Ted."

17

"I think we've finished with *White Rabbit* now, Howard," said Véronique, leafing through the piano book looking for a fresh challenge. "How about this one?" She pointed to *Three fine frogs*. "This one will really stretch you. The leaps."

"Do you think I'm making any progress, really?" Howard sighed.

Véronique considered. "You *are* a late starter but there's no reason why you can't have a good go at it. We're just laying some foundations of reading music, anyway. Angélique was in the same boat and look at how far she's come with her singing."

Howard winced involuntarily. "I suppose all the technical stuff comes further down the line, does it? I got squeezed by Sally's hand yesterday. Boy, there's some strength there – *The Beast with Five Fingers*. Anyway, if this wretched *Siege of the Roxy* goes on for as long as I think it will, I'll be playing at the Last Night of the Proms by the end of it."

"There's not much danger of that. By the way, I did have an idea about the siege." Véronique was blushing, "but I hesitate to mention it, really."

"Come on, you've got to tell me if you think it could help."

"All right but don't look at me." Véronique put her head down and her voice dropped. "You know the little red bucket?"

"The one we put in and out – yes?"

"Well, all things being equal. You know. After a day or two. The key will be . . . You know . . . "

"The key will be what?"

"You know, Howard. Don't make me say it. The key will be . . . You know . . . "

". . . in the bucket! Véronique, you're brilliant. In fact, I'd like to give you the honour of being the one to find it."

"No, I'm sure there'll be a better way of deciding who does that. Let's get everyone together and we can decide then."

"Okay, there's no rush. We'll be taking the bucket out at seven thirty this evening and putting some more wine back through so we can decide then. Now, shall I try this right hand first? The left hand looks a bit more challenging this time. I've got to say, you've given me something to look forward to."

*

"Cathy, it seems that the end is in sight now. We've had an idea. I've worked out that the key is going to end up in the little red bucket so all we need to do is find somebody who's prepared to search through the, ahem, waste products until they find it."

"Howard, as your immediate superior in the Lighthouse Agency, I nominate you to be that man."

Howard looked round and beckoned the Dynamix forward, "Right, Darren and Emma, here please. You've heard about *Operation Red Bucket* and as your immediate superior, I'm ordering you to search through the bucket for the key."

"Howard," Emma stood up to him, "isn't Sali our immediate superior? Anyway, if you make either of us do that, we're going straight to Ted Stringer. He's offered us money for any new developments in the siege and I'm sure he'd love to hear about that."

"Pascal?"

"What, Boss?"

"We've been through such a lot together, haven't we? Why, we're almost like brothers by now."

"What do you want?"

"I was wondering, for the sake of our friendship, will you take the plunge? For my sake and for the sake of the gospel? As a token of our fellowship? You know, like when Jesus rose from the table of the Last Supper, tied a towel around his waist and washed the feet of his disciples?"

"I'd like to do it, Boss, but I won't because I think it would be a true sign of servant leadership if you did it yourself."

"I must say I'm disappointed in you, Pascal. I thought we meant more to each other than that."

"Look, Boss, what I have done to move this forward is get some latex gloves and a clothes peg for your nose so whoever does do it is not going to be in too much discomfort, anyway." He fished the items out of his jacket pocket and placed them on the table.

"Folks!" Howard said, "We're getting ahead of ourselves. We haven't even got the wretched bucket yet. Let's go down and get that so that at least we know what we're up against."

"I for one have had enough of this absurd spectacle," snorted Cathy, "so if you'll excuse me, I'll return to my hotel room where my replenished mini-bars await me."

"Thanks for your support, Cathy."

With that, Howard followed Cathy down the stairs. She went out into the evening as Howard continued along the corridor, went into *Salle Deux*, climbed up onto the table and called in through the gap, "Slop time, guys. Let's have that bucket."

"Careful, Howard, it's a very full one tonight," said Paquito. "That wine you put through yesterday was rot-gut. There's no actual vomit but plenty of phlegm from hawking. Some big meaty floaters, too."

"Okay, just pass it through." The compressed bucket appeared. "Try not to bend it too much, Paquito. No, don't tilt it, for goodness sake. Right, I'll be back with the wine in half an hour or so."

"Throw in a couple more cans of Lynx if you can get hold of them, will you?" called Sally.

"I'll do my best but you've got nearly all of Darren's supply in there already."

Howard placed the reeking bucket at his feet on the table, climbed down and took it up again. Normally, his first stop was the gents lavatory where he would empty the bucket and rinse it thoroughly. In fact he did rush in there this time to retch into the basin but after that he went on with his steady return to the flat, taking care not to let the contents slop up the sides and over the rim. Opening the door at the bottom of his stairs with his elbow was a tense moment.

As he climbed the stairs he called, "Coming through, one bucket of . . . detritus. Spread some newspaper on the table somebody. Pascal, can you do that? There's a pile in the corner."

"A pile of what, Boss?"

"Newspaper, what do you think?"

"Sorry, Boss, I've got my mind on other things."

"Do we have to do this in the kitchen, Howard?" Darren protested, "we have to eat in here, don't forget. Why can't we just pour it out into the shower?"

"There's a better light in here for one thing. Plus, there are one or two, er, implements we might need – you know, bits of kitchen paraphernalia."

"Such as?"

"A colander. A sieve." Howard fetched each item out of the cupboard and put them on the table. "If we don't come across the key just by feeling for it, we're going to have to force the stuff through those."

"Come on, I'll make a start. It was my idea, after all." This was Véronique and she was business-like. "Gloves."

"Forceps," replied Howard, laughing with relief.

"I didn't say I was happy for you to treat it all as a big joke, Howard. Just give me the gloves and let me do it." She put the gloves on with a snap. "Now stand back. This is going to be messy."

"You're determined, Véro, and you have a servant heart – I like that."

"It was obvious no one else was going to step forward."

"If I were you, Véro, I'd just root around in the bottom first before I started on the solids," suggested Pascal.

"Stand back, both of you. Give me the colander: first of all, I'm going to pour all this liquid through slowly." Véronique did just that, holding the colander over the sink with both taps on full. "Right there's no sign of anything. Hand me the sieve, Pascal."

"One sieve, coming up."

"If anyone is squeamish, look away because I'm going to press these main faeces through one at a time."

Darren had his head through the open window and Emma was looking a bit green but she stood her ground and even seemed horribly fascinated, gazing with what appeared to be prayerful wonder.

"Couldn't you just break them up a bit and have a look inside, Véro?" asked Howard.

"No, I want to do a thorough job."

There was a clatter as Darren knocked a chair over on his way to the bathroom. He was just in time, as the others could hear.

"Go on, then, and . . . press." Now, the sound of earnest and dedicated vomiting could be heard from Darren in the bathroom. "Make sure you flush, please, Darren," called Howard. "Anything, Véro?"

"Not a sausage. I think they must have found some of that sweetcorn in the freezer, though, because there's plenty of that mixed in." She gestured at the sieve.

"I'm amazed that stuff has any nutritional value because it nearly always comes through whole. Don't you find that, Darren?" called Howard.

"What?" A washed-out Darren appeared in he doorway.

"Don't you find that sweetcorn nearly always comes through whole? You know, a bit like diced carrots when you're sick," This set Darren off again on a yearning dry heave.

"I admit defeat, said Véronique," snapping off and rinsing the gloves in the sink. "There's definitely no key in that lot."

"Oh well, I suppose it might take a day or two to work through – as long as it's not lodged somewhere in his stomach lining or in a pool of chyme in one of the convolutions of the large intestine. Better luck tomorrow, Véronique and thanks for volunteering to do this every evening."

"Not so fast, Howard," retorted Véronique, "we're going to do this fairly. It's going to be someone else's go tomorrow evening."

"Maybe the situation will be resolved by then," said Howard, crossing his fingers.

"Keep those taps running for a while – there are still a few bits swirling round, Boss. Oh, look, the sweetcorn has all collected in the plughole. Do you think it can be used again?"

"You're welcome to try, Pascal but you can count me out."

"What do you think, Darren," asked Pascal as Darren came back in.

"What?"

"This sweetcorn here – do you think it could be used again in a stew or a casserole or something once it's been through the bowels? Where's Darren gone, Boss?"

"I don't think he agreed with you."

"Maybe sweetcorn doesn't agree with him."

18

When Howard came out of the *Aigle d'Argent* he could see that, by now, people were moving freely in and out of the Roxy. More slogans had been daubed on the frontage both inside and out, including some personal remarks about Madame de Pigalette. There was a ladder propped up close to Darren and Howard's window and a younger person, presumably a student, was attaching the string from a banner to the letter *R* of *Roxy*. As he spread it out and began to look for somewhere to tie the other end Howard could see it read, *How many hats can a woman get? Ask Imelda Pigalette!* Gino carried in two cases of *1664*, one under each arm, right in front of Howard's nose and with barely a glance at him, even though Howard held the door open.

As Howard followed, he could see that another coffee machine had been added to his own behind the cash desk and that the corridor was scattered with cushions and blankets. There were already about a couple of dozen students lounging round, most of them smoking and there was a strong exotic scent in the air. Howard had to remind himself he was officially the victim of an invasion and that none of this could be held against him by Heseltine – at least not justifiably. He was pleased to see that, on the door leading to his flat, someone had pinned a sheet of A4 with *Défense d'Entrer* scrawled on it.

The moment he began to wonder about Emma in *Salle Une,* she came down the corridor, bedraggled and yawning and carrying a pile of sheets.

"They've, like, put me out, Howard? Where can I go?"

"Oh, hi, Emma. Yeah, I think they want to keep you out of harm's way. Hopefully . . . I mean, *it is to be hoped* that this isn't going to go on that much longer, so if I were you I'd plan to kip down in the kitchen upstairs."

"I was thinking about Sali's place up at the *chateau* – she doesn't need that any more, does she?"

"This is true – maybe we could look at that a bit later on. Transport would be a bit of a problem but you could come in with Véronique, I suppose. Anyway, better take your things upstairs for now."

Howard continued down the corridor and into *Salle Une.* Sure enough, Emma's place had been taken by nine sleeping bags laid out for the night to come. Somebody had recently daubed *In Loving Memory of the Siege of the Roxy* on the screen in red paint – it was still forming runnels down towards the platform.

In *Salle Deux,* a more permanent platform had been rigged up to allow easy communication with the projection room. Some planks had been laid across a small piece of hire scaffolding. Howard could see no reason why he shouldn't climb up and see how things stood in there. He immediately realised that nothing could be done from the outside to mitigate the stench which if anything had even intensified. He did notice, though, that a couple of bunches of flowers had been placed on the ledge of the hole in the wall and that a couple of scented candles and some joss sticks were burning in front of a framed newspaper article about Sally and *Shatto*. The projection room was a shrine – a holy grotto, a place of pilgrimage.

"Sally."

"What is it, Howard? Don't disturb me now – one of the students has put through a radio, you see, so I'm keeping up with developments on the out. It appears that a thousand militant students from the international politics faculty have turned the Roxy into a Republic – Ted Stringer was on a few minutes ago. He sounded quite excited about the whole thing. Some of the leading *enfoirés* are giving a free concert here this evening, he says."

"None of that's true, Sally. There's about thirty–five of them at the moment and they've done one or two slight, er, modifications but it's not really an organised thing."

"That's Ted Stringer for you. Good old Eddie! I know him of old you see, Howard. I can tell he's busy creating the event. There'll be a thousand people soon enough when word gets round, you mark my words. *Shatto* was just another coffee scrub until he came up with the name the other day in *La Rotonde*."

"You mean Ted is in on *Shatto*? He did mention it on air a couple of times earlier on, come to think of it. Is that even ethical?"

"Ha! You've worked that one out have you, Howard? Of course it's ethical – we would only ever use *Fairtrade* coffee grounds, you see. Ed is a good friend of Daddy's – he hasn't come up with any of the working capital to speak of but he is in a position to get the product *mentioned*, as you so delicately put it. This whole story has already been a terrific product placement for us. Oh, listen, here he is again. *Shatto magnate Sally Fanshaw.* Right at the start of the item! Good for you, Eddie."

"I see you've perked up again, Sally. That's good. How are things in there?"

"Yes, with E.S. on the case, this can only end in a most auspicious manner. How are things in here? Much the same, obviously. We found some sweetcorn at the bottom of the freezer, so that has been a bit of a change for a day or two. What's more, I've begun to find warm milk rather comforting, whilst the bread and butter can only recall one thing – the lacrosse pavilion at Brabourne Acres of a winter's Saturday. *Haec olim . . .* With such thoughts do I beguile the time. *Now, my co–mates and brothers in exile, Hath not old custom made this life more sweet?"*

"*Twelfth Night?*"

"No." Sally tutted." Look it up. A special consolation prize of nothing for getting Shakespeare right, though."

"*As you like it*, Sally. I'm delighted to see you're on top form. *Remember me when you come into your kingdom.* Speak later."

*

Back up in the flat, Emma and Darren were nervous. Darren had closed the shutters again, leaving only a chink through which he kept glancing down, giving a running commentary to himself in an undertone. Emma was brewing herself a second mug of instant coffee already, displaying tension in every fibre in spite of the earbuds shutting out the noise from the street. As for Howard, he couldn't decide whether to sit it out inside the Roxy for the day or go out on an afternoon's sightseeing or light shopping. Even though he was not responsible for the events unfolding around him he felt sure that some means would be found to pin whatever happened onto him. It seemed out of the question to join in with the protestors, but to stay in the flat seemed to him to force him into the role of the passive victim.

Howard tapped Emma on the shoulder and she removed one of the buds. "Yes? I was just making a coffee while I listen to *Vegan Praise Two*."

"Make that two coffees will you, please? Here," he took down his *Cymru am Byth* mug from its hook, "desperate times call for desperate mugs. I think I'll even have sugar in this one. Darren," he called, "will you have another?"

"Okay but just let me see what they plan to do next."

"Don't obsess. Coffee for Darren as well please, Emma. What are they up to?"

"I think they're trying to block the street. They're taking chairs and tables out of the *Aigle d'Argent*. Alain's trying to stop them."

"I don't think so," Howard was incredulous as he threw the shutters wide and looked across, "no, he's actually *helping* them." He called down, "Whose side are you on, anyway, Alain?"

"Ted's orders!"

"Look down there," Darren went on, "the traffic is backing up. People are trying to turn in the road, Howard."

"Aha! I thought so – they're actually blocking the street further up. It's going to have an effect on the boulevard in a bit – the *rue Jaurès* is a bit of a cut–through for the locals."

"They're taking our tables out as well. What's that they've got now?"

"Oh, I don't like that one little bit," said Howard, "that's a row of seats out of *Salle Une* – I've never seen them in the light before. They're not as dark as I thought. It's safe to say nothing's going to get past that heap of stuff now – not unless they bring a bulldozer."

As if on cue, at the other end of the street leading down towards the river appeared a city council earth mover, although for a moment it stood its ground and made no attempt to come any closer. With a rueful smile Howard remembered the Donald Duck cartoon that had started off this whole episode.

"I wish you hadn't have said that, Howard," said Darren, "they must have been listening. Look, here's Pascal coming – boy, that's all we need."

A minute later Pascal was up the stairs and flat out on Howard's bed. "Whew, what a night. I got wind of all this in a bar by *Pey Berland,* Boss. I was with some students."

"Why didn't you come and warn us?"

"It was too interesting. They started on beers and got onto fine wines about eleven. We were all out of it by one o'clock."

"So what's the plan?"

"The plan is what you can see down there. They kept on talking about somebody called E.S. I don't think there's anything else more organised, Boss. They did talk about a march on the City Hall but that's not for straight away. I think it all depends on what happens here going forward."

"E.S. would be Ted Stringer . . ."

"Thanks, I did manage to work that one out. They were listening to *France Inter* every hour on the hour and taking notes. I think they figured out there was a code word that kept on coming up all the time."

"Don't tell me – *Shatto.*"

"That's the one, Boss."

"That's a red herring. So there really is no concerted plan. It's all coming together down there though, isn't it?"

Howard could see that two complete rows of a dozen cinema seats each had been removed and placed either side of the barricade facing in opposite directions up and down the *Rue Jean Jaurès*. About half the seats were occupied by now. As he watched, another row emerged, carried with some difficulty by four men. It was placed facing the commercial district in front of the others. If this was to be a sit–in, at least it would be done in comfort. The crowd in the street was growing by the minute and now stood at maybe a couple of hundred – and it was still only coming up to ten.

"Put the news on Howard," Emma suggested.

Howard tuned in to *France Inter* on his ancient transistor. The lead item was about an earthquake somewhere near Jakarta but Ted Stringer was soon embarking on setting the scene about the Bordeaux story from inside the *Aigle d'Argent.*

"I'm currently trapped inside a bar directly opposite the Roxy where Alain the barman and I are in fear of our lives as a surging mob ebbs and flows around us, violently removing all the fittings and hurling them atop the makeshift barricade mere inches from the door." There was a light tinkle as of a wine glass breaking, "Get down, Alain – there goes yet another one of your plate glass windows! It is simply not going to be possible for the City Council to ignore this frightening incident as widespread looting begins and smoke drifts down the street. Madame de Pigalette cannot be seen to be idle – not with traffic at a standstill here in the centre of Bordeaux, backed up right to the boulevard in one direction and to the riverside expressway in the other . . ."

"That's not true, Boss. None of that is true – he's just making it up as he goes along."

"Shush. Ted might be about to tell us what's going to happen next if you listen."

"All right, I'll shut up then."

"Do."

"All right."

"Thanks."

" . . . the young *Shatto* tycoon? In a nutshell, that – that – and that alone is the crucial question the answer to which may spell the resolution of this stand-off. I leave you with that thought but, frankly, only time will tell. This is Ted Stringer in Bordeaux live from the *Siege of the Roxy*."

"Missed it, Boss."

"Don't worry, he'll be on again later: it's a rolling news network what with this going on."

The telephone rang and Howard picked up the receiver but said nothing, thinking it wise to screen all his calls. He was just about to hang up when an impatient voice was heard.

"Morgan, that's you, isn't it?" Daniel was terse, "you are to resign forthwith. That's an order – the trustees can ratify it later. There's no need for a vote this time because your complicity in all this is plain for all to see."

"Oh, hello Daniel. How are you today?" Howard flopped down on the settee. "Nice weather – a bit warmer than usual for the time of year. Not exactly, *Phew, what a scor* . . ."

"Never mind all that tosh. I've been listening to Ted Stringer on the news and quite frankly your position has become untenable this morning and you are to resign – as I told you, forthwith."

Howard had become used to these tirades. "Wait a minute. You're always saying my situation is untenable and saying *forthwith* and it always turns out to be tenable after all and life goes on. In this case I don't see how my resignation would do anything to change this situation. In fact, I think a steady hand and a cool head is called for. Sorry, a steady hand and a cool head *are* called for . . ."

"Right. I'm coming down there straight away with a draft letter of resignation for you to sign. Resolute, I sit at the wheel of my blue Jaguar and I fire up the engine, the draft in my hand and fury at heart. With stern determination, I engage first gear . . . "

"What, you haven't gone to the trouble of writing yet another letter of resignation?"

"No, it's the same one as all the other times. It may be a bit creased but it will still be valid with your signature attached."

"You're wasting your time. You won't get anywhere near the Roxy today, Daniel – you heard what Stringer said about the traffic down here. He did lay it on a bit thick but, still . . ."

"I'll get there somehow – you make no mistake about *that*. Expect me down there in twenty minutes – I'll put my foot down."

"Now you listen to me, Daniel . . . Oh, he's hung up. Hey, Heseltine is coming down here, Pascal."

"I know, I heard, Boss. I only hope the crowd decides to let him through." Pascal looked down into the street where there was now a quadruple row of cinema seats on either side of the barricade. A burning tyre was making a slow progress towards the waiting bulldozer – the engine was chugging away – and a small procession followed it, cheering and singing, *"Ah, ça ira, ça ira."*

Howard considered the scene. "High spirits. They may give him a bit of lip but they'll let him through. If he's got any sense he'll be dressed casually or they might rough him up."

"Véronique is about to come in, Boss. She must have come down under her own steam. They're jostling her a bit. Oh, no they're not, they're just ushering her through. Look, she's hating it."

In a few moments Véronique was climbing the stairs and came in, flustered. She sat down hard next to Howard on the settee and burst into tears.

"What's up Véro?"

"Oh, nothing really. You know how much I hate crowds don't you? But I felt I had to come in here before it builds up any more. I've been listening to Ted Stringer all morning and it's not going to ease up at all later on, is it?"

"No, it's going to get worse before it gets any better. Do you think it's wise for your Dad to be coming down here with all this going on?"

Veronique stiffened. "He's not is he? Oh, no. Give me that phone, I'm going to talk to Mum and try to put him off. There may be a riot if he shows up in his blazer."

"There's going to be a riot anyway by the looks of it," said Pascal. "I reckon there's getting on for four or five hundred people now and that's only outside. Listen to them playing their *djembes* downstairs."

It was true. Even though *Salle Une* was effectively soundproofed, an insistent rhythm could be heard and even felt through the walls from at least half a dozen African drums. In the foyer they were singing *Santiano* to the same beat – someone had got hold of the guitar from *Salle Deux*.

"I'd be surprised if there weren't a couple of hundred even inside the Roxy by now, Boss."

"Pascal's right. It's heaving down there," said Véronique, calmer now.

"Perhaps we should have a collection. Joke," said Howard.

"Actually, Boss, that's not such a bad idea. There's been such a lot of damage already and . . ."

"What do you mean, *already?*"

"All right, there's been an awful lot of damage full stop and it'll cost a lot of dough to get the place back in working order afterwards. Plus, who knows, they might set light to our seats out there later on or, you know, if they got drenched by water cannon, they'd be completely unusable."

"Yes, let's look on the bright side shall we, Pascal?"

"I'm only thinking aloud. Just think of it. Night falls and the isolated fires unite to an inferno. It'd only take one of those burning tyres to come rolling back and the whole lot would go up. If the wind changed, it might even set fire to the Roxy. In fact, there's no reason why they wouldn't just set fire to the place downstairs. A reckless crowd has a mind of its own."

"And the human imagination is such a marvellous thing, Pascal."

"I'm just looking and . . ."

"Looking and exaggerating and extrapolating. Don't."

Véronique was on the phone but saying very little. From time to time she would nod or raise an eyebrow. Once, she gasped and said *Oh, Mum!* When the call came to an end she made a gesture of hopelessness to Howard as she hung up. Without a word, she made for the door and clumped downstairs. Howard followed her out of the front door and into the bustling throng. Véronique was forcing her way through with surprising energy towards the end of the street leading down to the river and as she passed the bulldozer Heseltine's figure came into sight. He stood out in his blazer but a more disquieting detail was that he was brandishing a loudhailer. He approached with determination and brushed Véronique aside as she tried to reason with him. Feeling a wave of loathing directed from de Moulinet towards the window, Howard took a step back.

"I saw you!" cried Daniel into the loudhailer, "I'm coming up to your flat, Morgan. I intend to address the crowd from your window."

"Don't be a fool, Dad, they'll defenestrate you."

"Fiddlesticks, Véronique, I've always taught you to stand up for what is right and this is my hour. Clear the way, Morgan. If even one of your followers so much as touches me on my way through, I shall call in Madame de Pigalette and they'll soon learn what's what and who's in charge down here. Gangway! Gangway, I say, you rabble!"

"Hark at hoity–toity," called a voice from the crowd amid a volley of wolf whistles.

"Love the blazer!"

"Here, kitty, kitty, kitty."

It was a struggle, but Heseltine made it through into the foyer and struck out up the staircase with Véronique tugging at his sleeve and pleading. As Daniel burst in Howard made for the window and tried to block his way but Heseltine thrust him aside, flung open the shutters with a bang and switched on the bull horn.

"Boys and girls," he began with a roar, "Bordeaux has been my life and red wine beats in my veins. If you prick me, I bleed claret and on my couch I dream of the grape and the finest vintage. I was once as you are now although admittedly at your age I was already a junior director of my father's wine business, enjoying a salary roughly four times the national average. Nonetheless, even I had a 45 disc by Johnny Hallyday, although he did lose me by about 1965 . . ."

"Blue blazer, brass buttons!"

". . . you see, I too thrilled to the passion of Dalida while the music of Edith Piaf was like mother's milk to me." A relative calm had fallen as the crowd seemed to be enjoying the novelty of a distraction but Heseltine made the mistake of pausing for effect. A resounding raspberry was heard, causing a barrage of laughter. "Yes, you may well laugh, but some of us have worked hard for the continued prosperity of this city – I have attained through my own hard labour a certain ease of living which you in the younger generation seem to take for granted as of right. Yes, I do live in a *chateau* but so did Montaigne and you respect him, of course. Yes, I do drive a Jaguar but reliability is a great virtue in a vehicle in these days of mass–produced French rubbish. Look at you all, with your *Carrefour* jeans and your *Auchan* jackets and your, and your, your *hair gel*."

"What do you want, old man?"

"What do I want? Why, I call on you young whippersnappers to do the decent thing and disperse, of course. After all, *Four score and seven years ago* . . ."

"Dad, not the Gettyburg Address, I beg of you."

". . . *our fathers brought forth* . . ."

"My bum!"

A rhythmic rumour began on the far edge of the crowd and rose in intensity. It soon became clear that it was a chant.

The words began to solidify and take form, easily drowning out Heseltine's impassioned ranting. "Blue blazer, brass buttons; blue blazer, brass buttons."

"I'm not ashamed of my clothes. The finest tailors – *French* tailors, I might add – have laboured on these threads . . ."

At this, Howard was horrified to hear the pounding of heavy footsteps on the stairs and the heady rhythm of chanting now inside the Roxy as well as in the street.

"Debag him!" cried the first one through the door. It Paulo, closely followed by Gino. They started to do just that as Heseltine writhed on the flood. Over the brogues came the trousers and to loud cheers from the street, Gino hurled the elegant buff trousers down to be torn to pieces.

"You fools! Don't you realise those are *Fontenau Bags?*" shouted Heseltine, "those trousers cost me at least two hundred and fifty euros."

"Ha! There's no dignity in boxers, de Moulinet," scoffed Gino, "especially those. Tiny bunches of grapes! Let that be a lesson to you." He seized the loudhailer and led the chant to a still higher level in, "Blue blazer, brass buttons."

It was Véronique who picked up a pair of Howard's jeans from the back of a chair and handed them to Daniel – they were at least a size too small but did the job fairly well. Next, she tapped Gino on the shoulder and gestured to the loudhailer. Gino meekly handed it over. As she stepped to the window, Véronique's gaunt and angular figure seemed to intrigue rather than inflame the throng and as the chanting faded away to a murmur there was soon enough attention for her to speak.

"That was my Dad," she began, hesitating.

"Ha! I feel sorry for you, then, darling!"

"Shush! Let's hear what she has to say."

"That was my Dad. I'm not ashamed of that. He's got plenty of faults. I have too. So does Howard here. Everybody does. I support what you're trying to do. We all want to help the homeless. That's it. I love the Roxy too. We do our best. This hasn't got to be a personal thing. We all have different views. Dad's got his. I've got mine. That doesn't mean I can't love him." Véronique brushed away a tear and her voice broke a little. "Yes, I'm upset. You can see I'm upset. Listen, I'm going to lead him out of here. Let me through. He's my Dad. We can still protest. I'll join in, if that's what it takes. But we haven't got to hurt anybody. We haven't got to humiliate anybody. That's it. Thank you."

There was a murmur of approval and even some applause.

"You stupid girl," roared Heseltine, "look at you – you've made a fool of yourself yet again."

"I don't think so, Daniel," said Howard, "off you go, Véronique. I'll see you later. Daniel, you should probably sit this one out back in the vines."

"I'll leave that letter of resignation here, Morgan," said Heseltine, drawing a manila envelope from the inside pocket of his blazer. You should do the honourable thing and sign it. I've never been so humiliated in all my . . ."

"Dad, this isn't really about you at all, you know . . ."

"I'll deal with you later, Véronique. These losers have got inside your head. You were always a confounded dolt. Too soft: soft in the head."

"Maybe. Come on, Dad. I'll get you to your car. Where is it?"

"On the waterfront by the *Brasserie des Chartrons*. The irony," he said ruefully, "is that it's not even the Jag but one of the Mini Coopers. I took your advice about the traffic and selected a more manoeuvrable vehicle."

Howard watched as Véronique led her father down the stairs and he crossed back to the window to watch their progress. There were a few catcalls and a couple of people tried to start up the chant again but the mass of protestors was against them and they were allowed to pass through unmolested and in relative calm.

"Phew, that was a close shave," said Howard, "but I think we got away with it."

"You covered yourself with glory, Boss."

"Yes, Véro did really well. Still waters run deep and all that."

"I wonder how Ted Stringer is going to spin it though. Switch it on, will you, Boss."

19

Stringer was in full flow – *France Inter* had begun to cover the story in real time, it seemed. His tone was minatory, even apocalyptic, ". . . the ritual destruction by the howling mob of a pair of *Fontenau Bags* – the signature product of one of Bordeaux's leading trouser manufacturers. Martin Fontenau is of course a member of the board of *Shatto* and of the City Council which links him directly with the events unfolding here at the *Siege of the Roxy* where between five and six thousand unwashed and turbulent *sans culottes* have descended like a swarm of impudent lice to demand the liberation of the young and carefree *Shatto* mogul Sally Fanshaw on condition that the piffling and ineffective homeless breakfasts organised by the wheedling, whingeing Welshman Howard . . ."

"That's enough. Off." Howard could see which way the wind was blowing. He looked through the window. Maybe Ted had exaggerated the size of the crowd but by not all that many this time. There were easily three thousand people milling around with more arriving all the time as events took on a momentum of their own. To all appearances, every one of the seats from *Salle Une* had been removed, so three hundred people were seated in comfort facing in each direction both up and down the street and with at least as many sitting on the ground close by on blankets. The barricade in the centre was dense with bric-a-brac and at least five metres high, with lookouts perched on the heights.

"What can we do, Pascal?"

"I don't know. Play *Monopoly*? You've got a Bordeaux set, haven't you, Boss? You can't do anything about the crowd and there's no point in trying to reason with Paquito. It's a classic stand off, isn't it?"

"You could say that. They could break it up but if they bring in that bulldozer people are going to be hurt, make no mistake about it. The City Council can't want that – not with the European Year of Food coming up. All we can do is wait for *The Sifting of the Poo* and then think again, I suppose."

"Yes, it's your turn today, Boss."

"Funnily enough, I know that, Pascal. How could I forget?"

"Let's hope it's still firm. Are you feeling lucky today?"

"Life has been good to me so far; why should there be diarrhoea for the first time today?"

"That's a great philosophy, Boss. Look, Cathy is coming out of the *Aigle d'Argent*."

"Is Ted with her? No, but she's a little the worse for wear." Howard could hear Cathy's shrill voice cutting through the rumour of the crowd, *Namaste, namaste* it said. "Oh, look out, she's going through her greetings with the crowd. Gino, Jean–Pierre, bring her up here, will you, or she'll be starting up a conga or something."

"Shall I take the bottle off her?"

"It's empty. Just make sure she doesn't hit anybody with it."

"It looks as if she's a happy drunk, Boss. That's something, I suppose."

"Darren, coffee. Quick: strong and black."

"That's *unmilked* Howard. It's racist to say . . . "

"Strong black coffee, Darren. Now."

There was a loud bang and some curses from the staircase as Cathy made her laborious way up.

"*Namaste, namaste! Saudação, saudação! Bonjeu, bonjeu!*"

"Hello, Cathy, would you like a little lie down?" began Howard.

"*Namaste,* Howard. The day is still young – I've made it a rule not to drink before midday so I can start, like, another fresh bottle once I've finished this one from last night, you cheeky little pastor!" Cathy leaned down and squeezed Howard's cheek. It hurt.

"Put the bottle down, Catti – it's empty, anyway. You managed to give Ted Stringer the slip, I see."

"Ted! Oh, Teddie's gone live on air. As soon as he got a feed to Paris he dropped me like a lead balloon. Men! Don't get mixed up with them, Howard. They'll love you and leave you as soon as the day is long. Oh, is that a loudhailer? Let me address the crowd. *Friends, Romans, count . . .*"

". . . *ry men.* Let me see to it, Catti – it's not switched on, I don't think." Howard took the bullhorn and removed the batteries. "Testing, testing, one two, one two. Oh, I'm sorry, it doesn't seem to be working at all now. I say, moving on, is that really a *chateau de Moulinet 2000* you had there? That's the best vintage there's been recently. Could I interest you, though in a strong black coffee as brewed from instant coffee by our star *barista*, Darren?"

"Dazz, dearest Dazz – what a love! Don't change the subject though, Howard. I long to declare my love for Stringer from the rooftops. In fact, I intend to do it, loudhailer or no loudhailer."

"Maybe you'd like to hear what he has to say on the World Service instead, Cathy. He might send you a little secret message."

"I'd love to hear what he has to say on any subject, even on the world service whatever that is."

"No, on the *BBC* World Service, Catti." Howard took his transistor and began to tune through the short wave frequencies. He finally got a signal by leaning backwards through the window with the aerial touching the armature of the *Roxy* sign. The news was still full of Jakarta but soon enough Ted was on.

"Oh, Ted, Ted . . ." Cathy was sobbing.

"Be quiet, Catti. Just hold this will you, Darren." He sat next to Cathy, reached upward and put an arm part of the way round her shoulder.

" . . . where Madame de Pigalette has declared a major incident. If wine is king in Bordeaux, trousers are very big, too. In a deeply symbolic act, a pair of *Fontenau Bags* was summarily removed from the posterior of its owner and cast like pearls before the swine protesting here. First the gusset was rent and then the mother of pearl fly buttons flew to the four winds as the yielding honey–beige linen duck fabric was greedily torn it seemed to its constituent fibres and as student leader Dani Bohn–Kensit – *Dani-la-rue-Jaurès,* they are calling him here – led a chant of *Down with trousers* which momentarily replaced *Blue blazer; brass buttons.* It is hard to convey the force of such a course of action to those unfamiliar with Bordeaux *haute couture.* Many listeners will be wondering what is being done by those charged with bringing an end to the *Siege of the Roxy* as it were from within the camp. I spoke with Cathy Spedding of the Lighthouse Agency late last night and this is what she had to say."

Cathy's recorded voice was heard now: "Teddie dear, I'm sure everything is going to work out between ourselves." That panting laugh. "I'm quite prepared to wait, and once our current entanglements are over, we can make a new life down here. Open that bottle and let's drink – to us!"

Cathy had sobered up in a moment and was listening intently as Stringer went on, "So, you see that Ms. Spedding's attitude towards the Siege is a blindly optimistic one – she seems to have adopted an entirely passive role and to think that the situation is somehow going to resolve itself of its own accord. How she thinks she's going to facilitate a good outcome by coming to Bordeaux on what can only be described as a junket is anybody's guess, however. For the moment, her main concern seems to be *a pitcher full of the warm south with beaded bubbles winking at the rim.* This is Ted Stringer reporting from the *Siege of the Roxy* in Bordeaux, south-west France."

Cathy got up and started pacing round the room, "Howard, that, that *man* has, like, played me for a fool. And as far as the *Siege of the Roxy* is concerned, he has just set me up. *Let's whip it up*, he said, *come on, let's whip it up, woman! It's a sexy story*, he said. He must have recorded our conversation last night. *A junket* indeed! His casual companion in a drunken carousal – that's how he sees me. A moll – a mere drab. Some kind of fancy woman from Streatham."

"A fancy woman! I'm sure he couldn't think that, Catti, but at least we both know not to trust Ted Stringer in future and that's a useful lesson. He's played us both like a piano accordion. Plus, I suppose it's some comfort to know that not many supporters of the Lighthouse Agency will be listening to the BBC World Service in the middle of the day back home. Let's hope they don't put it on *From Our Own Correspondent* on Radio 4." Howard considered, "I suppose they're bound to do that though, aren't they? This is just the kind of thing they like."

"I'll have to get my head together with Cassi and make a vid about *inculturation* when I get back – that'll diffuse most of the, like, criticism in the churches when I explain what the culture of drinking is all about over here but as for the trust I thought I'd built up with Teddie . . . Hand me another bottle will you, Howard?" Cathy gestured towards Howard's assortment, collected in various encounters with the local growers.

"I think you've had enough for now don't you, Cathy? It's probably time to put our heads together and maybe get a press release of our own out. That might, er, *defuse* things a bit?"

Cathy was slumped on the settee, her canary sarong rucked up to her knees and even the little pineapple tuft of bleached blond hair crestfallen – by now she just looked as if she'd spent the night slumped unconscious in a bowl of peroxide. Her mascara had run and her lipstick was smudged. "I somehow think we should just maintain a dignified silence, Howard." She belched.

"Yes, I suppose there'll be plenty of time to make a fuller statement when it's all over."

"Howard, some slightly burnt toast and another black coffee, please."

"Fine. Then we can go down and have a word with Sally. It's been a long time since you spoke to her. In fact, have you spoken to her at all since you've been here?"

"I like to keep a light touch."

Howard realised that, apart from the brief contact at the church meeting, this would be Cathy's first visit to Sally in all the time she'd been in Bordeaux but he reasoned that you had to make allowances for the managerial side of Cathy's role.

The coffee was already done and as Howard was getting the toast ready, Cathy lay full length, moaning and tutting. He made one slice with butter and Marmite and another with strawberry jam to be on the safe side, then put on another couple of slices with the grill turned up full.

"Here we are, Catti – would you prefer jam or Marmite?"

"Neither – plain butter."

"Oh right – I'd better have these then. Unless you want, them, Darren? Emma?"

"Howard! I *am* vegan." Emma was outraged.

"Sorry, I forgot. Darren?"

"Has the bread got gluten in it?"

"I should think so. It's bread, isn't it? It's okay, I'll have them – I love gluten. I sometimes even have mock chicken curry from one of the Chineses on Chip Alley, sorry, on *Caroline Street* and that's *fried* gluten. Darren? Darren?"

*

When Cathy had finished eating and had a little nap they decided to go and talk to Sally. Cathy was still muttering imprecations about Ted and obviously nursing quite a hangover, so Howard warned her what to expect as they made their way downstairs and into the foyer.

"What's this all about, fancy dress or something?" called Gino.

"This is my boss, Cathy Spedding. Catti, Gino."

"Imposing. Statuesque."

"*Namaste*, Gino."

As they made their way along the corridor, Cathy scattered greetings in all her languages to the students sitting on cushions and blankets. A lot of them were in an elegaic mood after lunch and around thirty were sitting round a guitarist singing, *Chanson pour l'Auvergnat* while others were snoozing or were reading about the *Siege of the Roxy i*n the papers.

"Howard, you should really get these drains seen to," scolded Cathy as they passed the toilets. "Get a contractor – the punters will pay."

"I hate to break it to you, Catti but it's actually not the toilets – it's coming from in here." Howard threw open the door to *Salle Deux* and the full hot blast from the projection room caught them in the face.

"What a fu . . . furociously frowsty reek! Howard, it's far worse than I thought. I think I'm going to have to throw up," and she was gone, so Howard went down and opened the emergency exit and stood outside drinking in the fresh air.

Cathy came back about five minutes later. "I'm sorry, Howard but I had to go and, like, powder my nose." In fact, Cathy had freshened up her make up but there was a large greenish stain with some bits of half-digested toast on the light Ukrainian blouse she wore under the sarong.

"I think you've got a crumb there, Catti," said Howard, passing her his handkerchief. "Excuse me, can I borrow this?" He took a bottle of water from one of the students lounging on the floor a little further down the corridor. "Here you are, Catti, this may help a bit."

"I must confess I'm a little overcome? I think the serious nature of the situation has been brought home to me quite hard in the last couple of minutes?" Cathy was dabbing away the worst of the debris. "Let's like, get this over with shall we? Help me up onto that scaffolding. Sali! Sali!" She began coughing and retching into the handkerchief. "Howard, it's like the Black Hole . . ."

"We've already had that discussion thanks, Catti. Quite a few people actually died in the Black Hole of Calcutta. I've forgotten how many but Sally knows."

There was a rustling from behind the projector followed by two or three muffled thumps. "Sally's asleep – shall I wake her?" asked Paquito.

"If you don't mind, Paquito. I've got our boss here and she's a bit sensitive to the, er, atmosphere so I'm going to try and get her back up into the flat as soon as we've touched bases with Sally for a couple of minutes."

"Right you are Howard. Sally! Sally! You've got some visitors."

Howard beckoned Cathy forward. "Don't hold your nose, Catti and try and speak normally if you can. Come on, bright personality. You know, motivational."

"I'll do my best, Howard: wish me luck. Sally! A big *bonjeu* from all of us at Milton Keynes. I'm sorry I haven't been in before but I've had to deal with the press down here first."

"Yes, I'm up to speed. I heard Ted Stringer on *France Inter,* you see. He hasn't been giving the Lighthouse Agency a very good write-up actually and he was quite scathing about you in particular – about some of your outfits especially. He's nicknamed you *Pineapple Poll* after the Gilbert and Sullivan ballet skilfully assembled by the late Sir Charles Mackerras as early as 1951! Yes, I hear you gasp, Catti," Cathy was hawking into the hankie, "I'm always surprised at that myself. One would hardly have thought Mackerras would go on from that light confection to be the leading British champion of Janacek? I know! A fine Mozartian too. Are Howard and Pascal with you? Ted's named them Livingstone and Stanley. Some of his slots have become quite scathingly satirical about missionary work in general I'm afraid."

"Just Catti and me," called Howard, "Hello Sally. Glad to hear you're on top form again. Is there anything we can bring you? More Lynx?"

"I tend to think things have gone too far for even Lynx to be of any use don't you, Howard?"

"Yes, it's really quite striking how far things have gone."

"I can only imagine what it must be like for someone who hasn't got used to it. As far me, I've got used to some of the different stenches and can only smell Paquito's feet now. They're practically rotting away and he will insist on going barefoot in here. And that weeping sore – the pus oozing down is something to behold! May I have another word with Cathy, Howard?"

"I'm afraid she's just slipped out for a moment, Sally. She needs to see a man about a dog. I don't know if it's something you said. It was quite graphic, after all. Anyway, maybe I can help?"

"No, it's quite all right – I'll wait. You see, what I have to say is by way of being a manifesto of sorts. After my wobble I have become more resolute by far."

"Actually, she's back. It was quite a short visit." Cathy was ashen apart from two great patches of poorly applied blusher. "Sally says she has something quite formal to tell us, Catti."

"I'm all ears. Should I take notes?"

"There'll be no need for that. What I have to say is admirably brief and it's as follows: *Ahem, I, the honourable Sally Fanshaw, being of sound mind and body do declare my unequivocal support for the immediate reinstatement of the homeless breakfasts at the Eglise Evangélique de Bordeaux Centre, otherwise known as the Roxy Christian Centre. I do solemnly declare my respect for Madame de Pigalette, Mayor of this city but remain committed to the alleviation of the suffering of my fellows. I must speak truth to power and light a candle in the darkness, you see. The gospel of our Lord and Saviour Jesus Christ requires nothing less.* I put in that last sentence as a sop to you, Howard, you see. A little something for the Lighthouse Agency to work on, too, I thought, Catti."

"*Speak truth to power! Light a candle in the darkness!* Such wisdom in one so young!" breathed Cathy.

"Could you run through it again please, Sally? How did it go? *I, Sally Fanshaw . . .* I can't quite remember how it carries on. It's very memorable, mind you, but I didn't . . ."

"There's no need to trouble your little mind about that, Howard for I've written it out, you see. And not only so but with an eye on history, I intend to write a separate one in fine calligraphy for all six of the copyright libraries the moment I get out of here. I'm addressing you now, Catti. Would you be sure to give the original of this text to Madame de Pigalette, please? A photocopy to Ted Stringer. You may go now."

"But Sally, I've hardly had a chance to touch bases with . . ."

"That will be all thank you, Catti."

Howard stepped forward and leaned in. "Oh, Sally, is the poo bucket ready? We could make an early start, perhaps."

"Howard," Sally scolded, "we observe a strict routine and we ablute in turn at six thirty on the dot."

"Better wipe the dot, then. Joke. That's fine, Sally. I'll be along a little later."

As Howard and Cathy made their way back up to the flat, Cathy was sobbing and dabbing at her eyes with the soiled handkerchief.

"Yes, it was quite a moving statement, wasn't it, Catti?"

"It's not that. I'm like, overcome because I feel I've let her down – as if she somehow knew I'd ramped up the tension. She barely had a single word for me. She's rejected me. I've come all this way and I've wasted my womanly charms on Teddie Stringer instead of seeing to my duties and Sali has seen through all that. That's how it feels, anyway."

"I admit that's probably the right explanation, more or less, Catti, but she was possibly just keen to make sure her statement gets out there. There you are, that's something you can do – phone it through to Ted. Hang on, I've got his mobile number here somewhere." Howard was rummaging through the heap of receipts in his inside pocket. "Here it is."

"Oh, Howard I wonder could you do it please?"

"Go on, Catti – at least It'll give you a chance to see how things stand between you and Ted. He may just be playing hard to get with all that stuff on the media. You know, testing you out."

"Give me the text, Howard. There are still one or two things to be done with it. I need to take a photocopy before you get it to Madame de Pigalette. Have you got Reg's number as well?"

"Why do you need to give it to Reg to do? I can translate that just fine, Catti and it won't cost you about three hundred euros plus VAT. I'm not completely hopeless, you know. Even Darren and Emma could . . . oh, I suppose not."

"I'm afraid that won't cut it, Howard. We should have asked Sally for an authorised version, come to think of it, but Reg will have to do it now and put an official stamp on it to show that Mary has seen it."

"What do you mean? Who's Mary?"

"Everything official needs to be stamped Mary – I thought you'd know that Howard."

"The word is *Mairie*, Catti."

"And that's exactly what I said, Howard. Do keep up."

"Whatever."

Back in the flat, Howard started warming up the photocopier and a quarter of an hour later, after several paper jams and a change of toner, some smudged copies were ready. He was careful to remove the original from the glass and hand one of the copies to Cathy.

"I expect Ted will be over in the *Aigle d'Argent* having his tea, Catti. Maybe Reg will be with him. Do you want to come and see? I don't think you've tasted a nice chilled white Bordeaux yet, have you?"

Cathy perked up for a moment but then subsided as another wave of nausea broke over her. "Not just for the moment thank you, Howard. I think I'll have a little lie down instead. I had like, a funny turn earlier on. I think the *coq au vin* Teddie stood me yesterday evening disagreed with me and I'm still feeling a bit queasy. That or the toast just now. Are you sure that bread was fresh? You will take it to him, won't you?"

"All right. If you insist, I'll go and see what I can do and by the time I come back it'll nearly be time for the *Sifting of the Poo*. I'm dreading that – I swear to you, if they've got the runs or Paquito's piles are playing up . . ." Howard turned round but Cathy was gone. A few moments later he heard the toilet flush, refill and flush again. Howard shuddered.

*

Outside, the crowds had swelled still further and there was a carnival atmosphere now because the bulldozer had been taken away although there was a minibus of C.R.S. riot police at either end of the street. Howard knew they had a routine of appearing in full kit and forming up in intimidating line behind a phalanx of shields for some little time before a charge so he made the same assessment as the crowd and was confident that an attack was not on the cards for the time being. It was hard to estimate how many people were in the *rue Jaurès* by now but he thought it unlikely that there were fewer than five thousand. A couple of street dancers with a ghetto blaster were entertaining a semicircle of admirers and elsewhere there was even a fire eater.

Howard made his way to the boulevard to draw out some euros to pay Reg. When he got back, the *Aigle d'Argent* was heaving with people spilling out of the door and Alain mouthed his thanks for the extra custom as Howard forced his way in. He was too busy to come over but Howard held up sixteen fingers and Alain nodded his understanding and gestured to the back room where Stringer and Reg were seated in front of their brandies.

"Ah now, Mr. Howard Morgan in person. You're quite the international celebrity now, Howard. Rather notorious because of your controversial role in this, I fear, Howard."

"Thanks for that, Ted. That's home–grown British irony, by the way. I mean, *thanks for nothing.* I'm here purely on a business errand."

"Ah now, there's no need to take that tone – as a gentleman of the press, I've just been helping the story develop ever since Catti gave me the green light and by the same token I can just as easily influence the telling of the tale when day is set. Isn't that so, Reg?"

"Yes."

Alain pushed his way through the throng with Howard's *1664.* "One *Seize.* This one's on the house – I haven't seen so many people in since the World Cup final. Enjoy!"

"Shan't! Glad to oblige, Alain. Actually, Reg, I came to see you with this – for translation," Howard showed a photocopy of Sally's text.

"Original."

"I've got the handwritten original here in this envelope. That's got to be handed over to Madame de Pigalette, I'm afraid."

"Give." Howard handed it over. "Typewriter." Ted picked up a portable typewriter from the floor by his side and passed it to Reg who, spreading out his fingers, removed the cover.

Reg rolled in a piece of paper. "This is old technology surely, Reg?"

"Best." Reg tapped away for a couple of minutes. "Done. Two fifty."

Howard stared at the few lines of typing. "Is this good for official use? It all seems a bit casual." Howard had become used to sitting in waiting rooms and standing in queues sometimes for hours at a time for even the most minor administrative task.

Reg took a tiny box out of his briefcase and stamped the document. "Seal. Three seven five."

"He's not cheap but he's good, Howard. He keeps his comments to the minimum for fear of litigation but I've never seen his translations invalidated in court or even seriously questioned."

"That's fair enough I suppose. Will you accept a bank transfer for the money, Reg?"

"Cash."

Howard rummaged in his wallet, handed over the money and turned to Stringer, "Do you by any chance know where I'll find Madame de Pigalette, Ted? I know you've been in close contact all through this."

"*Rotonde*."

"Ah now, Reg is quite right, Howard. What he means to say is that Madame de Pigalette is in conclave at the moment in *La Rotonde* where you will find her enjoying a pre–aperitif in preparation for the assault many of us are confidently expecting, nay predicting, will take place later on this evening. They won't let you in to see her, of course – not dressed like that and not with your reputation preceding you – but I'd be quite happy to deliver the document in question myself. It so happens that Reg and I are invited to the conclave."

"Do you think, I'd trust you with that, Ted? There'd be nothing to stop you going with it as an exclusive. I shall hand it to the floor manager, ask for a receipt and if possible watch as he hands it over to Madame de Pigalette."

"Suit yourself, Howard. May I tempt you to another brandy before we make our way round there, Reg?"

"Yes."

Stringer laughed. "And if I were to tempt you to another brandy, would you accept it, Reg?"

"Yes."

"He has a very fine legal mind, you notice."

"What a stupid distinction! I'll just leave you two to it. You deserve each other." Howard pressed back through to the entrance and out into the street. As he approached the C.R.S. van in the direction of the commercial district, the occupants began to climb out but Howard was relieved to realise that it wasn't for his benefit although their pointing showed he had been recognised. They were stretching and flexing, so maybe things were moving forward at last and some time earlier than Ted had predicted. Howard walked a little faster and was soon at *La Rotonde* where he made as if to walk past the doorman into the glittering interior.

"I'm terribly sorry, sir. There are no denim jackets allowed in here and even if there were you would need to wear a tie."

"I haven't got any ties and I only want to hand something to Madame de Pigalette – she is in there isn't she? It's something important about the *Siege of the Roxy*."

The doorman looked Howard up and down again, "Yes, I can see that you wouldn't have ties. I have a selection but I still can't let you in, though. Neither can I confirm or deny the identity of any of our clients although by way of answer, may I refer you to the standard of the City of Bordeaux billowing on the flagpole up there. It denotes residence."

"May I see the manager then, please? I need to get a document to Madame de Pigalette. It's urgent."

"I'm afraid I am not empowered to call the manager to the door, sir, although I am able to convey an object to him. We have a runner for that. Maxime!"

"Sir."

"Maxime, this gentleman has an object which he would like to convey to Madame de Pigalette through Monsieur Arlette."

"Certainly, sir."

"I'd like a receipt, please."

"Maxime, would you be so kind as to obtain a handwritten confirmation of your having passed this document to Monsieur Arlette, please?"

"Certainly, sir."

Maxime was back only a couple of minutes later and handed the receipt to Howard who glanced down and saw with satisfaction that it bore Madame de Pigalette's flamboyant signature familiar to all in Bordeaux from the mayoral quarterly bulletins. The messenger waited expectantly so Howard gave him a five euro note and did the same for the doorman. "You've both been very helpful. Well, you've been efficient."

"Thank you, sir. I wonder, sir, if I would be correct in my surmise that you are pastor Howard Morgan of the celebrated *Eglise Evangélique de Bordeaux Centre* otherwise known as the *Roxy Christian Centre*?"

"Yes, that's right."

"I wonder if I might have your autograph on this serviette please, sir?"

20

Howard decided to saunter the long way back by the waterfront and made his way up onto the *Pont de Pierre* where he stopped to contemplate the river and the city. The sun was setting and the reflections of the ornate lamps were winking in the water while the twin spires of the cathedral could also be seen as though under the Garonne. Further down the estuary, he saw a sailboat making its way out to sea. If only there were more time – other lives would be possible. *Now is the time for the sifting of the poo,* he said to himself. He wondered if this was why he had left a good job in banking with great prospects because of his French just to look through someone else's waste for a key that might not even be there at all.

As he rounded the corner into the *rue Jaurès,* Howard was horrified to see that the C.R.S. were now formed up in full gear and ready to move. An uneasy calm had fallen on the crowd in the street and there was no organised chanting although quite a few taunts could be heard. The mood was tense because from a practical point of view the crowd was kettled, apart from the narrow roads leading off the *rue Jaurès* which would be quickly blocked and dangerous if any trouble began.

"Hey, isn't that Morgan over there?" A random voice from the crowd. "Howard, what are you going to do if they move in?"

Howard remained silent and people seemed happy to let him through so he was quickly back at the Roxy and in the flat a few moments later.

"Come on, Boss – we've been waiting for you. You can't put the evil moment off any longer, you know."

"Have you got the bucket?"

"Come off it Howard," said Darren, "you know it's part of the deal to pull the bucket through before you sift."

"All right. Pass me the gloves, Emma. Are you coming down with me, Catti?"

"I think I'll give it a miss thanks, Howard but I wouldn't miss the *Sifting of the Poo* itself for the world."

"Right you are. Okay, folks plenty of newspaper and I'll be back in five."

Downstairs, Howard could see that since he came in, preparations had begun for a siege within the siege. The cash desk was being moved bodily to block the double glass doors while some of the fittings from the toilets had been ripped out and were coming through to be piled up behind the counter to give it more weight. The doors of *Salle Une* were in the process of being removed and would presumably be added, too. Howard had to remind himself once again that he was no longer in charge and not responsible for anything that took place.

"No, Daniel. I am adamant." Howard could hear Sally's voice as he came into *Salle Deux*, "I don't care what any of you thinks. I'm in it for the long haul. You've heard my declaration and I won't back off from it at any price. Not now it's written."

Howard was surprised to see that not only Heseltine but also Suzon and Véronique were there. Suzon turned to Howard with a helpless gesture, "There's no reasoning with her, Monsieur Morgan. We've tried everything."

"This is all your fault, Morgan. People are going to be crushed; people are going to suffer; people are going to be killed in the crush; people are going to be injured and writhing in the rumpus. *Quelle Horreur!* What do you have to say for yourself, eh?"

"Poo. That's all I have to say."

"Oh, Howard. I'm so disappointed in you," murmured Suzon.

"I'm sorry, Suzon but I'm only here for one thing. I've been dreading this all day but I fully intend to go through with it. Paquito," he called, "Sally! Have you gone?"

"Of course they haven't gone, Morgan," Daniel was angry, "you know full well they're still in there."

"Yes, we have gone, Howard. I'm afraid it's a bit pungent this evening – what I used to call as a girl a *round poo* before I discovered the word, *diarrhoea,* you see."

"Well, I'll do my best with it, Sally and I'll come back down with some supplies once I've emptied the bucket. I think I've got some kaolin and morphine in my bathroom cupboard."

"That would be very welcome, Howard. Send these people away – they are trying to deter me from my great purpose but you've had a chance to meditate on *La Déclaration du Roxy* so you know I shall not, I shall not be moved."

"Yes, it was very good. Very clear. Come on you lot, up to the flat," said Howard as the bucket squeezed through. There was a yellowish slime sidling down one side but he managed to avoid touching that. They made a strange procession as they moved along the corridor – a priest bearing a weird host at arm's length in a red bucket and his acolytes following, Véronique in a little black dress, Suzon in lime silk and Daniel in his blue blazer. The crowd in the corridor turned away and hid their faces but more in disgust than from any feelings of awe and wonder.

"Why are you not turning into the lavatory, Morgan? The sooner we get this over with the better. *Quelle horreur!* Left wheel."

"If you took more notice of the news bulletins you'd know we have a special thing we do every day, Daniel. You'll see. Come on up. *Thou art gone up on high; thou hast led captivity captive*," he sang in a reedy tenor.

"What's Handel's *Messiah* got to do with this?" growled Heseltine.

"It just struck me as strange – what we're doing, so it seemed appropriate. Boy, it's at times like this I wish I had a censer!"

"Why not just stop saying all these stupid things then, Howard?" asked Véronique, exasperated.

"A *censer*, Véro, not a censor!"

"I'll swing for you, I swear it, Morgan!"

"I haven't actually got a censer, though, Daniel, so you can't. Anyway, we're there now so we can begin."

As they entered the kitchen Howard began to intone, "Dearly beloved, we are gathered here this evening for the ceremony of *The Sifting of the Poo*. Let none enter into this Sifting lightly or without due consideration," Howard was laughing but it was with a touch of hysteria and his hands trembled as he began to lower the bucket onto the table, causing a wave to build up and a little cloacal matter to slop heavily over the side. "Folks, let's not bother, shall we? We're three days in and there's not much hope of finding anything this late."

"Do the deed, Boss. We're all watching and holding our breath." Pascal held his breath.

Howard looked more closely into the bucket and his stomach turned. On the surface was a lightish yellow scum gathering around some thick toenail clippings and some great dun plaques of fungal nail but the predominant colour was the amber of rich urine made luminous by the setting sun's rays through the half–closed shutters and through the sides of the translucent red bucket. The contents had separated and below the upper layer was the mottled ochre of diarrhoea made granular by specks of lingering sweetcorn. Gobs of catarrh seemed suspended in aspic between the two. Trying to avoid thinking about Paquito's weeping sore, the pus from which was undoubtedly present on some cotton wool balls he could make out, Howard made sure his sleeves were rolled up and was steeling himself to plunge his hands in when there came a loud grating against the wall below the window.

"Darren, go and see what that is, would you? I'm getting ready to operate."

Darren opened the window and peeped down between the shutters, then recoiled into the room with a jump but leaving the window wide open. Now, from both ends of the street a rhythmic beating could be heard over the defiant shouts below. It was clear that the C.R.S. were beating their shields and were preparing to charge within the half hour.

"What is it, Darren? What have you seen?"

"It's a ladder. Someone is trying to climb in. I'm sorry, Howard but it's . . . it's Ted Stringer."

Stringer's combover appeared at the window as Cathy lunged forward calling, "Teddie, Teddie."

"But hush, what light through yonder window shines . . ." Ted began. As his torso appeared, it became clear that the large black object he was carrying over his shoulder was a video camera. Howard made as if to close the window but Stringer allowed his elbows to come to rest on the sill and prevented him. He leaned into the room.

"Right, everyone: best behaviour. Are you ready for this, Reg?"

"Yes."

"You can't do this, Ted," yelled Howard. I'll pour this bucket over you if you don't get down, I swear."

"Ah now, Howard, while that might make for great television, it would be a poor public relations exercise for you and for the Roxy." He adjusted an earpiece. "As it is, we go live in seven, six, five, four, three . . . Good evening, this is Ted Stringer reporting live from the *Siege of the Roxy* in Bordeaux,

France for Channel 4 news and FR3 and on BBC Radio 4 and the BBC World Service. What you are about to witness is a ceremony they've developed during the siege known as *The Sifting of the Poo*. They are looking for the key which will allow them to liberate the hostage, the honourable Sally Fanshaw, the *Queen of Shatto – Shatto* being a cosmetic coffee scrub available in all good supermarkets. Howard Morgan is the man with the gloves and he is about to plunge his hands above their wrists into that bucket full of what I can only call *the Remains of the Day*. How are you feeling, Morgan? Is this a humiliating moment for you?"

"Wait till I see you after this, Stringer . . ."

". . . and you'll fill me in on the emotions you are feeling in an in–depth interview: thank you. Yes, it is an intense moment, isn't it? Also present are the other members of the *Eiffel on my Feet* team from the Lighthouse Agency, yearning to be reunited with their colleague. Cathy Spedding of the Agency is here, having changed into the national costume of the Philippines. What have you to say, Ms. Spedding?"

"May I say, *Namaste* to your listeners on the World Service, Ted? And indeed, *Mbote, Salamu, Saudação* and of course *Bonjeu.*"

"Some church members are here, too and are fervently supporting Howard Morgan as he reaches down into the more solid mass of . . ."

"Actually, this is nearly all liquid, so I've made the decision to go directly to the sieve," Howard explained to the camera with the air of a TV chef. As he crossed with the bucket to the sink, Stringer craned around the corner of the window with the camera.

"It's a red plastic sieve, to match the colour of the bucket," said Stringer. "Morgan holds the sieve low in the sink in one hand and with the other pours in some of the contents of the bucket. It takes a moment to pass through the mesh – obviously, some of the excrement is more solid than Morgan thought. May I say to the viewers and listeners that the stench is indescribable: the reek of stale urine is fighting it out with (there goes Cathy Spedding of the Lighthouse Agency, running from the room) what I can only call . . . What would *you* call it, Morgan?"

"Ignore Stringer, Boss. Just forage in there. Concentrate on the task in . . . bucket."

"What do you think I'm doing, Pascal?"

"Concentrate: I thought I saw a dull glint then, Howard," Véronique leant forward, clasping her nose with thumb and forefinger, "there in the bucket."

"What, this bit of sweetcorn?" He picked it out and held it up to the camera.

"No, that's a bit of sweetcorn. What I'm talking about is just there – look." Véronique indicated a larger gobbet with the dull lustre of brass.

"Yes, yes, I think you're right! Look – here it is!" Howard picked out the key, ran it under the tap and held it up in triumph to the camera. "I did it! We can set Sally free and take it from there!"

"Howard Morgan," for some reason, Stringer had a look of triumph, "now that the eyes of the world are on you, how does it feel, if I now reveal, as I now can, that I bring news from the City Hall team as assembled at Bordeaux's leading restaurant, *La Rotonde*? News that Madame de Pigalette has been pleased to accept Sally Fanshaw's demands in *La Déclaration du Roxy* and has issued a proclamation which rescinds the ban on the homeless breakfasts? You see, there was no need . . ."

"You mean there was no need to go through this . . . *The Sifting of the Poo* . . . I've been had. I'll get you for this, Stringer."

Stringer pulled the focus tight on Howard's face. "Yes, ladies and gentlemen – this is the face of humiliation. The face of Howard Morgan. Howard Morgan has finally grasped the dreadful truth: there was no need for him to rummage in the poo at all! Congratulations, Howard Morgan, you have just contributed an anthology piece to the world's video archive – the ultimate blooper, one might say. You there, hold this, and turn it on me." Stringer handed the camera to Pascal. "I am now in a position to declare the *Siege of the Roxy* officially at an end. As I hand you back to the studio, this has been Ted Stringer live from Bordeaux. Thank you, and goodnight. . . and . . . cut. Did you get all that, Reg?"

"Yes."

"You mean you put me through all that for nothing?" Howard was incensed. "You might have . . ."

"Ah now, Howard, you've no call to complain. I think this was your desired outcome? Reg and I came into *La Rotonde* shortly after you left to find the conclave most amenable to Sally's elegant and wise missive. Madame de Pigalette was always quite well-disposed to what you are trying to do here. It was passed *nem con* in the end, although it did take a while to coax Brian Filcher down from his high horse." Stringer turned round on the ladder and gestured to the street, "Look, people are already beginning to disperse. They were never going to spend a whole night out in the cold at this time of the year – not with the C.R.S. threatening to move in. That's right, isn't it, Reg? Reg?"

Howard looked down. It was true, the crowd was evaporating: into the *Aigle d'Argent,* down the side lanes and gullies, in both directions past the C.R.S. who were themselves stowing their kit and climbing back into their buses. Reg was already making his way into the bar with his briefcase and typewriter, his coat collar raised against the chilly evening air. Soon, there were only about fifty people visible in the street, some sitting smoking on the cinema seats, others in little groups chatting. The barricade was abandoned like a wrecked galleon, ghostly in the glare of a C.R.S. searchlight, casting weird shadows on the deserted buildings.

Howard called down, "Hey, is nobody going to help me carry some of those seats back in here? You lot have gutted the place."

"Not our problem, mate."

"You've had your fifteen minutes, Morgan: suck it up."

"Ah now, speaking of fifteen minutes of notoriety, Howard, I think it's time we went and freed the sainted Sally from her captivity. *Stone walls do not a jail make nor bars of iron a cage,* but they are not very pleasant all the same. Come and help me carry this ladder in and we can get up there. I'd like to record a couple of interviews with her a.s.a.p. – both in French and English, you know. She's the ideal hostage. From that point of view I mean."

"What about *us*, Teddie?" Cathy was gushing, fluttering her bleached eyelashes.

"*Us* being you, Darren and Emma? Listen, this is the best I can do: I'll record your comments but I won't guarantee to use them, I'm afraid. As for *us, us,* I'm afraid I'm spoken for." Howard could see Angélique loitering in the entrance to the *Aigle d'Argent* and looked to Stringer with raised eyebrows.

"Indeed. Angélique – the light of my life. We met only this morning by the barricade where she was loitering like a lost spirit. Come on, Howard. Let's get started. The sooner we get these interviews done the sooner you can start clearing up. If I know Madame de Pigalette, she'll want the street swept of all that rubbish and all your precious fittings will be at the dump if you don't hurry. They're doing garbage collection by barge on the river now – did you know that? They'd make short work of your stuff in one of those."

A few minutes later a ladder was propped up next to the projection room door. Howard climbed up as Pascal steadied it below. He took the key and as he turned it there was a heavy clunk as the four points of the security lock came free.

"Sally, Paquito! The *Siege of the Roxy* is over!"

"I know, Howard," replied Sally. "We heard it the radio just a moment since. You must feel like a perfect fool – although I imagine that's a familiar sensation for you by now."

"No need to rub it in. One of you push this door, please. It's all right, I'm standing to the side."

At that, the massive door swung open and Howard nearly jumped off the ladder to the ground not because of the door but as the stench from within hit him with full force. By the light of the sixty watt bulb, Howard could see Sally was pale and bedraggled while Paquito held back, crouched like Caliban behind the canvas curtain.

"It's all right, Paquito, you can show your face. I promise there'll be no consequences. We're just glad it's all over."

"*Lazarus, come out!*" shouted Pascal from the foot of the ladder.

"Do you want a hand or can you manage, Sally?"

"What a silly old question! I'll be just fine – I've been running through some Pilates exercises interspersed with a little elementary yoga in there," said Bunty as she climbed down after Howard. "You'll need to help Paquito, though – I think he's seized up."

Emma moved forward as if to embrace Sally but thought better of it while Darren gave her a firm and pucker handshake then wiped his hand on his jeans.

Cathy said, "We always knew you could, like, do it, Sally."

"So did I, apart from my briefest of brief wobblies, about which Howard will, of course, maintain radio silence. Now, Ted," Bunty was brisk and in charge, "you'll be wanting an interview, I expect. Is it TV or only radio? French or English?"

"Ah now, it so happens we'll need *four* interviews, Sally. One of each in both languages. There'll be a fee, of course. We can do something in more depth later on: we're in talks about a

Radio 4 *Profile* so it'll probably be a few thousand pounds, all in. You may need to get an agent."

"I already have an agent – or, rather, the family does. I shall plough a paltry amount like that back into the business, in any case. Speaking of our little concern, I do hope you brought some *Shatto* with you or at least some dummy packaging. It's time to make hay. Time to *clean up* one might say."

"What do you take me for, Sally? I wouldn't forget a thing like that: I've brought both sizes. They are waiting up in Howard's flat, displayed as a still life on the table and ready for the camera. I expect you'll be wanting some to help you make yourself presentable for the lens?"

"*Shatto?*" Sally made a disgusted face, "you must be joking. Nothing would induce me to touch that muck. Who'd ever think about putting coffee and grape pips on their face? That's a rhetorical question, by the way. Good old-fashioned soap and water for me every time. I'm a classic English rose, you see. Howard, lead me to your shower and put out plenty of towels, then we can get on with the interviews in your flat. Oh, and plenty of coffee. To drink."

"Oh, Sally I've got a question that's been bugging me if you don't mind before you get on."

"Yes, what is it, Howard?"

"Whenever I mention speaking truth to power and lighting a candle in the darkness people groan and roll their eyes but when you say it people go, *Such wisdom in one so young!* Why is that?"

Sally thought for a moment and looked Howard up and down. "You have to be prepared to walk the walk, Howard."

21

"Something something Acapulco – we are flying down to Rio!" Cathy was gay and there was an end of term mood in Cornflower as she took the familiar road to the airport. "Roxy Music – *Virginia Plain*. It's all ended so well, Howard. There's been such a lot of positive feedback from the churches. The punters have stepped up to the plate once again and they are, like, filling our coffers to overflowing?"

"I think the summary is a bit more mixed than that as far as the Roxy is concerned, though, Cathy," replied Howard. "There's been a huge amount of damage and the whole thing has done nothing to make things better between me and Daniel de Moulinet. I don't suppose there's any chance of a grant from the Lighthouse Agency to help us with some of the bigger repairs, is there?"

"Ah now, Howard. Oh, I'm, like, really really sorry, that thing with Ted Stringer has, like, left its mark on me too, you know. I'll need a couple of Tequila Sunrises or Pina Coladas when I get to Brazil just to clear my head?"

Cornflower was toiling round the ring road in the direction of the Bordeaux–Merignac turn-off, rocking gently from side to side this time. Pascal was in the back pressed heavily into the back door of the car on some of the longer bends by a couple of Cathy's suitcases and some of the holdalls and carrier bags she had acquired during her stay.

"Come on, old girl – you can do it."

"There's no need to get personal, Howard. This trip has taken it out of me, it's true – particularly finding out that Ted Stringer was about to get engaged to that woman, Angelica, was it? All the same, I'm not finished just yet."

"I was talking to the car again, Cathy. Your luggage is a lot heavier this time what with all that plonk and those outfits. I hope they don't make you pay a penalty for all that extra weight." Cathy made as if to speak but Howard cut in, "I know – evangelism: the punters will be only too pleased to cover it."

"These are fine vintages, anyway, Howard – Stringer may have left me flat but he did point me in one right direction during my stay. Now, as it happens there is nothing that can be done to help you financially at this time because, despite the money rolling in, it's all spoken for or otherwise tied up, whatwith keeping the Milton Keynes operation ticking over. There is, however, another investment opportunity I think you may be very interested in indeed? There may well be some, like, trickle down from this – in fact, I'd be very surprised if there weren't some green shoots."

"Oh yes?"

"Yes. Now, how does this sound, Howard?" Cathy smacked her lips, "an all-expenses-paid tour of the British churches in Larry the limo. A first-rate public speaker. So, only the best hotels with the best-stocked mini bars. A large rally –

with a big collection, naturally – at each of the venues. A card-reader – you know, for credit cards and so on." Cathy made a dollar sign. "Going round talking about the *Siege of the Roxy*, naturally. Probably about twenty stops – just the capitals and the biggest cities – London, Bristol, Glasgow, Edinburgh, Birmingham, Belfast – probably even some of the cities in the North of England, whatever they are, and maybe even somewhere in Wales, given your involvement . . ."

"Cardiff. My *involvement*, eh? Do you know, I must say that sounds really like a very interesting proposition indeed, Cathy. It would help give me some closure on the whole business. It's all been so traumatic."

"That's just what I thought. I've been keeping a pastoral eye on you and so Vicki's suggested the tour and we've both felt it's an idea that could be developed still further from Milton Keynes while the initial few rallies are going on. For instance, after the British leg we had in mind a whistle-stop continental tour of some of the places where we work, probably flying in and out of Stansted this time – possibly even in a private light aircraft. No stinting on the standard of accommodation, mind you, because I'll be along. Paris of course, Tirana, Stuttgart, Vienna, Budapest, Rome, Madrid – there'll be fully qualified interpreters, naturally. Some of the Hungarian reds are definitely worth sampling, I've found?"

Howard was all ears. "D'you know, that's what I call a mouth-watering prospect, Catti! These last few days I've been discovering it's marvellous being part of the Lighthouse Agency team."

"The feeling is mutual – it's great having you on board, Howard. Then, after the European leg, maybe we could cast the net a little wider. There is still some public relations work to be done in Phuket and Rio de Janeiro because of the false starts with the Ditsies and after what happened with Ivor Morris and now the Johnstones who have been given the sack for negligence? Come to think of it, even international headquarters in New York would like to hear a few vignettes about what's been going on in Bordeaux, I'm sure, to say nothing of the Sydney and Auckland offices. Now, Howard, how does all that sound as a package to be going on with?"

"It's a great plan, Catti. It's coherent. A sure-fire hit and *so* dynamic. Ground–breaking, even. Earth–shattering. Granular. Agile." Howard shifted down through the gears and took a ticket for the short–term car park, easily finding a space at this time in the morning.

"I knew you'd like it." Cathy rummaged in her bag and leaned across to Howard. "Now, here on this card are the Lighthouse Agency bank numbers – I know I can trust you with these after all we've been through together over the last few days, Howard. Once you have used them, you are to like, destroy the card? Is that clear? Eat it if necessary. There are only four of these in existence at any one time: mine, Vicki's, Suzi's and one in the safe at Milton Keynes. Destroy after use – do you understand? There's a procedure – we print a new one that goes directly into the safe and the one from there comes to me and it all goes round again."

Howard glanced at the laminated card with *Top Secret* at the top in bold red letters. "I understand perfectly." He kissed the card. "Thank you for reposing in me your sacred trust, Catti. You know I won't let you down."

"The top number is the sort code and the bottom one the account number. The long number beneath is the I.B.A.N. – the International Bank Account Number. The printer had to continue it on the other side of the card, as you can see. You need to be very careful with that one because the scope for error is huge but nothing serious can be done without it outside the United Kingdom. You know: souvenirs and suchlike."

"Understood. Such wisdom!"

"You are to book business class with all the trimmings, mind," Cathy wagged an admonitory finger, " No frugality on this, of all things, Howard – you know: V.I.P. lounge, priority boarding, complementary newspapers – the whole shebang. *The worker is worthy of his hire. So,* Larry the limo will be there waiting at Heathrow. No doubt there will be a crowd of well–wishers after all the media attention. We can put the word out about the arrival time and maybe people will begin to gather spontaneously even if we don't like, lay on some coaches. Which, of course, we will!"

Howard nearly said *complimentary* but instead enthused, "Brilliant! It's great working with you, Catti. When shall I book it all for?"

"There's obviously no point in hanging around – we need to strike while the iron is hot, so I reckon tomorrow morning or early afternoon will be fine to make a start. The media is notoriously fickle – well, you've seen that with Ted Stringer and I." Howard winced, but bit back the correction. "We really don't want this story to go cold on us?"

Howard was gloating now, "That's all great, Catti. Leave it all up to me – I'm onto it." Maybe this was the way in to a coveted place in the Milton Keynes set-up, perhaps in a post involving international logistics. He decided he could even reconcile himself to being called Howi or Howzz.

"Good. That's settled." Cathy leaned back. "So, four tickets in the names of Sally Fanshaw, Darren and Emma. I've forgotten what their surnames are but you can find that out easily enough, I expect. Make Sali the lead passenger, though. This will be great experience for her before she goes up to Oxford?"

"That's only three tickets, Catti." Howard was salivating now, eager to clinch the deal.

"Oh, did I forget to say? Brian Filcher has agreed to spend his sabbatical doing it for us. That's a *coupe de grace* for the Agency."

"Hey, guess what Pascal?" called Howard in French as he got ready to put Cathy's bags on a trolley. He was blowed if he was going to help her into the terminal.

"What's that, Boss?"

"You know the homeless breakfast? It looks like it's just you and me on Monday. So, we need more bread and butter – oh, and milk."

Printed in Great Britain
by Amazon